10 × 12/13 LT 10/13

WITHDRAWN

Taos Chill

BOOK ONE IN THE CARMEN AND CHILL
MYSTERY SERIES

Taos Chill

Linda Lea Castle

FIVE STAR
A part of Gale, Cengage Learning

GALE
CENGAGE Learning

Detroit • New York • San Francisco • New Haven, Conn • Waterville, Maine • London

GALE
CENGAGE Learning

Copyright © 2009 by Linda Lea Crockett.
Five Star Publishing, a part of Gale, Cengage Learning.

Set in 11 pt. Plantin.
Printed on permanent paper.

LIBRARY OF CONGRESS CATALOGING-IN-PUBLICATION DATA

Castle, Linda Lea.
  Taos chill / by Linda Lea Castle. — 1st ed.
    p. cm. — (Carmen and Chill mystery series ; bk 1)
  ISBN-13: 978-1-59414-754-8 (alk. paper)
  ISBN-10: 1-59414-754-X (alk. paper)
  1. Women authors—Fiction. 2. Taos (N.M.)—Fiction. I. Title.
PS3553.A81433T36 2009
813'.54—dc22   2008049396

First Edition. First Printing: March 2009.
Published in 2009 in conjunction with Tekno Books and Ed Gorman.

Printed in the United States of America
1 2 3 4 5 6 7 13 12 11 10 09

ACKNOWLEDGEMENTS

This book is a work of fiction, though many of the bizarre and humorous incidents are based in truth. I want to thank my sister, Vicki, an award-winning artist, for venturing into the world of Taos for up-close-and-personal research. And a special thanks to Logan for giving me such a great idea.

This book is lovingly dedicated to The Lord. Without His blessings I am nothing; without His Grace I would be lost. I am thankful I am saved. And of course to my family, those bound by blood and those bound by love. You know who you are. May the Lord Bless and keep you.

CHAPTER ONE

Ontario, California, 2005.

"A movie deal? They offered her a movie contract? On that tell-all piece of fiction?" Officer Hugh Blaines—"Chill" to friend and foe alike—splurted a mouthful of bitter coffee over the papers strewn across his desk.

"Rumor mill says she is going to take it."

"That little witch!"

"I thought you should hear it from me first. Word is they are going to try and get Kevin Costner for the lead." Captain Eloy Martinez scrubbed a hand over his two-day growth of beard. A hostage situation had kept the two of them busy for over forty-eight hours, but at least everyone was alive.

"Kevin freakin' Costner? Please, Eloy, take my piece and kill me. Just kill me now." Chill laid his gun on the desk.

"Chill, you have got to calm down before you meet with I.A. today."

"Internal Affairs can kiss my lily white butt." Chill surged to his feet. "They have been looking at me for six months now, ever since that damned book came out—"

"Chill, I know you're not dirty—"

"That makes two of us." He shoved aside a stack of police reports, scanned the surface of the desk, opened his top drawer, shuffled through the contents.

"What did you lose?"

"Cigarettes."

"You stopped smoking last year when we nailed Jetne Sisco and his sister."

"Yes, well I started again about the time my former partner turned author. I hit two packs a day the morning she was on CNN. Maybe I'll switch to unfiltered. It will be quicker." Chill slammed the drawer shut. Not one damned coffin nail in sight.

"You are going to kill yourself if you don't calm down and learn to deal with your partner—"

"Ex-partner."

"Your ex-partner's book—fictional book," Eloy added firmly. "You are going to stroke and die a long, lingering death."

"Not if you do it for me . . . really, Eloy, just give me one right in the brainpan. Come on—put me out of my misery."

Eloy snorted. "Don't tempt me."

They had gone through the academy together. Nearly fifteen years ago they had been full of piss and vinegar, ready to change the world.

Things had changed—a lot.

Chill shoved aside a stack of manila folders and saw the edge of a photo. He knuckled it out into the open. It was the young woman who was the real hero in the Jetne Sisco case. Plump, dark-haired, with prominent crooked front teeth, and round dimpled cheeks, Lily Platero had testified and put Jetne and Selma Sisco away forever.

"Chill, in all fairness she told the interviewer the book was fiction. She told him her book wasn't based on any real person."

"Yes, she did, and then she winked. She winked. Do you know what a wink means to those barracudas in the media? It's a special signal, Eloy. And let's not forget what else she did. She wrote a tell-all book about a dirty, wife-beating, coke-snorting, evidence-faking cop named Drew Maines. How could anybody have possibly thought she based that low-life fictional character on her real, live partner, Hugh Blaines? I mean Drew Maines

10

and Hugh Blaines—not a bit of similarity there."

"I know it has been tough on you—"

"Tough? How could it have been tough? First the D.A. wanted to go over all my old cases but he assured me he didn't believe I cooked the evidence. Now Internal Affairs is investigating me for—how did they put it?—my own benefit, to put out any fires before they start. Uh-huh, right. And I'm Little Red Riding Hood. But you know what the worse thing is, Eloy? I can't face my accuser because it is all whispers, speculation and beer-foam gossip. Perps give me that crap-eating-grin, my fellow officers watch me like a pit-bull who turned on his master. Every time I walk into the squad room, all conversation stops."

"So what are you going to do? You know I've got your back. Just tell me what you need."

Chill flopped down in his lopsided chair. The door of the office opened and an ashen-faced rookie stood there, clinging to the knob for support.

"What do you want?" Chill growled.

"It just came over the radio. A crash in the canyon. The car caught fire. It was—it was Lily Platero. She's dead."

Taos County, Taos, New Mexico, 2007.

Chill unwrapped a piece of gum and folded it into his mouth. He chewed like he was chomping a tough steak, fingers drumming on the steering wheel while he inched his way up the road. Eighteen months ago he had turned in his badge, given up his lease on a cramped, expensive apartment, loaded his Ford Explorer and headed east.

He had gambled in Vegas, stood in jaw-gapping awe on the vermilion rim of the Grand Canyon in Arizona, fished frigid, crystal-clear streams in Colorado, and now he was stuck in traffic in what looked like the snow-covered artsy-fartsy capital of the world.

"Hoorah for me," Chill grumbled.

Today had not been a good day. The warning citation he'd gotten hadn't done anything to get his knickers out of a twist, and even though the female cop had been professional and friendly, he was damned sure he hadn't been going fifteen miles over the posted limit.

"But who can argue with a woman?"

His stress level—the one he was continually trying to lower—was climbing like a thermometer in a hot oven even though there were icicles glittering from the low hanging eves of the tile roofs.

How could he be in gridlock in a one-horse town with only one main street? Chill was giving himself TMJ chomping on a stick of Teaberry chewing gum.

His attention shifted like quicksilver to the bumper on the car ahead of him. A faded decal about the joy of turning on and dropping out caught his eye.

"The sixties were good to this place."

His gaze slid over the pedestrian traffic. This delightful little burg seemed to be populated by an equal mix of aging hippies and New Age cowboys.

The horn on the car behind him blasted his eardrums, sending his blood pressure up two points. But the impatience was contagious, flowing from the driver behind him right into his brain.

"Come on. Move it, buddy. It's just a little slush for pity sake. I'm from California and I can drive in snow," Chill roared, but the car in front of him didn't move an inch. It was obvious he wasn't going anywhere fast.

Bored, frustrated and battling his type A personality, his eyes drifted over the adobe buildings dusted in white confectioners' sugar, looking like life-sized gingerbread houses. Chill wasn't into feng shui or color coordinating, or other girly-man stuff, but he had to admit the colors of stucco and snow made a fabulous backdrop for the bright colors of abstract paintings displayed in gallery windows. And above it all was an expanse of endless orange tinted sky.

"Orange? What the—?"

Chill peeled off his sunglasses and gave it another chance. A clear blue-gray, cloudless sky stretched out above the low buildings as far as he could see.

"I never get tired of looking at a sky like that."

The cars suddenly surged forward. He stomped the accelerator, then slammed on his brakes just short of connecting with that aging bumper sticker. The whole process took about a minute and a half. Okay, it was a stupid passive-aggressive action, but he felt better lurching forward even if it was a short trip.

He rolled down his window and craned his neck to scan the next few blocks, searching for an opening—an escape route—another road.

Craft shops, galleries . . . a sign for a bed-and-breakfast caught his eye, but no obvious way to peel away from the bumper-to-bumper traffic. Eloy had made him do a little deep breathing whenever they got gridlocked in California. He did it now. The air was crisp, sweet, fresh and invigorating, full of wintry flavors.

All right, he had to admit it. California couldn't hold a candle to this tableau. This was true late autumn in the Rockies, the kind of weather travel writers went all gaga over. He sucked in another deep breath and held it for a minute, tasting the season on the back of his tongue.

Chill stopped drumming on the steering wheel and leaned back in his seat.

Why was he in such a hurry? Maybe this bit of New Mexico was worth sitting in traffic for.

Life was good. He had cashed in his retirement and he was doing okay for the time being. His bank account wasn't obese but it was plump enough. This could be a nice little stopover—a place to spend the winter—a place to relax and try to forget the reasons that drove him east.

After all, that was one beaut of a sky.

Having made the decision to enjoy the place, Chill turned on his blinker, inching his way toward the street where a fanciful sign promised the best B&B in town. He had made a little progress when a streak of blue automobile appeared in his rearview mirror. The compact car overtook him and veered right, doing a close approximation of a ninety-degree angle.

Chill slammed on his brakes, lurching to a stop just in time to avoid a collision. The car flew by him in a shower of melted road slush, but not before he marked the damage to the front end.

"Geez, lady, I can see why your fender is crunched." Chill tossed his gum out the open window and unwrapped another piece. He patted his shirt pocket, relieved to feel the hard outline of an unopened package. Man, he was glad he didn't smoke anymore—women drivers like that required at least a pack per day.

Carmen Sofia Pollini glared at the man in the SUV when she heard him slam on his brakes and yell at her.

"Male driver," she yelled back without slowing. She was late and didn't have time for out of state drivers rubbernecking their way through town. She grimaced. Wouldn't it have been just too ironic if she got into another accident on the way to see her insurance adjuster about her fender?

"Not even I could have that kind of a bad karma."

She sped down the road and turned left, then she zipped into the small parking lot beside the insurance office. She slammed on her brakes. Her little compact skidded on the slush and ice, finally coming to stop more or less in between the rapidly disappearing yellow lines.

"Stay!" She ordered her canine companion, looked again at her dented fender, cursed under her breath and then gingerly made her way inside, hoping she didn't fall as she had at the bank. It was difficult to argue over a bounced check when one's butt was sporting ice and dirty snow.

"This day is going to get better. It has to." So far she had found out her checking account was overdrawn, and then the icing on the cake had been having a car wreck after paying a sultan's ransom for a few gallons of gas.

Yes, her day had to improve. Nobody had consistently bad luck, not even her.

Fifteen minutes later Carmen had to reevaluate that optimistic opinion. It had been cold outside; it was absolutely frigid on the business side of her insurance adjuster's desk. Her insurance agent, Tom Hardwick, a balding man with ill-fitting dentures and a penchant for nubby cardigan sweaters with leather patches on the elbows, stared back, his eyes shards of icy disdain.

"But you don't understand. It was not a moving violation. Not really." She tried to explain for the third time.

"You are not listening, Ms. Pollini." His flat voice cut her off. She wasn't feeling the love.

Carmen flopped back in the office chair and discovered the hard way there was not an ounce of padding under the generic gray upholstery. Feeling like a child brought before the principal, she sat up straight, resisting the urge to rub her spine. Tom was not a pleasant man at the best of times. Today, when a winter storm was due to blow in and she had just had a fender bender with Jake-the-snake, the local Rapid Express Delivery driver, Tom Hardwick looked like he might be catching a cold. He was definitely not a happy-chappy.

"Ms. Pollini—" Tom Hardwick's mouth turned down at the

corners while he dragged out the S*s* in a reptilian hiss. Through slitted eyes he stared down his narrow nose at her from behind his desk. She half expected a forked tongue to coming flicking out of his mouth. And what was with him and that desk? It was bare—so neat it set her teeth on edge.

"Let me try and explain this to you one more time. You were in control of the car, the driver of the Rapid Express Delivery truck was in his truck. The two vehicles collided. For our purpose, that is an auto accident, and it is also considered a moving violation. Your policy clearly states you have a one-thousand-dollar deductible in such cases. I cannot change your coverage to suit you when your bad driving has led to property damage."

"But the damage probably won't be more than one thousand dollars, and I was actually parked at the pump. Do you hear? Parked. At the pump."

He stared at her, unblinking, over the black plastic rim of his glasses while he closed the manila folder with her name on it, laying his pale hands palm down upon it as if she might try to snatch it away.

"Then evidently all the expense for the repairs will be out-of-pocket for you. There is nothing I can do. My hands are tied."

Those smooth hands looked pretty free to her, but she could see it was useless to protest. Carmen Sofia was going to have to pay for her own repairs—except she had checks bouncing all over the county and nothing remotely resembling money in her account to pay them with.

"I think you should expect to see a rate increase as well," Tom Hardwick added with a twitch of his mouth. "The home office will be sending you notification shortly."

"My rates will go up? Why?"

"There was that road rage and the other incident we had to pay out. Your home-owner's policy had to cover the medical bills on that one, but since your coverage is bundled it is monitored by one office."

"I did not have road rage. How many times must I explain this? The guy tried passing on the right." She waved her right hand. "You know, the right side, on a single-lane road. And as for the other."

He held up his hand like a traffic cop. "In any case, you have had two moving violations in three months. There will be a rate increase—a rather substantial one I would imagine."

"Oh, I could just kill Jake-the-snake. The man is making me miserable. It takes him days to come and pick up my manuscripts when I have a deadline. He tosses my parcels at my house. They usually look like he took the time to soak them in the Rio Grande, and most of them are covered with what looks like tire marks. Now I'm going to have to come up with a thousand dollars because he rammed my car? It isn't fair! You just don't know what I've been putting up with—it's like he has some personal vendetta against me. I swear the man is keeping a log of what each package weighs and where it is going. He clearly has issues."

The agent frowned and gyrated his head like a cobra preparing to strike.

"I have no control over the R.E.D. office or their employees. If it is as bad as you claim, then you should file a formal complaint. According to the police report, you were equally at fault in the case of the accident because your car was not parked properly at the pump. Now if you will excuse me—"

"The police report was written by Sheriff Jim Dunn—surely you've heard all the rumors about him and his attitude about women. The Taos Telegraph says he is a gnat's whisker away from suspension because of his sexual—"

"Ms. Pollini, it is none of my business, but you should refrain from unsubstantiated gossip that could result in litigation.

People still do sue for slander, you know. And you might want to think about taking an anger-management class."

Carmen Sofia swallowed and gasped for oxygen. "Anger management? You think I have a problem with anger control? Why would you say that?"

"Oh, I don't know. The incident for one. What you did is considered perverse and out of control by most sane individuals. I'm just saying you might want to consider getting professional help before you do something really crazy."

"I think I'd be better off getting a new insurance agent, Mr. Hardass, I mean Hardwick."

He didn't rise to the bait. Instead he heaved a long-suffering sigh and said, "Surely, this can't be a financial hardship. Your books are doing quite well—they are in all the bookstores. Evidently there is a large market for that sort of writing."

She wanted to smack him, but that would only prove his theory that she was a hothead who wrote romance. It was bad enough she had this silly insurance policy that didn't pay squat. Worse, she was unaccountably broke. Carmen wasn't going to give Hardwick the satisfaction of telling him that her royalty checks were way overdue and that her literary agent, Ethyl Gatz, was not returning calls or E-mails. It didn't matter how many books Carmen had in stores if she didn't get paid for them when they sold. Her name might be out there, finally, and she might be visible, but visibility didn't pay the bills.

"I'm having a small cash flow problem," she mumbled, embarrassed and frustrated because phone calls, E-mails and letters to the Gatz Agency had gone unanswered for many weeks.

But at least tomorrow Ethyl was scheduled to be at an Albuquerque writers' conference where Carmen Sofia was speaking and autographing books. She would finally be able to speak with Ethyl and get this mess cleared up. Maybe the mail had gone wonky or something.

"Then I suggest you take steps to remedy the temporary blockage of revenue, because you have a car fender to repair—and you may have to assume some of the financial responsibility for the R.E.D. truck's damage as well." Tom's voice dripped sarcasm. "In any case, I hope you can do it without losing your temper."

"I do not have a temper. I really don't understand why you continue saying I do. Everything I have done, including the—uh . . . incident—was justified, clearly thought out and necessary." Carmen Sofia shoved her arms into her coat, ignoring Tom's disapproving look as she stood up.

"Necessary? Really, Ms. Pollini, I do wonder how your mind works."

"I'll bet you do." She dashed out of his office and across the parking lot through a combination of hail and snow. Typical New Mexico fall weather—like the old joke said, if you don't like it, just give it two minutes; it was likely to change. And judging by the fast-darkening sky, it was going to change for the worst.

She hurried to her car, sliding once but regaining her balance before she went down in the thin crust of dirty snow. Flakes were just starting to fall when she put her fingers on the door handle.

The pungent aroma of boxer hit her full force when she opened her car door.

"Tyson, have you been passing gas—again?" She looked over the back of the seat at her pet.

Dark brown canine eyes glittered as the stout-bodied boxer yawned, stretched and hopped into the front passenger seat to give her a full-on, attentive stare.

"You have got to stop this—breathing methane gas is dangerous. I swear, one day you are going to blow something up—probably me."

She rolled down the window, ignoring the cold bite of icy air. Taos, Santa Fe and Questa were expecting the first big snowfall of the year. The weather report said they could get as much as a foot overnight. She flipped on the wipers, clearing the windshield, but it was covered again before the arm repeated its arc across the foggy glass.

Carmen Sofia eased out onto the main street, already sliding on a surface that would freeze and become black ice by evening. A sleek sports car flew past her, honking twice before it disappeared around the corner. She was startled when melting snow sprayed her windshield. The wipers struggled to remove it.

"See, Tyson, that guy is obviously driving too fast for road conditions, but if I did anything about it, I would be accused of road rage. Sheesh, what a day. The bank, Jake crunching my fender, Hardass and his attitude about my insurance, and now a kamikaze sports car—I'm going home before something really bad happens."

She hunched over the wheel and concentrated on the road. It was twenty miles back to her house. Twenty miles between her, a glass of wine and a warm fire.

Twenty miles to her haven of solitude where nothing ever happened.

Wind-driven snow and hail buffeted Carmen Sofia's compact car when she dipped into the canyon. She wrestled the steering wheel against the wind sheer until the road sloped up again and the strain on her wrists eased.

Nearly home. She could practically smell the pine smoke of her fire now.

But when she caught sight of her road, she groaned. Cars, vans and a few tricked-out motorcycles were lined up along both sides of the dirt avenue. Her house, like those of her closest neighbor's, sat on several acres of pasture grass. People in Taos County didn't live right on top of each other; they had space and highly prized privacy—until Penny hosted a party. Most of the more than thirty vehicles were parked in and around Carmen Sofia's driveway, blocking the entrance to her drive, sidewalk and house. She couldn't even see her front door beyond the second row of cars.

If the weather turned worse as fast as the weatherman promised, and if the past behavior of Penny's guests was repeated, then the party would go on until the storm blew out.

"It could be days, Tyson," Carmen groaned. "Why does my closest neighbor have to be a starving artist with a ton of talent and too many weird friends?"

Tyson did not answer that question; he was too busy trying to help Carmen negotiate through the thick piles of snow, his nose pressed to the windshield, his hot breath causing the window to fog even more.

Penny Black's monthly bash was the social event of the art community that stretched from the ski lift in Red River to the Plaza in Santa Fe. Everyone, from the old school to avant-garde newbies who lived in converted buses—off the grid on the canyon rim—came to Penny's parties. Carmen had met Vicki Sweazea, and even R.C. Gorman before he passed on, at one of these gatherings. Usually Carmen didn't mind the parking nightmare or the influx of visitors, but today had been anything but the usual.

Carmen drove to the end of the road and turned around at Millie Hyde's gate. The crusty octogenarian was one of the last true ranchers in the area. She lived in an eighty-year-old house with a hundred rolling acres stretching out behind her. The Taos Telegraph, Carmen's pet name for the rumor-mill, said she owned a lot more land towards Red River. Millie lived with an aggressive watchdog and an old-west attitude, which she swore was the explanation for her longevity.

"And, if I may point out, her watchdog is the motive for guests to stay far from her driveway, Tyson. You could take a few pointers from Annie, you know." Carmen drove slowly, scanning the crowded lane.

Tyson wasn't much of a watchdog but he was a great listener, although Carmen was afraid to gloat too much about that trait. Maybe it was just another aspect of his peculiar ear-fetish.

Carmen spotted an unoccupied space on the shoulder of the road. Funny, she could've sworn there was a vehicle there a moment ago. She could just squeeze her car into it if she was careful. Unfortunately it was not too close to her own driveway. She would have to walk through the deepening snow.

She parked the car and got out, slogging through the white stuff with Tyson gingerly picking his way beside her. The hail had stopped, but it was starting to snow harder, leaving a white crust inside her deep footprints.

When she reached her own drive Tyson halted, his hackles standing at attention. He growled low and deep in his chest. Big flakes of snow collected on his dark muzzle, giving him a comical appearance, but the snarling and flashes of sharp, white canines convinced Carmen he wasn't fooling around.

"What is it? Snow making your feet hurt? Sorry, but you have to walk. No way am I going to carry you. I'll get a fire going and you can thaw out on your rug."

Tyson only snarled more. She stepped around his stiff body and peered around the trunk of a Loblolly pine, one of a half dozen that grew in her front yard. Only then did she see the cherry-colored Rapid Express Delivery truck parked in her drive. It had a crumpled left fender—bits of blue paint matched the smashed right fender of her car.

Jake had *cojones* the size of baseballs; she'd give him that. But if he thought he was going to come and complain to her again about the volume of mail going to New York, or bully her right here in her own house, well, she wasn't going to stand for it.

"That's it, Jake," she yelled. "I'm not going to have it. Do you hear me?" She stomped up to his truck and looked inside the open cab. It was empty. The keys were in the ignition. "Where are you, Jake? You damned deliveryman terrorist! Don't hide. Come out and face me like a—like a R.E.D. driver!"

A retro-hippie couple walking up the road toward Penny Black's place stopped and looked her way. Carmen Sofia mugged a face, then slopped through the soft snow to her sidewalk, muttering oaths under her breath all the way.

Tyson stopped growling when they were nearly at her front door. Now he whined, a mournful sound that made the hair on Carmen Sofia's neck rise. She followed the line of his sight, taking a few tentative steps. It couldn't be a rattler; they hibernated during the winter.

It wasn't a rattler, but it was another kind of snake.

The snow fell hard in big fluffy flakes, a confectioners'-sugar frosting on everything.

Including Jake. Jake-the-snake, known for the fanged reptilian tattoo on his hand that disappeared up his sleeve.

Sprawled face down in front of Carmen Sofia's front door, stiff as a board, dead as a doornail, gone to that big delivery truck in the sky was Jake, the R.E.D. deliveryman.

CHAPTER TWO

Snow had collected in white slashes in the folds of Jake's red uniform jacket and in the creases of his dark dickie pants. She bent down on one knee to see his face. One cheek was submerged in crisp, white snow.

His eyes were open—at least one eye was open. The other was hanging out of the socket, looking like something from a gross joke-shop specializing in Halloween horrors.

His lips were blue.

Strands of his dark hair were wet; others were starting to freeze to his forehead.

The finality of death rolled off him in icy waves.

Tyson whined again before he came to stand beside her in the snow-frosted mud at the edge of her concrete walk.

"No, Tyson. I don't care how many times you saw it done on TV. I'm not going to check for a pulse. Uh-uh, no way am I going to handle a dead guy."

The wind blew snow against Jake's nose and chin, giving him a white beard and mustache.

"Why did he die at our house? It must've been a massive coronary, and when he fell on the cement he broke the bones in his face, and his eye fell out. . . . I wonder how quickly they will get someone to take over his route." She sucked in a breath when the reality of what she had just said washed over her. It was petty and stupid to care about the condition of her packages, and cold and callous to hope the next guy had more concern for her manuscripts heading to her agent and her publisher. But that was precisely what she had been thinking.

"You're right, Tyson, I must be in shock. I don't even know what I am saying."

Jake-the-snake was dead.

Dead on her doorstep.

She needed to call someone. It was way too late for 911, he was beyond resuscitation, but she should phone the police. Right on cue, the sound of police sirens penetrated the fog of her shock.

Tyson gave one deep bark.

Carmen Sofia looked up to see flashing lights winking through the white veil of heavy flakes. Relief washed over her.

The police would know what to do with Jake's body. They were professionals; they were equipped to handle this sort of thing. She was a writer. Corpses were something she inserted to eliminate sagging middles, not something she found on her porch.

The police car halted beyond the triple-parked cars in front of Carmen's driveway. Good-ol'-Sheriff-Jim Dunn hauled his top-heavy body out of the white Crown Vic with his jaw set firm as a coyote trap, his small round eyes locked on Carmen Sofia. He stumped his way through the snow, cussing all the way.

"What the Sam Hill is going on, little lady?" Jim stalked up to her, his stubby legs encased in tan trousers, the deep snow soaking his pant nearly up to the knees. He hitched up his belt as far as his eleven-month-pregnant-belly would allow.

"We had a phone call about a disturba—" His gaze slid over Jake's body. "Oohoweee! What have we here?"

Carmen Sofia's confidence in the law shattered like a thin rime of ice on the Rio Grande. Her navy wool pea coat wasn't thick enough to protect her from the weather or the chill in the lawman's beady little eyes.

Jim bent over and touched two fingers to Jake's neck.

Carmen Sofia swallowed—hard. Tyson whined.

The lawman straightened, hitched up his belt again, cocked his hip and said, "You want to tell me why in hell you went an' killed ol' Jake?"

Carmen Sofia's pulse sent hot darts of pain shooting into the nerves behind her eyes. This couldn't be happening. This was 2007, for pity sake. There were laws and procedures, even here in Taos County. Making idle threats in the heat of the moment and an itty-bitty past incident with the law just couldn't be enough to get her arrested.

"Could you loosen the cuffs a little?" Carmen wiggled her butt and tried to adjust her position in the backseat of the police cruiser. The air smelled of tobacco smoke and something worse she didn't want to think about.

Maybe Tyson's gas wasn't so bad.

The cold metal bracelets cut into her skin. She realized with a jolt that she hadn't truly captured the reality of cuffs in her last book. One-size-fits-all did not apply when the person putting them on was trying to make a point.

Sheriff Jim Dunn had definitely been making a point.

Carmen Sofia couldn't feel the tips of her fingers anymore.

Would she ever type again?

Would she spend the rest of her life in the hoosegow, behind bars, typing in a stark, poorly lit prison cell as the years and the best-seller's lists went by? Or would she become a literary darling from behind bars? Would Geraldo do an interview? Would Barbara Walters make her a special? Would TMZ write her name on the board?

She mentally shook herself.

"Focus, focus," she whispered to herself.

Good-ol'-Jim's piggy little eyes bored into her from the rearview mirror.

At least she thought he was looking at her; it was kind of hard to tell through the expanded metal barrier that separated the front and backseats.

"Jim . . . er, I mean, Sheriff Dunn, you can't really believe I killed Jake-the-snake—I mean the R.E.D. driver? Why would I?"

A twitch at the lower corner of Jim's left eye signaled that he was thinking. It was a slow process. Carmen Sofia found herself leaning forward, mentally coaxing him to put thought to word. Finally his fleshy lips parted and he spoke.

"Well now, there was that little altercation in town today, wasn't there, little lady?"

The Taos Telegraph had been working again. Carmen never understood how the smallest event could be worthy of gossip, but things like barroom brawls, car wrecks and gallery closings traveled twice the speed of light in Taos County.

"Altercation? Oh, you mean the little fender bender? That was a scratch, really, hardly a reason to kill a man, Sheriff. Surely you can see—"

"Tom Hardwick up to the insurance office allows as you were very upset—even made threats against poor ol' Jake. You've got a bad temper, Carmen Sofia. We all know it. Tom says you were making threats about your agent—some woman named Ethyl Gatz. And the manager of R.E.D. says you have made complaints against Jake, says the poor man was so harassed, he started a list of what you sent and where. Out of control temper will do it every time. I've seen murder committed for a whole lot less, little missy."

Yep, the Taos Telegraph again. She wondered if Tom Hardwick had Jim Dunn on his speed dial. Thank the Lord party lines were no longer in use, or everyone in the county would know all about her upcoming visit with her literary agent.

"I do not have a bad temper. I—"

"Or it could'a been a crime of passion. Yes sir. Ol' Jake was quite a ladies' man. Girls find those exotic tattoos real excitin'. Maybe you and him had a little history, eh? Could be that you are the jealous type. You write all that lovey-dovey, stuff don't you? How do I know you didn't get all het up over Jake and some other woman and decided to put an end to it? You wrote a book about a murder, didn't you?"

"Yes, *Recipe for Revenge,* but I never—"

"Now you just keep quiet back there, missy. You understood the Miranda I read you, didn't you? Anything you say I gotta repeat in court, so you'd be smart to keep shut-up until you get yourself an attorney."

He pinched his fleshy lips together, hunched over the steering wheel and focused on the road.

Carmen flopped back against the seat. In her head Joaquin Phoenix, dressed all in black just like Johnny Cash, sang "Folsom Prison Blues."

"I'm going to fry."

"Just relax your hand and let me roll your finger."

"Sorry. I'm a little tense."

"Understandable." Victoria Smith, the only female officer in the county, pressed Carmen Sofia's index finger onto a pad of black ink.

Carmen looked away and found her gaze met by a man she had never seen before. His eyes were the color of sea foam, his face a map of the Rockies—all high peaks and sweeping ridges. Thick, unruly hair, streaked from hours in the sun, stuck out at odd angles as if he had just run impatient fingers through it. His nose was too big, his chin too square, his muscled body too wide at the shoulders, yet he exuded the grace of a predator, which was the only word Carmen could think of at the moment. It sure wasn't a pretty face that stared at her without a bit of embarrassment, but it was without a doubt one of the most interesting and masculine faces she had ever seen.

His eyes flicked over her like a predator's too; sizing up his prey, looking for a weakness so he could close in for the kill.

He was . . . arresting.

She giggled at the unintentional pun in her inner monologue. The man frowned at her. Had she offended him?

Something about the way his blunt, sun-bleached brows pinched together made her believe he didn't offend easily.

"Are you okay?" Victoria tilted her head as if Carmen was a tick off plumb. She glanced toward the man.

"Who is that?" Carmen couldn't believe that even in the middle of this crisis her writer's curiosity would not rest.

"An ex-California cop interested in a job." Victoria didn't even look up. In fact she ducked her head as if the guy's stare bothered her as much as it did Carmen. The harsh fluorescent lighting gave her blond hair greenish highlights.

"That's not the kind of guy I'd expect Jim Dunn to hire. He wouldn't hire someone who looks sharp and gives off waves of masculine strength."

Victoria looked up. "You're a pretty smart cookie. He wouldn't and he didn't. Hugh Blaines' C.V. found its way to the county commissioners' meeting, so it didn't go through Jim Dunn at all."

"Oh, I can just imagine what Jim will say when the Taos Telegraph gets wind of that." Carmen grinned.

Victoria frowned at her. "Huh?"

"Oh, nothing." Carmen had forgotten that Victoria was not an old-timer around Taos. "What do you mean his C.V. showed up?"

Victoria paused in mid-finger-roll. "You didn't hear this from me, but Hugh Blaines' bio and NCIC record were faxed directly to the meeting room. Wouldn't surprise me if the commissioners took one look at the guy's credentials and hired him before the day is out."

"That begs the question."

"What question?" The officer started rolling inky fingers again.

"Why would a guy like that work in a place like this unless he had some deep dark secret he's trying to hide?"

Victoria arched a brow. "Everyone has secrets. Some of them are worse than others. Anyway, he's a very experienced detective."

Of course that begged another question: "Is he being offered a job to work under Jim, or was the notorious Taos Telegraph right again? Is Jim Dunn about to be fired? Are all those accusations about his conduct true? Is Jim about to go down?"

"When I finish printing you, I'll escort you to a holding cell." Ignoring all Carmen's questions Deputy Smith pressed the last digit on the paper and rolled it slightly.

"When do I get my phone call?" Carmen had done the research; she knew the drill. She had one call. If she followed the television scenario, she would use it to find a lantern-jawed bail bondsman to spring her before the ten o'clock news. That was how it always played out on the channel three movie of the week and in all the cozy mysteries she read. Of course in books the suspect usually jumped bail, got chased by tattooed bounty hunters named after jungle cats, then ended up doing hard time.

Carmen's knees turned to rubber.

Victoria glanced up. "Hey, stay with me. We're nearly done, and this concrete will leave a mark if you keel over. Besides, I don't think you'll have time to make your call. Jim was fuming when he got off the phone with your father. I think your dad is probably already out front posting your bail, but you didn't hear that from me—or anything else we talked about, got it?"

"My lips are sealed." Carmen Sofia heaved a sigh of relief to know her dad was on the way. Right along with his flawed, flirty, Italian genes, Tony Pollini had also inherited protective, heroic, wonderful fatherly genes.

"Thanks, Deputy Smith."

"No problem. I think the bail will be high, considering the charges." Victoria finished the last print and handed Carmen a paper towel. It looked inadequate to absorb the amount of dark ink clinging to her fingertips.

"What are the charges?" Carmen wiped her inky thumb with the paper towel.

"Didn't Jim tell you? You're being booked on suspicion of premeditated murder."

CHAPTER THREE

"Baby-girl, what the hell happened?" Tony maneuvered his big, ecologically unfriendly SUV through the thick accumulation of snow in the parking lot of the police station.

"The good news is I got the whole process right in *Recipe for Revenge*. The bad news is that Jim put cuffs on me and tossed me in his squad car as if I were a hardened criminal. Thank goodness Millie came down and took charge of Tyson, or he probably would've had animal control come pick him up and lock him in the slammer, too. Guilt by association, you know. The law is mean and unforgiving in Taos County, Pop."

"The bastard. Jim Dunn needs to be given an attitude adjustment. The sawed-off fart should've been drummed out of his job a long time ago. But what I meant was what the hell happened with the R.E.D. driver? Was he really dead at your front door?"

"Yep. Dead as a doornail." She twittered a nervous laugh. "It was pretty gross, Pop."

"I'm getting you a lawyer."

Carmen Sofia Alvarez-Pollini's head swiveled around. She stared at her father. He had a great Italian face, generous nose, suave chin and a big heart. But he tended to make snap decisions.

"Whoa, Pop. I had nothing to do with his death. He probably had a heart attack and fell down. Jim will find that out and I'll be in the clear. I have a deadline, a conference and an important

32

meeting with my agent. We don't need to waste time or money I can't afford on an attorney."

Tony paused a second too long before he said, "Of course not, baby-girl. If you can't afford it, then you can't afford it."

"Pop, don't you do anything, you hear me? I mean, anybody who knows me at all knows I'm not the murdering type. I kill people in print, not actual fact. I don't want you taking off like a loaded cannon and I don't want you spending money on my behalf." Carmen slouched in the big seat, staring blindly out the dark tinted windows.

"You take all the fun out of being a father, Carmen. I can afford to spoil you. Why don't you let me?"

"I'm an adult, and I can stand on my own two feet. Thank you, but I don't need your help. I am innocent."

"Sure, yeah, of course you are, but everyone knows what a temper you have. Everybody in town remembers what happened during the incident. . . ." Tony let his words trail off. Then he cleared his throat and said, "Everybody in town knows you've been complaining about the way Jake has been banging up all your manuscripts. I'm worried, Carmen. I think you need a lawyer . . . some big-name attorney."

"Gee, won't anybody in town ever let me forget what happened? Besides, I think lawyering-up would only make me look guilty."

"Lawyering-up?"

"Hey, when you've been in the joint, you learn to talk the talk." Carmen felt gritty and hardened, in a county-lockup sort of way.

"I called your mother."

"Drive another nail in my coffin, why don't you? If Mom starts meddling, I *will* be behind bars. You know she goes over the top."

Carmen's head pounded when she thought of her mother.

Maria Alvarez—she had dropped the name Pollini when she divorced Tony—couldn't even speak to her ex without fur flying. Not that Carmen blamed her mother. Tony had a roving eye and bad judgment when it came to willing women. He was on his third wife—Tiffany. Middle initial Gold-Digger—a year younger than Carmen. Maria was volatile and unforgiving. Tony had hurt and humiliated her with his betrayal, and the divorce had been a hot topic on the Taos Telegraph for many months. The only thing that got her more irate and irrational than the subject of her ex-husband was anybody threatening her only child.

As a singlet, Carmen fought a continuing and often losing battle to be left out of her hot-blooded parents' drama.

"So, tell me what Mom thinks and how much you two fought over your differing opinions."

Tony grinned. "She thinks you should have some female attorney she knows—one who stays at La Señora and is known for her hard stand on women's rights. She defended two brothers in California who murdered their parents. It was all over CNN."

"Good character recommendation. And how long did you two fight?"

"We didn't fight at all," Tony said with a somewhat sheepish tone.

"Really?" Carmen perked up. Maybe things were looking up.

"Well . . . we didn't have time to argue. She hung up on me."

"I should've known."

A short while later, while the SUV was purring its way toward Carmen's house, Tony got a call from Tiffany. After a monosyllabic conversation he snapped his cell shut, made his apologies, dropped Carmen off outside Millie's fence and drove away. Within moments Millie's loud-mouthed blue heeler, Annie, had

34

alerted everyone within a quarter mile that there was a Barbarian at the gate.

Farther up the lane, Carmen saw the door of Millie's ranch house open. Tyson flew out, slinging rooster tails of fresh snow behind him as he pounded down the drive toward the locked gate and his jailbird master.

"How you doin'?" Millie yelled and waved, trailing behind the boxer in her knee-high vintage cowboy boots. She plowed through the snow like a woman half her age.

"I'll live. Thanks for watching Tyson."

As soon as Millie unlocked the gate, Tyson hit Carmen's thighs with his snow-crusted paws, slathering her with boxer drool and affection.

"No problem. Jim Dunn never did have a lick of sense, his eyes are too close together. I should be thankin' you for givin' me the chance to get his goat by takin' Tyson. You sure you're okay? I saw the ambulance loading up Jake's body—seeing your first dead body can be a real shock."

Carmen shuddered. So how many bodies did a person have to see before it was no longer shocking? And how many had Millie seen? Carmen wondered.

"It was kind of gory. Not like I have been portraying death in my novels, but I'll be fine." Carmen pulled her pea coat tighter around her body.

Millie studied Carmen's face for a moment and then she said, "Yes, I expect you will. Just remember, there are some people who need killin'. Leastwise that is what my daddy told me, and I never knew him to be wrong. Could be that Jake needed killin' and somebody knew it."

"Killed? But what makes you think he was murdered? He probably had a bad heart or clogged arteries or something. God knows, he shoveled in enough biscuits and gravy to feed a third-world nation. I'm sure that is what the autopsy will show."

Millie raised a brow. "Looked healthy as a bull to me this morning when he was yelling at you in town over his banged-up fender."

Carmen stabbed the burning piñon log, sparks exploding off the tip of the black iron poker in a glittering shower of gold and red. The gray, snow-laden clouds of day were vanishing into the black cloak of night. Tyson was stretched out on the wooly sheepskin rug near the hearth. He sighed and smacked his lips in canine splendor.

"Glad you are home, huh?" Carmen replaced the poker in the black wrought-iron rack. She flopped down in the soft leather chair and put her feet up on the matching hassock. "Me too."

She picked up her cup of hot tea and wrapped her fingers around the mug, absorbing its warmth. Try as she might, she couldn't get Millie's words out of her mind.

Some people need killing.

Millie was rough, tough and lived by the old-code-of-the-West, but her comments about dead bodies and Jake made Carmen wonder if there was more beneath that leathery skin than just a crusty widow-lady.

A thump outside brought Carmen's heart to her throat and Tyson scrambling to his feet. He growled and stared toward the darkening kitchen.

"It's probably just the wind. It is still storming, you know. Settle down or you'll have me jumping at every little creak and groan. It's been a bad day. Let's just kick back and chill."

Tyson gave her a boy-are-you-stupid look and padded into the kitchen, his nails clicking on the Saltillo tile with each jaunty step. She leaned back in the overstuffed club chair and closed her eyes. If she couldn't see him, she would be able to ignore his silent nagging.

A loud bump against the outside wall of the house brought her to her feet, slopping hot tea over her hands in the process. She set the tea aside and followed Tyson's path into the kitchen, flipping on every light she passed. She grabbed a paper towel and dried her damp hands.

Tyson growled, giving her another of his eloquent looks.

"Okay, okay, I'm going to check outside."

Tyson moved toward his doggie door, growling louder, the short bristles on his shoulders rising.

"I'm telling you there is nobody out there. It is just the storm. Now stop trying to scare me. I already said you could sleep on the foot of my bed, you don't have to sell me on how great a watchdog you have become."

Tyson growled again, then erupted into a rapid series of barks, all the while staring at the door.

"Okay, so maybe you did learn something from Annie. But I don't believe you heard anything. I'll prove it to you." Carmen opened a kitchen drawer and grabbed a heavy wooden rolling pin.

"Just in case." She raised the hefty utensil and took a step. She flipped on the back porch light and opened the door.

An icy gust of wintry air took her breath away. The snow had stopped, the clouds had blown away, and now the mercury was plunging. The porch light revealed a blanket of downy snow, soft mounds, changing her familiar patio into an abstract landscape of rounded edges.

Tyson growled louder and dashed outside into the snow. Carmen shivered and braced herself to step into the full brunt of the wind. Tyson barked again. He was just beyond the arc of light from the porch, in gray shadow.

She followed him. Then she realized he had his nose in tracks.

Fresh tracks.

Somebody else's tracks.

They were big. A man's footprint. The stride was long. So a big guy with long legs had been at her backdoor.

In just the last few minutes.

"I think we should we follow them."

Tyson gave her a look that would have withered a less secure woman, but to his credit he did stay at her side while she followed the line of prints—for a short distance, where the porch light still provided a weak bit of shimmering illumination.

She had the rolling pin raised and ready to strike.

Then she saw it.

Propped against the wall of her house was a package with a scarlet R.E.D. label attached to the brownish envelope.

"Now I know what Jake was doing here." Carmen Sofia told Tyson while she scooped up the package. Jake may have died making his final delivery, but those were not his fresh tracks in the snow.

An icy chill danced up her back, spurring speed. She slooshed toward the comforting glow of the porch light, Tyson at her heels. The wind started to rise, brooming snow around her feet, swirling around the light giving everything an air-brushed effect.

She had just reached the door when she heard a sound. Out of nowhere a hand grabbed her shoulder. She screamed into the howling wind.

CHAPTER FOUR

Chill's cop-radar was on full alert. Something was just not right in this little backwater town. First he had received the call out of the blue from the Taos county commissioners' secretary asking him to meet them for coffee to discuss the letter of interest he had sent them. Trouble was, he hadn't sent them any damned letter of interest or anything else. And just how had they gotten his cell phone number?

After he had spoken to the men, he had gone to take a look at their setup, where he had watched while a woman was booked for murder before the autopsy on the victim was even started. Kind of an ass-backward way to investigate as far as he was concerned. There were four kinds of death and homicide was only one of them.

Odd didn't begin to cover it.

"They sure do things differently here in Taos County," he mused aloud. "Letters of interest write themselves, and the sheriff has psychic abilities about the C.O.D."

Chill got in his Explorer, started the engine, unwrapped another piece of gum, popped it in his mouth and headed back to the B&B he had checked into.

"If I had one ounce of sense, I would've packed my bag and headed down the road." But he hadn't, instead he had paid a full month in advance.

The charm of the B&B, and the bizarre offer from the county commissioners, had got him curious. He didn't have any schedule to keep or time clock to punch. He was indulging himself and allowing the little mystery to pull him in, because the worst possible thing had happened: Chill's curiosity was piqued.

It had been the single biggest reason he had been a good cop. He just couldn't walk away from an unsolved case.

But this wasn't his case.

"Not yet anyway," he murmured when he eased out onto the road. All he had to do was to accept the job offer. Then he could satisfy his curiosity and start replenishing his bank account at the same time.

Why not? Why not snuggle into this scenic patch of heaven and spend the winter? When spring came, he could pull up stakes and continue his meandering journey east.

He turned on the wipers to clear away the droplets of moisture that beaded when he turned on the defroster. Then he let his mind take over while he drove on autopilot.

It was late. Chill hadn't eaten since breakfast. He was ready for a cold beer. He couldn't stomach hard liquor—never could—but he did like a cold beer now and again. He thought he'd try the restaurant that shared the courtyard with the B&B where he was staying.

The Blue Coyote sported a sculpture by Luis Jimenez. Chill had the pleasure of seeing his stuff at a show in San Diego a few years ago. The artist had a free-wheeling style: big, bold sculptures of caballeros, coyotes, all done up in airplane paint. They were stout, impressive and invited kids and adults to touch them.

"A cold bottle of Dos and a plate of hot red chili enchiladas. Yep, that's the ticket." Chill was looking forward to discovering all of Taos County's secrets.

Carmen swung the rolling pin in an arc. She intended to brain her assailant but she missed, spinning around, and staggering with the momentum of her swing.

"Easy there!" Millie let go of Carmen's shoulder and hopped backward, avoiding Carmen's weapon. The old girl was agile as a lynx. "You about took my head off. Are you all right?"

"You scared me to death. Millie, what are you doing in my backyard?"

"I . . . uh, I thought I saw someone." Millie glanced around. Only then did Carmen realize Millie was carrying her shotgun.

"You saw someone? From your house?" Carmen wasn't sure she could even see Millie's gate from here. The old girl must have eyes like a red-tailed hawk.

"You are nervous as a cat. Good thing for me you haven't got good aim. What have you got there?"

Carmen followed the line of Millie's gaze to her hand. She had forgotten all about the parcel. She turned it over and read the label. "It appears to be Jake's last delivery. Now I know what he was doing at my house. Ironic isn't it? This one is not decorated with tire marks."

She turned it over in her hand, inspecting every inch of it. The package was clean and uncreased. Her address was printed in neat block letters in black marker on what had started life as a brown grocery bag.

"Hmm, someone who prefers paper instead of plastic. I'm surprised it is not even wet."

She turned the package over and checked it twice. There was no return address, only the shipping label from R.E.D.

Just like all the others she had been receiving.

A cold finger traced a line up her spine.

"Millie, I don't want to be rude, but I'm freezing out here. I need to get back inside."

Millie regarded her from old, suspicious eyes, but she nodded and said, "Sure. I wouldn't want you to catch your death."

"Thanks for coming over."

"Any time." The old woman disappeared into the frigid night. Carmen hurried inside and shot the dead bolt. But even with the solid wood door barred and locked, she didn't feel safe. The package in her hand gave off a palpable aura of menace.

"Another one, Tyson." She ripped the paper off with shaking hands. Inside was a foil box from an upscale Albuquerque store, Sinfully Sweet. Scented pink tissue paper covered a skimpy, lace-covered confection of sensuous black satin. An embossed card rested at the bottom of the box. Carmen Sofia read the message.

From your secret admirer.

"This one would give Victoria's Secret a run."

Smashing the lid back on the box she went into the hallway and opened the closet door. A stack of similar boxes covered the floor. She added the box to the hip-high stack.

"You know, Tyson, this admirer of mine is generous as well as creepy."

The gifts were coming more often now—more than two a week. At first she hadn't paid much attention. Fans would occasionally write a letter, some of appreciation, some the inevitable query about how they could become published. It hadn't been a big deal—until now. Carmen Sofia hadn't made any effort to keep her address private. It was no secret in Santa Fe, Taos or Red River that she was a novelist. Anybody could find out where she lived with little effort. Especially with the Internet, all anyone had to do was to punch in a zip code and phone number, and they could get a map to their favorite actor or author's home.

Nobody had ever paid much attention to a homegrown writer, not when there were Hollywood producers and stars aplenty.

Val, Julia, Sam and Katharine, even several A-list movie

producers were sprinkled between Red River and Albuquerque; a mid-list writer was dull fare on the menu of exotic celebrity. Even Jessica had done a movie here before she started spending so much time watching football.

Carmen was practically anonymous—until about six months ago when she had started receiving gifts, all sent by someone who signed the cards as her secret admirer. Cards and little bits of jewelry had come first—silver charms intended to go on a bracelet. Then it was a frilly robe, chaste, almost prim. But little by little the gifts had become more intimate—suggestive, risqué; the kind of gifts a lover might choose to give his partner. That was when she realized she had a bone fide stalker.

"This is not funny anymore, Tyson. I should report it, but Sheriff Jim Dunn would twist it around and suggest something kinky was going with Jake. Even though I'm sure his death was an accident. I better keep my mouth shut, at least until this blows over." She shut the closet door, wishing she could just as easily shut the door in her mind and block out the stack of gift boxes.

Tyson and Carmen both jumped when the phone rang. Her heart was pounding in her chest when she reached for the receiver.

"Hello?"

"*Chiquita?* Are you all right?" Carmen strained to hear her mother's voice over the clanging of pots and pans in the background.

"I was going to come to the jail, but your father said there was no need of us both. He says it is all a mistake. Is that true, or did he lie to me?"

"Yes, Mom, it is true. This is all a big misunderstanding. The autopsy will clear it all up. What's up?"

"Your father." Maria suddenly spat a string of rapid-fire Spanglish. Carmen could almost smell the onions, garlic and chili through the phone lines. "He wants you to hire some good-ol'-boy attorney but I don't agree."

Carmen's temples began to ache, a steady pain in tempo with her heartbeat. It was always "your father" and "your mother." The divorce had taken away their given names. She only half-listened while Maria listed the reasons Carmen needed a female advocate.

She knew her parents were truly concerned, but she was metaphorically the bone between two dogs. Once upon a time the air had thrummed with their passion and love; now it vibrated with animosity.

"So, do you agree?" Maria's sharp question yanked Carmen's attention back to the moment.

"What?"

"I said, I have set up a telephone appointment for you. She will call you on your cell phone tomorrow. *Chica,* this is a smart woman. She stays here at La Señora when she is in town."

La Señora del Destino had been the Alvarez family *hacienda* for many, many generations. Now it was converted to a B&B, the top floor Maria's living quarters, the wing beyond the open patio housing Maria's restaurant, the Blue Coyote. When Maria and Tony's marriage had dissolved like sugar in the rain, Maria had sold their big rambling house out of town and moved into one of the two dozen bedrooms in La Señora. Tony had moved on to another woman and a condo.

La Señora del Destino could accommodate more than thirty guests, and the Blue Coyote could feed hundreds, which Maria did daily. Carmen was well aware that her mother had used work to see her through the heartbreak, but along the way her menu became the favorite for those seeking authentic New Mexican cuisine. Alvarez family recipes were now a staple for anyone wanting a true taste of the southwest.

"Carmen, I told her to call you before the conference." Maria's voice was soft but firm. Carmen ignored her pounding temples and tried to focus on the topic at hand.

The conference. Albuquerque. Tomorrow.

Carmen groaned.

"With all that is going on, I forgot about the conference. I'm not even finished with my talk."

"You'll make the time to speak with her, yes?"

"Yes, I'll talk to her—but that's all. I don't need a lawyer. This is some kind of stupid mistake. Jake had a heart attack or a stroke. He was a smoker, you know. I don't need an attorney." She looked at the stack of gifts in the closet.

"What do you need, *Chica?*"

Carmen knew she was being a wimp, but the sincerity in her mother's voice had gone straight to her heart.

"Have you got an empty room?"

"For you?"

"Yes. I feel . . . I don't know. Sort of homesick." It was a lie, but Carmen didn't intend to tell Maria about the gifts or her stalker—not yet anyway.

"*Chica,* La Señora del Destino is your home—it will always be home to any Alvarez. I will have room number three ready and a nice meal waiting for you."

"Thanks, Mom."

"*Por nada, Chiquita.*"

Within five minutes, Carmen had Tyson, her laptop and a too-full suitcase stuffed into her backseat. Feeling like someone was watching her every move, she backed out of her drive and shoved down the accelerator. Her little car fish-tailed, and she fought the steering wheel in the fresh powder all the way to the highway.

Carmen's car bumped out onto the highway and she glanced down at the gas gauge. It was hovering dangerously near the red E. Wasn't this where she came in?

"Great, no gas, bounced checks and missing royalties. I'm screwed." She was so intent on her present pickle that she didn't see the other car. A blaring horn snapped her head around.

She caught a glimpse of a big SUV before it swerved into the other lane to keep from hitting her. It had been a close call, and although she hated to admit it, it was entirely her fault. Carmen took a deep breath and focused on the road. For the second time today she was headed toward a place she hoped would give her sanctuary. If she could just get to La Señora without having another fender bender, then she would consider herself to be blessed.

"What would be the chances I could be arrested twice in one day, eh Tyson?"

Inside the SUV Chill spewed a string of epithets. He had swerved just short of hitting the car as it whipped out onto the road.

It was dark, and it had only been a matter of seconds when the car was in his clear line of sight, but his years of training and experience had enabled him to recognize the car from his earlier near-miss in town today.

"Someone should lock that woman up." Chill dug out a new pack of gum and indulged in two pieces. He drove just under the speed limit, and traffic was light, probably due to the snow from earlier in the day, so he made good time, his SUV rolling in and out of the canyon smoothly. The moon was out and Chill was enchanted by the silver blue snow on either side of the ebony ribbon of highway. It was all backlit by a shimmering moon, highlighting the fresh, untouched powder, dotted by majestic pines and clumps of juniper.

"I could learn to like this place. In spite of its female drivers."

Chill flipped on the radio and hit seek. A Spanish station

came in loud and clear. He didn't understand the lyrics, but he didn't need to. The mellow guitar and soothing baritone voice washed over his edgy nerves. This definitely was the land of enchantment—the slogan he saw on every license plate. The pace of life was already bewitching him; he could feel his blood pressure going down with each mile he drove.

"Yep, this is a nice, sleepy little town where the only bodies are those that expire from natural causes. I'm going to like spending the winter here."

Carmen had driven like a madwoman, but it hadn't done her much good because she had ended up behind a camper with out-of-state plates. Floridians weren't used to snow and ice. The maddeningly slow pace had hitched up her anxiety level. When she finally made the turn and saw the weathered wooden La Señora del Destino sign, she was near tears.

It had been too much. The accident, Jake, the package with another gift from her so-called secret admirer. Her nerves were pulled so taut she was afraid they would snap like a worn rubber band.

Of course it was Murphy's Law that the parking lot at the B&B was packed and she was forced to circle the block once to find a space near the entrance to the Blue Coyote. Carmen inched her car into a small space beside the trash Dumpster, barely leaving her enough room to wedge her door open.

Tyson squeezed out the tiny opening and gave her a look that would peel paint.

"Don't start, just don't start. Give me a break and I'll find you some goodies in Señora's kitchen, okay?"

Carmen clutched the handle of her suitcase and snagged the strap on her laptop, while praying she didn't slip on the ice. Her baggage was heavier than she thought, and she was winded by the time she used the employees' entrance to the Blue Coyote.

The bright, modern kitchen was the usual mixture of chaos and order, the smell of chili, garlic and tradition spicing the air. She swallowed a deep breath, savoring the feel of it on her tongue.

This was home—comfort food—sanctuary and acceptance, all rolled into one.

Hefting her burdens, Carmen moved through the kitchen toward the spacious open patio that connected the La Señora del Destino and the restaurant. Hand-cut stone pavers covered the wide expanse. The plastered adobe walls were decorated with hand-painted tiles in scenes from the Spanish Colonial era. A tall, ornate central fountain, created out of one single pillar of hewn stone, reached toward the night sky. For many generations, Carmen's mother's family had spent their evenings under the stars here, sipping wine, discussing the events of their day. Now it was Maria's private domain, a shortcut between the two businesses, a place where only family trod between the buildings.

Carmen loved the patio. In the hottest days of summer when the earth was dry and parched, it provided a cool environment. Now, though everything was blanketed by snow, she only had to close her eyes to picture it: the trumpet vines and honeysuckles in bloom, hummingbirds—which her Spanish ancestors called flying jewels—flitting from bush to bush, taking turns sucking nectar from the heavy flowers while the fountain burbled a sweet song.

Tyson barked. The summery scene her memory had conjured was shattered. Carmen had been standing unaware of the biting cold, gazing with unseeing eyes at the fountain that looked like a frosted cake.

"Okay, okay. I know it's cold. . . . I was just—I had a moment." She shifted her laptop to the other arm to take the strain off her shoulder before she hurried across the patio to the entrance leading to the B&B section of La Señora del Destino. The big carved door had swelled a bit and it was hard to open, but she managed to turn the knob, and using her butt to bump against it, she got it unstuck.

Tyson slipped past her and headed straight across the lobby to bound up the steep, winding stairs. She backed through the door, yanked it shut and lugged her stuff to the second floor.

Room number three was unlocked, the small wrought-iron lamp beside the tall old bed turned on. Light glowed on the polished furniture, the wood smooth and dark with age and the touch of Alvarez hands. Carmen inhaled the scent of burning pine logs wafting up from the fireplace in the lobby.

"No place like home." Carmen flopped her burdens on the bed. She rotated her neck and shrugged her shoulders to remove the fatigue and tension of the day.

The suitcase practically exploded when Carmen flipped the latches. She shook everything out, found hangers for her things, inhaling the attar of the old cedar-lined closet. She kicked off her boots, wiggling her sock-covered toes into the thick carpet.

"Heaven."

She opened her laptop and powered it up. Cross-legged on the century-old bed, she scrolled through her E-mail. There were hundreds of messages, mostly ads, and announcements from a few writers' groups she kept up with via the Web. One message was a congratulatory one-liner from her publisher.

"Wow, *A Hot Brand of Love* has made the best-seller's list of both big chains, Tyson." Her heart did a little tumble of satisfaction when she read the E-mail again aloud.

Tyson was curled up beside her and did not deign to recognize the significance of his master's success.

"It would be nice if you got a little excited for me, bub."

He farted.

"Swell. Keep that up and it is the floor for you."

Carmen saw another E-mail from her publisher. They were sending a model to Albuquerque; she was expected to pick him up in the morning before the conference.

"Damn, damn, damn." It was too late for her to get out of it. She had no choice; she would have to do it. That meant leaving nearly an hour and a half earlier than she'd planned to make the drive and meet the plane.

The niggling worry about her lack of money returned with the force of a slap to the head. At the moment she didn't have enough cash for a full tank of gas. Her credit cards were not in bad shape, but she didn't have the money to make the minimum payments this month. With no end to her present situation in sight, she wasn't going to charge any more.

Her temples started to pound again. She bit down on her lip and continued to scan, read and delete the spam.

The next E-mail caught her attention like a fishhook to the eye.

"You bitch. Plagiarism gets little girls hurt. Did you judge a contest and think my story was too good to pass up? Or did your agent suggest it? Either way, you are a thief, little girl. You will make a public statement within 24 hours, tell the world you stole my plot, my writing and my book. If you don't, there will be consequences—people will get hurt, especially you."

CHAPTER FIVE

Carmen was stunned. She read the E-mail message three more times. If the word *plagiarism* didn't get the attention of an author, nothing would.

The E-mail address was not familiar. Carmen's finger hovered over the delete key, then moved to the reply key.

She could fire off a response and set this nut-case straight. She had never stolen an idea or a plot.

"No. If I answer, it will open up a dialogue with a crazy person. Who do they think they are, Tyson? I work hard for my plots, and I would never take a story idea from my agent . . . sheesh."

Carmen flopped back on the thick, down pillow and stared at the ceiling. Her life seemed to be spiraling out of control. She did a slow burn.

"I don't want to keep this garbage on my laptop." But she didn't feel right about deleting it either. If she only had a printer.

"Mom has one." She scooted off the bed and ran to her purse. Beneath her wallet, next to her lipstick and keys, she located the extra flash drive she carried. Blowing the lint off it, she shoved it in a UBC port and saved the E-mail. Then she pulled it out and with the laptop humming, Tyson snoring, she jumped up and padded down the carpeted stairs toward Maria's office next to the dining room. The trip was longer than the patio shortcut between the kitchen and the back of the lobby but she was still in her socks.

"Maybe nobody will notice."

The restaurant was in full dinner-rush mode. Dim lighting, burning candles and soft music provided atmosphere. Waiters in crisp white shirts and black trousers glided efficiently from one table to the next, serving Maria's classic dishes. Carmen noticed her special table near the office was set up for one diner, a candle flickering inside a red glass orb.

Maria had thought of everything. The room, Carmen's usual table—probably even her favorite drink and meal were waiting for her.

Hunger grabbed her unaware. She hadn't eaten all day, and her brain was sending urgent messages. She ignored the hollow emptiness in her belly and opened the door to her mother's office. It took only moments to pop the drive into her mother's running computer and print off a copy of the threatening E-mail.

When she was finished, she read the message again, feeling weak. Carmen sagged into the office chair. She had been going all day on adrenaline and aggravation. Now she was crashing, her body limp with fatigue and lack of food. Her vision was blurry, and she felt lightheaded.

"Food and a tall blended margarita are in high demand." Carmen ran her fingers through her tousled hair, plucked a tissue from the holder on Maria's desk to wipe her face. She had removed the last traces of makeup and probably looked a little rough around the edges.

"Good enough in dim lighting." She tossed the tissue, grabbed her printout and headed for the dining room.

Chill's room in the B&B was great. It was warm, inviting and full of venerable, masculine furniture. He hated all that spindly artsy stuff that made a guy wonder if it would hold his two-hundred-plus bulk. Yep, he liked this place, the price, the food, the people—except for a few oddball kamikaze drivers. He was content.

Content enough to accept the job offer.

He had been mulling it over and somewhere between the police station and La Señora del Destino, he had come to a decision.

He was going to hang his clothes in the closet and become the sheriff of Taos County. At least temporarily. Truth was, he was just passing through, but a winter on the job in a small town would be quiet and cushy.

Chill pulled the business card out of his pocket and flipped it over. Several of the county commissioners had written their first names and phone numbers on the backside. He dialed the first one.

It was a quick conversation. He accepted if they could come to terms. They made a monetary offer, he countered, they negotiated, and within five minutes it was a done deal. The contract, with a termination clause that was comfortable, would be delivered for his signature tomorrow.

"Time for a congratulatory chow-down, Sheriff Blaines," he told his reflection in the beveled mirror.

Chill changed into comfortable jeans—the kind that let a guy eat his fill—and a mock turtleneck that was faded and soft. Then he headed down the stairs, his steps light and bouncy, at least he felt light and bouncy, and even if it was a girly-man thought, he kind of enjoyed the sensation.

After all, he told himself, he was secure enough in his masculinity to be in touch with his feminine side. Eloy would surely burst an O-ring laughing if he heard Chill say it, but then again, Eloy was still giving himself an ulcer fighting crime in California.

Chill paused at the bottom of the stairs and the spacious lobby area. A fire burned in the stone hearth, a flat-screen television was on, the volume low, inviting anyone who passed to flop down on the comfortable sofa and watch a while.

His gut growled and he focused on the smell of food somewhere beyond. A few strides brought him to the arched doorway of the dining area.

A single table was already set up with a burning candle—a little hokey, but kind of nice—water and silver.

"They must be expecting me."

When he checked in, the girl at the desk assured him he would fall in love at first bite. The food at La Señora del Destino, she said, was beyond description. Tonight he was going to have the biggest combination plate they offered. He would judge for himself if the food was great.

And tomorrow he would start a physical regimen. Chill wasn't one of those cops who let themselves go flabby, potbellied and out of shape. He was going to set an example while he was here. He would be a trim, fit sheriff.

His hand was on the dining chair when he felt a soft bump, the kind any heterosexual male knew was delivered by the curves of a woman. He whirled around, but the smile he had ready to use on the female in question dried up on his face.

Looking up at him with wide eyes was the woman he had watched getting fingerprinted. She must have recognized him, too, because all the color leached from her face leaving her sort of sickly gray.

"You!" she breathed.

"Uh-huh, me," Chill agreed.

"Why are you here?"

"I'm living here—in La Señora. I was told Maria makes the best food in town."

"That's true. My mother is a great cook."

"Maria is your mother?" Chill noticed her color was getting worse. She had that fuzzy, unfocused look in her eye, and she looked so familiar, not just from the police station, but somewhere else.

About that time he realized she was the kamikaze driver, her dark eyes rolled up into the top of her head and she went limp. He grabbed her around the ribs, pulled her boneless-rag-doll body to his while the paper in her hand drifted to the floor.

"*Madre de Dios!* You fiend! What have you done to my daughter?"

CHAPTER SIX

Chill held the unconscious woman in his arms while the entire atmosphere of the restaurant shifted around him. The soothing ambiance had evaporated. Now waiters, eyes dark with indignant rage, left their customers, and Maria, reputed sorceress-of-chili, flew toward him with a sharp bit of cutlery gleaming in her hand. She was speaking Spanish, which he didn't understand, but the snapping eyes and tone told him everything he needed to know.

"Carmen! *Dios! W*hat have you done to my daughter? Carmen!"

Chill let two of the waiters take the light burden from his hands and he moved half a step back, the distance he calculated was out of slashing range.

He watched while the men patted' her hand and dabbed her face with a dampened cloth napkin.

"Carmen?" Maria touched her cheek, murmured soft words in Spanish. Just like in the movies, the fallen woman's eyes fluttered open. Candlelight spilled over her face.

They were pretty eyes, deep chocolate, full of intelligence even while she was fighting off the lethargy of having been out cold. Long, feathery lashes gave her an innocent yet exotic expression.

Chill looked from mother to daughter and back again. There was a strong resemblance between the two women, even if Maria didn't really look old enough to have a grown daughter. He should've known immediately. He was getting soft, in both body and mind. It was a good thing he was going back to work.

He studied the women, putting his flabby brain to work. They both had smooth olive skin, sleek ebony hair and high rounded cheekbones.

Pretty women.

Angry women.

Chill realized with a jolt that everyone in the restaurant was staring at him, looking at him as if he had sprouted horns.

"What did you do to make her—" Maria began.

"Now wait a min—" Chill held up his hands and took another half step back. It was a very, very long knife.

"Mom, it wasn't his fault. I haven't eaten all day. In fact, I think I skipped dinner last night. I was feeling lightheaded. I think I just fainted from hunger. I'm okay."

"Carmen, I own a restaurant. My own daughter is fainting because she is hungry? *Dios.*" Maria stood up, mumbling in Spanish while the waiters helped Carmen.

Chill wondered how many of the penguin-wannabes had crushes on Maria or Carmen, or both. Neither smooth feminine hand sported a wedding ring.

Carmen was dusting at her trousers when Chill noticed the paper. He bent down to retrieve it, his eyes focusing on several words. Maybe his brain hadn't turned to mush after all, because without intending to, he found himself scanning it, noting it was sent yesterday.

"That is mine." Carmen snatched the paper from his hand.

"Someone sounds real unhappy with you." Chill was pleased to realize he sounded like a cop.

"Lots of people have been unhappy with me today, or haven't you heard? I have been in a wreck, gotten arrested and fainted in public. It would seem no public humiliation is to be unobserved."

He resisted the urge to smile—but just barely. She had a mouth on her. He liked spunky women. "Yeah, I saw you earlier today—you kind of had your hands occupied at the time."

Her eyes narrowed and her pallor was fading. "Ha, ha. Is your intelligence as sharp as your wit? And since we are on the subject, what were you doing in the police station—fines, outstanding warrants, getting bailed out for reckless driving?" Her color was coming back.

"No, not really, but since you bring it up, I'd recommend you take a few defensive driving lessons. That stunt you pulled on the highway today was dangerous."

She glared at him, took a breath as if she was about to speak, but shook her head and remained silent.

One by one the waiters had gone back to serving, and the guests were settled. Maria had graciously given them all a free drink. Business as usual. Chill started toward the table with the solitary setup when he and Carmen collided once again.

"Excuse me." She lifted a brow, the perfect picture of haughty righteousness.

"No need to apologize."

"I wasn't apologizing. I was trying to sit down at this table so I can eat."

"This table?"

"Yes, this table. This table set for one."

They were practically snarling at each other when a disembodied male voice called out from the kitchen.

"Carmen, someone is on the phone for you."

Carmen gave him another menacing glare—well, about as menacing as a Yorkie snarling at a Doberman would be, then she went to the phone. He watched her, ignoring the dark looks from the wait staff. She went pale again, curling the telephone cord nervously around her fingers.

For a moment her knees seemed rubbery, and Chill found

himself moving toward her, expecting her to faint again. His newly roused cop-radar jangled a million volts a second the closer he got. Something was definitely out of whack with this woman.

First she was arrested for murder when the dead body on her step could have died from a dozen natural causes, then the E-mail she didn't want him to see, and now she looked as if she were staring down the sights of a hunting rifle.

Maybe this sleepy little county had more going on than he first thought.

"Carmen, you sit and eat." Maria forced her into a dining chair that had been brought into the kitchen, ending the boundary dispute over the back table. Right there on the counter Maria put a large plate of red chili enchiladas, topped with melted longhorn cheese and one egg, over easy. A wicker basket full of hot sopaipillas and a jar of honey waited nearby.

It was Carmen's favorite meal and she was starving, but her mind rebelled at the thought of food.

"I need a margarita. A big one." She felt as if she had aged ten years in this one day.

"Eat first. I will get you one."

Carmen nodded, too numb to do anything but obey. Maria's cooking was superb, but honestly, she could've been chewing leather for all she tasted. Still, she forked it into her mouth, chewed and swallowed.

By magic a blended margarita in a tall, frosty glass with a salted rim appeared. She tipped it up and drained it.

"Carmen!"

"Keep them coming, Mom."

Chill beckoned the waiter, who still eyed him as if he were a scorpion. "That was the best chili con carne I ever had. I wonder, could I give my thanks to the chef?"

"It is not permissible." The man's diction was perfect, his expression bland, but Chill perceived the unmistakable tone of menace.

"Aw, come on. I just want to pop to the back for a minute." Chill shoved his hand into his jeans and pulled out his battered money clip. "A tip to the chef would be all right, wouldn't it?"

The waiter paused for a moment and then, with narrowed eyes and a tight, artificial smile, he said, "This way."

Chill followed him, his ears straining to separate the sounds of voices from the customary clangs and bangs of a busy kitchen.

He was soon rewarded when he distinguished two soft female voices. Carmen and Maria were at the shiny stainless-steel counter near a door. It didn't bother him one bit to eavesdrop. He told himself it was strictly professional, that he needed the practice.

"I should be slamming down shots of Tequila, Mom. I can't believe this day. First I had to deal with Jake and the fender bender, then my insurance agent lorded it over me, taking pleasure in telling me I have to pay for everything, and my rates are going up to boot. Then Jake went and died on my property. Now Millie tells me someone has vandalized my house."

"*Que?*"

"That phone call a few minutes ago. It was Millie. She said she drove by just now and saw a shadow. She went back to check and all my windows are broken."

"I will call your father to go and see." Maria was already poking the buttons on the phone.

"There's more, Mom. I didn't want to tell you but—"

"Then maybe you better tell me." Chill's radar was never wrong. This woman was at the vortex of something, and he was going to find out what.

CHAPTER SEVEN

"Who are you? I mean, everywhere I go, you suddenly appear. The police station, my favorite table and now here in Maria's kitchen," Carmen snapped. Another margarita had appeared. She tipped up the glass and drained it, running her tongue around the salty rim when she was finished. "Don't tell me you are a stalker—you go completely against type."

"Thanks . . . I think. Actually, I'm Hugh Blaines, my friends call me Chill."

"Well, Mr. Blaines, you seem to be everywhere I go. Why is that?" Carmen tapped her empty glass, with her index finger. Maria frowned and hesitated only a moment before she picked it up.

"It's a done deal, so I guess I might as well tell you. I'm the new sheriff of Taos County."

Silence fell over the kitchen like the final curtain over a bad off-Broadway play.

"You are going to be taking Jim Dunn's job?"

"Not going to be. I already did. And I'm pleased to say I'm staying at La Senora del Destino." He held out his hand to shake with her after the introduction. She stared at his hand as if it was the slimy tentacle of a space alien.

"Mom, you rented a room to a cop?"

"He didn't tell me he was a cop, he told me he was retired." Maria's gaze flicked over his face, sizing him up . . . for the kill? "Not that it matters. I rent to anybody who is polite, and he was very polite. You said you were retired. Why did you lie?"

"I was retired at the time. I just agreed to take the job this evening, by phone."

"Odd time to conduct a job interview," Carmen quipped. "See, Mom, the Taos Telegraph was right about Jim Dunn's job. So if that is true, then I'll bet the accusations of sexual misconduct are also true. I can't wait to see the look on Tom Hardwick's face." Carmen took another swig of her fresh margarita. She realized somewhere in the farthest reaches of her brain that she was getting tipsy, but the lobe that was supposed to control her mouth had gone to take a little tequila-induced nap. "Yippee! The windbag Dunn is finally going to get his!"

"Carmen. . . ." Maria's voice held a warning.

"No, no, it's true, Mom. I told old Hardass that Jim Dunn, the pig, was getting fired. It's all because of that lawsuit—"

"Carmen, really, I think—"

"No, no, Mom, listen. It's about time that horrible man got what he deserves. Somebody should've killed him years ago."

"Just like somebody killed Jake?" Chill asked mildly.

Carmen was tipsy, not brain-dead. She blinked in surprise and clamped her lips shut.

"That's enough, Mr. Blaines. I do not allow interrogations in my kitchen. And Carmen, you're going to bed. Now, sir, if you will excuse us." Maria nodded at a man in a long white apron, and quicker than Chill could say chili-relleno with Spanish rice, Carmen was being bustled from the kitchen. He followed at a respectful distance, watching as the trio swayed up the stairs, somewhat bemused when they went to room number three.

"Right next to mine. How convenient."

Chill pulled the shearling coat tighter and hunkered over the steering wheel. It was cold, and now treacherous black ice was beginning to form, but this errand couldn't wait for daylight.

He strode into the police station and found one lone officer manning the radio and the desk. He looked sleepy and uninterested when he saw Chill.

"What's up?" The young cop asked.

"Your butt, if you have any sense." Chill was grumpy, and it translated into his words.

The officer did rise from his chair, now very interested.

"Look, I don't know—"

"Much. Yes, I can see that. Now here is the deal. I'm your new boss, and it would be in your best interest to impress me. So what you are going to do to impress me is get a cruiser warmed up and find me some sort of a badge. In the meantime I want to see all we've got on a woman named Carmen—"

"Carmen Pollini? You are investigating Carmen Pollini?" The officer was far less concerned with Chill being his new boss than he was with Carmen—Pollini? Her mother's last name was Alvarez. Oh well. Chill would sort that out later.

"Show me the file. Now."

Twenty minutes later Chill was in a warm Crown Vic that could use a good cleaning.

It was his firm opinion many things could be discerned about a man by the way he kept his police vehicle. Chill didn't think much of Jim Dunn. This car reeked of smoke and the backseat smelled suspiciously like old vomit. He didn't want to get involved in a broth of rumor and speculation about Dunn— with his history he was more than willing to give a guy the benefit of the doubt—but any man who let his vehicle get in this shape had issues.

Chill popped a piece of gum in his mouth and rolled down the window, mentally making a note to get the car detailed and deodorized.

While the rookie had been getting the car ready, Chill had done some quick research about Carmen, which had been easy when all he had to do was access her Web-site. Of course that was only her promotional view of herself, it could be all hype. For a little truth in advertising he tapped in her name and pulled up a previous arrest. He quickly skimmed her file.

"Okay, so little miss romance writer has a prior and a history of violence."

Already Carmen was heading south on his list.

"A writer with a smart mouth and an attitude problem. Fiction writers. Can't trust 'em an inch." He thought about the old charges and the fact that she had entered a guilty plea. She had a smart mouth and a short fuse . . . but she hadn't tried to bargain her way out of the charges.

"Interesting. But she's still a writer."

Although if he had to pick the romance writer out of a lineup, Carmen would not have been his first choice. Truth be told, Chill expected anyone who wrote romance novels to be a cross between Barbara Cartland and Barbara Walters—not the trim, feisty young woman in faded Levi's and socks who had fainted into his arms.

But a writer was a writer. People who lived in a fantasy world were on his black list, along with a few others like murderers and rapists.

Chill ground his teeth together and patted his shirt pocket, searching for a pack of gum. He had no use for any individual who made their living by making up lies and calling it fiction. He'd learned his lesson when his ex-partner had become a media darling. In fact, he hadn't read a book since he'd had his nose bloodied in print, even if it was called fiction, while rhyming his name and using real cases thinly veiled.

Chill missed reading, but he refused to admit it to anyone, even Eloy.

He jerked his thoughts from the past and focused on the present corpse. Going just on opportunity and prior behavior,

Carmen Pollini looked good for a murder—if indeed the coroner found it was murder. Hell, the guy could've just dropped dead, or maybe he had a history of health problems. Still, Chill wondered if maybe that was why Dunn jumped the gun and arrested her before he got an autopsy report.

"I would sure like to know the details of her prior."

The incident in her youth might have been the first of many meltdowns. Maybe her rage had been escalating and nobody had seen the signs. Or maybe she had been a model of control since that first brush with the law and something—something to do with the victim—tipped her over the edge.

"Like a fender bender . . . or threatening E-mails."

He pushed the accelerator down and made the turn off the highway. Chill drove up to Carmen's house, taking note of a dozen things all at once: there were no close neighbors, the house was dark, set well back from the road, and the country lane didn't boast a single lamp or light post to drive back the stygian night. There was a moon, but the cloud cover was thick.

He left his headlights on and got out, shining a flashlight at the ground in front of his feet, sweeping it back and forth, while the pristine snow crunched under his tread. If there had been previous tracks, the recent snowfall had wiped them out.

The driveway had a lot of visible tire tracks; no surprise there, since they were deeper and it took longer for the powder to eliminate them.

Chill walked toward the house, encountering the yellow police tape near the door. He swung the light beam across the front of the house, checking the windows. Nothing odd caught his eye. The drapes were open, the windows intact.

Not wanting to screw up a crime scene before he could see it in the daylight, he didn't want to use the front door. Instead he headed toward the back of the house. Then he wondered if the scene had even been processed. But surely Dunn wouldn't have arrested Carmen without having a CSU come in. However, Dunn was sloppy. If it had been Chill's call, he wouldn't have arrested Carmen, but he wouldn't have allowed her or anyone else back into the house, until the autopsy report was in.

In the glow of the light, Chill saw two sets of footprints. He wasn't a mountain-man-tracker, but they were fresh—made since the last smattering of snow had stopped. Thanks to the frigid temperature, the outlines had frozen hard. One set was big; one was smaller. They seemed to come and go from the same direction.

When Chill was at the backdoor, he found another set of small tracks and dog tracks coming out of the house and then returning.

"Carmen," he mused. "And a dog."

He aimed the light on the back of the house and into the fluffy drifts beside the wall. Something glittered like diamonds.

"Glass."

Every window had been shattered, pieces lying in the snow. The small glass in the kitchen door was gone.

"Not something that could be seen from the street."

Chill had listened to the recording of the incoming 911 call. The voice was muffled—the caller obviously didn't want to be identified and thought somebody could or would know them. "And they said they saw all the windows broken."

Then Carmen received a call from her neighbor, telling her that she saw the broken windows while driving by.

He was standing there thinking, processing the implications of that when he heard a car motor, a door close with a soft thud, then crunching footsteps coming closer.

He switched off the flashlight and waited.

The sound grew louder. On the backside of the house where the headlights couldn't reach it was dark; not the kind of dark you find in the city where lights blazed a block away or a shopping mall brightened the horizon, but dark like the inside of a black sack.

The steps were even, steady, measured. Chill took in a breath and stilled himself, the heavy police issue flashlight held chin high. As the steps drew in front of him, he snapped on the flashlight. He found a pair of dark eyes staring back.

"Don't move a hair. I'd hate to have to shoot you." Chill spoke softly, but his tone was rough as unpolished granite.

CHAPTER EIGHT

Carmen was trapped in a world of razor-sharp ice and blizzard-like snow. She tried to scream when she saw Jake's body frozen like a Popsicle, but no sound came out. She tried to run, but snow piled up around her feet and kept her frozen to the spot.

She ripped herself free of the nightmare and sat up in bed, groggy and thick-tongued. The clock beside the bed read eleven. She had only been out for a couple of hours, but she felt the lethargy of long, hard sleep weighing down her limbs.

"The margaritas. It was the margaritas."

Carmen was not a heavy drinker. She did enjoy a good Rita, but too much tequila left her feeling like she had been hiking across the desert with a mouthful of sand. Her head hurt, her stomach was queasy, and in a few hours she had to be in Albuquerque fit to give a talk to aspiring writers and her loyal readers.

"And I won't give them short-shrift."

She powered up the laptop and opened the file to her partially finished talk.

It took a few minutes to find the dangling thread of her thoughts, but soon she had her rhythm going. She typed fast, ignoring everything but the words telegraphing from her brain to her fingers. Carmen heaved a sigh of relief to know she was prepared.

"Finished." She would go down early tomorrow and use Maria's printer again.

Now that she was up and her synapses were firing, she wasn't a bit sleepy. Of course she could go find a snack in the kitchen; being the owner's daughter had its perks.

"But I can't go tramping around and disturb the other guests."

Her gaze fell on the page she had printed earlier. Anger, curiosity and dread mingled. Carmen stared at the laptop for a full minute before she finally opened her E-mail program.

Another message was there.

You bitch, you ripped off my plot. You won't get away with this. Make a public statement. Admit your guilt, or what I did today will be nothing compared to what will happen. I swear, you will suffer the consequences.

Carmen sat back and read the message again.

"Today." What had the author of this E-mail done? Had the writer broken her windows? Or had he or she done much worse?

"But why kill Jake?"

Unless she was being set up to take the fall for murder.

"No, I'm being paranoid."

She had heard enough horror stories at conferences and retreats to know an accusation of plagiarism wasn't an unusual event. There were a finite number of plots in the universe; it was inevitable that someone, somewhere would see similarities in books when no plagiarism had been committed. Carmen had always taken this possibility very seriously. In fact, she never critiqued other writers' work or judged contests for that very reason.

"I have been covering my butt, Tyson." He got off the foot of the bed and padded over to her chair, where he sat down. "And I still have some nut hounding me."

Her research was solid. Her record of when she started the first outline was dated. She could prove her plot and character ideas were original, as well as how long she had been writing on each project from start date to contract.

"It's nothing to worry about," she told herself while she zipped through the rest of the messages. When she was finished, she closed out the E-mail program.

"But I will print it out tomorrow before we leave."

She powered down and shut the laptop, and all the while she had the uneasy feeling she was being watched.

"Stay right where you are," Chill ordered.

"Who in the hell are you?"

"I'm the Taos County sheriff."

"No you're not." The man brought his hand up to shield his eyes from the light.

"Yes, I am. And I said don't move. Who are you? What are you doing here?"

"I'm Tony Pollini, and this is my daughter's place. Look, it is too damned cold to stand out here playing cops and robbers while you pretend to be Jim Dunn, though why any man in his right mind would want to do that is beyond me. I'm going inside and unless you intend to burn out my retinas with your light-saber, Han Solo, I doubt you're going to stop me."

Chill smiled in the dark. So this was Carmen's father. He could see why she had a mouth on her.

"Fine, but no sudden moves," Chill said. Then he heard the sound of a key fitting into the lock.

"Yeah, sure. Don't get all excited on me, Deputy Dawg, but I'm going to flip the lights on now."

Chill almost laughed out loud. This guy was a cocky male version of his feisty daughter. He hoped that Tony was a straight arrow, 'cause it would really pain him to have to arrest the guy.

Light flooded the room. Chill walked over broken glass that snapped and crunched under his feet. He stood in an ordinary-looking kitchen. Tony, a man of middle years with dark eyes and salt-and-pepper hair cut high and tight, was glaring at him.

"So what do you mean you are the sheriff of Taos?" Tony asked.

"I just took the job."

"About time. That scut Jim Dunn is a bad apple. Now, since you are the new law-dog in town, would you mind telling me what you are going to do about the vandalism to my daughter's house?" Tony held his arms out and turned in a half circle.

Glass littered the floor, the counters; even the lacy white tablecloth was covered with shards. Chill frowned. He had seen a lot of vandalism, windows broken by BBs, rocks, bricks and by snatch-and-run burglars, but this didn't fit any of those categories.

Tony left the room, his steps muffled by carpeting.

"Those sorry sons of. . . ." Tony's words trailed off. Chill followed the sound of his voice into a bedroom. It was a nice room, feminine but not frilly, painted a subtle, barely-there lavender. There the nice part ended.

All the windows were shattered, spots of damp marred the cream-colored satin bedspread.

Tony's face was flushed. Every few minutes he would utter an obscenity. Chill let him vent as he followed him through the house, his brain mentally cataloging everything he saw, touched and smelled.

"Damn," Chill said.

"What?" Tony frowned, waiting for Chill to answer.

"So far there hasn't been one pink boa in this house."

"Oh, so you are one of those, are you?" Tony's words had a sharp, flinty edge.

"One of those what?"

"One of those self-proclaimed critics who dogs on romance and romance writers. Listen, I'm damned proud of Carmen.

She is talented, smart and writes books that entertain and sell like gold futures, so don't say one deprecating word about her within my hearing."

"Easy. It was a joke."

"Really? Then you need to do some work on your funny bone."

Chill found a piece of gum and refrained from making any more comments. Damn. Tony was as touchy as Carmen. He hoped everyone in this county wasn't like them. Otherwise, he might be moving on before spring.

He shoved his annoyance aside and studied the house. It was a calm, peaceful house, full of wood and antiques. It had an almost masculine feel to the decoration. Photos of Carmen and a dog—no pink-skinned poodle but a short, mugged-faced tank-of-a-canine with a wide chest and intelligent eyes—were everywhere.

That explained the dog tracks in the snow.

Chill paused and took stock of all he knew so far.

Carmen was a romance writer—bad point. Dog-lover—good point, in her favor. Bad temper—scratch one up on the bad side. Arrested by the former sheriff as the number-one suspect in what might or might not be a suspicious death. Could be a very bad point.

Chill realized he didn't really have squat. Carmen was a victim of vandalism; that was a fact, but he didn't even know if Jake the R.E.D. driver had keeled over from too many pinto beans and tortillas or if he had been bitten by a rattlesnake.

Okay, so Chill had to admit, the only reason he was even looking at Carmen was because Jim Dunn had jumped the gun, and Chill had a personal case of heartburn with her from the get-go because of what she did for a living. Facing that truth made him feel small—so small, he was itchy and uncomfortable inside his own skin.

A cop—a good cop—didn't indulge in personal grudges. He had to be on-the-job tough and detached while he worked the case and sifted through the evidence.

Chill had always been a good cop. The niggling worry that he might've changed put a small round ball of acid in his gut. It sat there and burned.

He and Tony had finally come to the living room and a tidy book-filled study at the front of the house. Not a sliver of glass lay on the gleaming wood floors. The vandalism had not been a drive-by shooting, unless the perp was out riding his pony in Carmen's backyard. And, in his opinion the damage definitely couldn't have been seen by the neighbor driving by.

So what was the story? A 911 call that was suspicious, followed by the call from Carmen's neighbor. Had she made both calls? Why lie and say she had seen the damage from the road?

Questions were niggling at Chill's mind. He didn't like questions; he liked answers.

"For Pete's sake!" Tony exclaimed, drawing Chill's attention. Carmen's father stood at the front closet, with his hand gripping the doorknob. He stared, with his mouth hanging slack, at a pile of boxes, all open, flung carelessly across the floor, as if somebody had tossed the house. Mingled with the cardboard boxes and tissue paper were soft, transparent garments dripping in lace and satin, each one a different jewel hue.

"And just when I had forgotten all about pink boas. I must say your daughter has interesting taste in lingerie."

"Don't piss me off." Tony flashed him a look. "Besides, think of what you are saying. If this stuff was hers it would be in her bureau drawer, not in her front closet. Carmen has never worn one piece of this stuff, I can guarantee it." Tony shook his head as if Chill was dumber than dirt.

Chastised, Chill stepped a little closer and picked up one of the garments. All the stereotypes about romance writers came rushing back. This was some hot underwear—just the kind of stuff he expected would show up in a romance novel. Not that he would ever read one—he wasn't that in touch with his feminine side and Tony had a valid point.

He squatted down and picked up a black lace teddy. A white card fluttered to the floor.

From your secret admirer.

"What is that?" Tony didn't trust him; that was plain to see.

Chill picked the note up by an edge, trying not to contaminate the paper with his own prints. "It could be the answer about why she is keeping them here instead of her dresser drawers. Can I keep this?"

Tony frowned. Chill could see his mind turning on the question.

"Unless you think she has something to hide. Then, of course, you should remind me that this is not your house, and only Carmen can give permission," Chill goaded—it worked every time.

"Carmen hasn't got any secrets. Go ahead and keep it."

God bless the gullibility of a loving father. It made Chill's job so much easier.

Chill went into the kitchen, and after opening a few cabinets, found a plastic bag. He slipped the card inside and ran his thumb over the edge to seal it.

Tony might not think Carmen had any secrets, but Chill would have to disagree. He had just met the lady, but he was convinced she was one big question mark with a closet full of skeletons.

The day dawned cold and gray with an anvil of northern clouds threatening more snow. Carmen Sofia had dressed against the weather, wearing a thick, cream-colored woolen dress in a sleek princess cut, expensive, by an up-and-coming Santa Fe designer.

High-top boots with fluffy fake-fur tops kept her feet warm. Her hair had been swept back and twisted into what she hoped was a sophisticated chignon. She had walked Tyson early, taking him out into the patio for his business. Maria didn't mind him in the B&B, but Carmen tried very hard to keep his presence a secret from the other guests. Tyson either stayed in her room or in the patio, and since he had never been a barker, it worked out great.

So far, she was sure nobody even knew a dog was on the premises.

Carmen had a great Spanish omelet and enough coffee to make a corpse dance a highland fling. A quick call to Tony had taken care of her immediate cash-flow problems. She hated to ask but he was thrilled to float her a small loan and take care of Tyson while she was in Albuquerque.

Her dad might have been a less than exemplary husband, but he was a terrific father. She loaded Tyson into the backseat and got into her car and pulled out onto the highway. Only light slush remained on the roads, and they had been sanded.

Traffic was light, and within fifteen minutes she whipped into the parking lot of Tony's pseudo-southwest-designed condo and turned off the engine. She hopped out and opened the passenger door. Tyson leaped to the asphalt, which had been shoveled free of snow. He trotted around, sniffing the air, peeing on tires, ready for adventure.

"Come on. Tony is waiting."

Tyson obediently heeled while she jogged up the red brick steps. The door opened before she even knocked. Tony was dressed in a black knitted turtleneck that hugged his trim form, casual jeans and western ropers.

"Pop, you look great." She stood in the open doorway. Tyson scampered inside as if he had been invited. Carmen followed him and kissed her father on the cheek.

"So do you. Actually you look like a character out of *Dr. Zhivago.*" He paused for a moment with a crooked grin. "Tiffany would tell me that she never heard of Dr. Zhivago and lecture me about the generation gap."

"I'm definitely not my stepmother, even though we were in school at the same time. I read the book, Pop, and I saw the old movie. I take it as a compliment that you assume I know something about your generation's pop culture."

She glanced around the ultra-modern foyer. Something was different, but she couldn't put her finger on exactly what. Then she realized. The place was quiet, the usual cacophony of bad rap music was not shaking the picture windows or vibrating the expensive crystal in the bow-front cabinet.

"Where is Tiff?"

Tony looked at his wristwatch. "About Telluride, I would guess. She left me. Said she had fallen in love with her yoga instructor."

"Ouch."

Tony shrugged. "These things happen."

"You don't look too broke up about it."

"She was too young for me—which you already knew." His smile slipped. "But I didn't call you to cry on your shoulder. Come on. We don't want to be late." He tossed his keys up in the air and caught them.

"What do you mean, we?"

"I'm driving you to Albuquerque."

"Why?" Carmen's stomach knotted with tension. Whenever her father tried to be spontaneous, it usually turned into a disaster. His last unplanned act had been marrying Tiffany.

"Because I want to drive you to Albuquerque. I'm a better driver, and it looks like it is going to snow again. Now, come on. Let's get your bags and put them in the SUV."

She had to admit, traveling in that gas-guzzler was more

comfortable than her small compact, but still. . . . "Pop, I'm not going anywhere until you tell me what's up."

He picked up the TIVO control and punched a button. The big flat screen flickered to life. The handsome Albuquerque anchor appeared, straight white teeth flashing while he read copy.

"Taos police arrested popular New Mexican author Carmen Sofia Pollini in connection with the death of Jake Harris, a local R.E.D. delivery man."

A picture of Carmen, taken from her book's dust jacket, flashed on the screen.

"Further details at noon."

Tony flicked the TV off.

Carmen swallowed hard. She had wanted to see herself on TV, but she'd kind of hoped it would be with Matt Lauer talking about her book selling a million copies.

"I didn't expect it to make the news. I thought they would at least wait for the autopsy." Carmen's stomach lurched. "When they find out Jake died of a coronary, people will still remember my arrest."

"You really believe he had a heart attack?"

"That or a stroke or something. Who would kill Jake?" Carmen said, but the E-mail flashed through her mind. She shoved it aside. Nobody was trying to set her up for murder. She was just being paranoid.

"The damned media never waits for the facts. Chances are they won't think of trying to interview you at the conference in Albuquerque, but just in case, I want to be with you—to run interference if needed."

"What about Tyson?"

"He can hang out with me. We'll do some shopping at the local pet store. Christmas is getting close."

"Pop, it is not even Halloween yet."

"Yes, I know. The Christmas stuff is on the shelf right next to the Halloween kibble. Makes it easy for an old guy to shop when they put all the holidays in one place."

"Pop, I don't want to impose—besides I have an errand to do on the way to the convention center."

"No problem."

"You don't even know what the errand is. How can you say it is not a problem?" Carmen tried to smile, but she knew it was more of a grimace.

"It doesn't matter what it is. You're my baby-girl. I will do whatever you need. I'm here for you."

"Okay, get your stuff. I'm supposed to stay for a couple of days." Carmen felt blessed to have two great parents.

"I'm all packed. It took a little longer than usual. Tiffany had left me a little message."

"What sort of message?"

"My clothes were draped over the banister, and the shrubs on the back balcony." Tony looked more embarrassed than annoyed. "I had to do a little laundry and tidy up a bit, but I'm ready."

Carmen Sofia surprised herself by smiling. "Sounds kind of childish."

"Yes, that describes Tiff all right—childish—high maintenance—self-centered. I swear there are times I really miss your mother. Let's go. What time do you have to be there?" Tony pulled up the sleeve of his sweater and glanced at his watch.

"We have to leave now. That errand I mentioned—I have to pick someone up at the airport."

"Who?"

"A model." They walked side by side, Tyson had already dashed to Tony's blue SUV and was waiting, his stubby tail wagging. Carmen was certain he understood every word they said. The little devil was probably contemplating picking stuff off the shelves at the pet store.

Tony raised a brow. "And. . . ."

"The marketing department has decided to have a model with me at book signings. Anybody who buys a book gets a snapshot of themselves with him."

"Who is it?"

"I don't know. I've met a few of the professional models at conventions but I only got the E-mail last night and it didn't mention a name."

Tony's dark brows shot up higher. "And they are doing this because?"

"Because the marketing department thinks provocative book covers sell more books than words."

"What kind of idiots are they?"

"Don't get me started, Pop."

Tony flicked the blinker on and glided by a slower car. "I went out to your house last night, like your mother asked. While I was there I met the new sheriff."

"Oh." Carmen stiffened. She had tried to push that to the back of her mind while she mentally rehearsed what questions she wanted to ask Ethyl when they met at the conference hotel.

"Sharp guy, tough looking. A far cry from Jim Dunn."

"So, what happened?"

"Your windows are broken, just like Millie told you."

Carmen looked at the sky. She hoped it didn't start snowing any time soon. If the weather turned lousy, it might mean lower attendance at the conference. She knew the local chapter had worked their butts off to organize it, and she hoped it was a big success.

"There was glass all over."

Carmen had been in the zone and only heard bits and pieces

of what he had said. "I meant what happened with the new sheriff. He seems kind of full of himself."

"We uh. . . ." Tony glanced at the rearview mirror and accelerated a bit.

"Pop, are you blushing?"

Tony cleared his throat and passed another car. "I might be. Carmen, we found all that sexy underwear in your front closet."

Carmen's stomach tightened into a hard, painful ball. "The sheriff saw it too?" She felt her cheeks growing warm. That sleazy stuff was not something she wanted her father or any other man to be looking at and thinking it was hers.

"Yeah, he saw it."

"Pop, you don't think I bought that, do you?"

"Of course not, don't be silly. I never thought that. Besides, he found a card."

Oh, great. The new sheriff had managed to poke his nose into her privacy and see an E-mail and the provocative gifts in one day. How long would it take him to concoct some crazy scenario with her as a crazed murderess? Maybe losing Jim Dunn was not such a good thing after all.

"Just who is your secret admirer?"

"That is a secret I don't have the answer to."

"What the devil—?" Tony wrenched the wheel to the right, the big SUV swaying. "Crazy fool!"

Carmen saw a low-slung black Italian sports car fly by them. Santa Fe was home to a lot of rich people who drove expensive cars.

"More money than brains," Tony grumbled. Then he settled down to concentrate on the road. The big SUV sailed along the highway. The dark tinted windows enveloped Carmen. It was great; kind of like being cocooned in a plush, military tank. Tyson had claimed the entire backseat as his own, his doggie snores competing with the radio station Tony was listening to.

Carmen tried to think about her talk, but nagging thoughts about her missing money kept intruding. She had another contract waiting unsigned on her desk, but she hadn't accepted it yet. Carmen didn't want to think Ethyl was doing something she shouldn't be, but until she had a face-to-face meeting, she wasn't signing any new contracts or letting the Ethyl Gatz Agency broker any new deals.

"Penny for your thoughts." Tony flicked the blinker and passed an eighteen-wheeler.

Just how fast was he going? Those truckers didn't meander, and Tony seemed to be sailing by each one they encountered.

Carmen swiveled in her seat and looked at her father. "Do you think I'm morally bankrupt?"

"Is this a funky way of asking your old pop for a bigger loan?" Tony smiled at her. He had got in on the ground floor of a Santa Fe lab that did paternity tests and DNA research. The small company had made millions almost overnight.

He sold most of his stock and retired the next day, a very, very rich man. Soon after that, he started running around on Maria.

"No. It means I just realized I'm more concerned about money than human life. That doesn't speak well of me."

Tony stifled a laugh. "How so?"

"All I can think of is my empty bank account after I just found a man dead on my doorstep. How shallow is that?" Carmen frowned. "Maybe I should be blaming you, Pop, since you obviously didn't instill me with the proper values."

"Hey—no cheap shots. I don't know what happened to Jake, but as your father, I have to admit I'm having a little trouble feeling too much sympathy for the guy. I have heard from more than one person that he was verbally abusive and threatened you after that accident. In fact, one guy said he thought Jake came close to hitting you. You aren't a saint, Carmen, but stop beating yourself up and use your head. What exactly do you think would've happened if Jake had found you there—alone—and he was still ticked off over the wreck?"

"I don't think anything would've happened. He was a jerk, Pop, but all the poor guy did was leave one last package—"

"What?" Tony flicked her a glance before he turned his concentration back to driving. "What package?"

"I found a package at the backdoor yesterday evening. That must've been what he was doing there. He didn't come to yell at me. He was just doing his job. He left the package and then he died."

"Look, Carmen, I don't want to be a know-it-all, but if that package was related to Jake's death, even a dullard like Jim Dunn would've taken it into evidence. And besides, you say you found it at the backdoor. He died at the front. Where is that package now?"

"It was one of them in the closet."

"From your secret admirer?"

A chill traced up Carmen's spine. What if Jake hadn't left the package? Then who did? Had her stalker been at her house?

"Yes. It was another unwanted bit of fluff from my secret admirer."

What if Jake hadn't died of natural causes?

CHAPTER NINE

While Carmen silently stewed in her own juices, her cell phone began to ring. She finally found it at the bottom of her purse and flipped it open.

"Hello?" Her voice was a dry croak. The more she considered the unthinkable possibilities surrounding Jake's death the harder it was to breathe.

"Yes, this is Gloria Tewblu. Your mother gave me a call—great lady—wonderful cook. I understand you are in need of some legal advice."

"I—I'm not sure if I am or not." Carmen thought of the murderous brothers this woman had defended in California.

"Tell me what happened, Carmen. May I call you Carmen?"

"Yes, of course, Miss Tewblu."

"Fine. Now in your own words, just tell me what happened."

Carmen recapped the salient points of her arrest, trying to believe it was all just an accident, that Jake died of natural causes, but the door had been opened and couldn't be shut so easily. Her father was right. The police would have taken everything that Jake could possibly have touched, and there was no logic to him having left a parcel at the backdoor and then going to the front. That package had been left later. No wonder it was clean and dry. Did Millie realize that right away? She was a smart lady. But if she had, then why didn't she say something to Carmen? Or was the shadow Millie said she saw the stalker leaving the package?

"I think I have the picture. Jake Harris was a bit of a handful, but tell me about finding the—uh—corpse."

Carmen swallowed hard, the image of Jake's half-frozen body, his damaged eye, popped into her mind.

"When I got home, Penny's monthly art party—"

"Who is Penny?"

"Penny Black, is one of my neighbors—an artist. Anyway, her party was starting. I had trouble finding a place to park. I had to walk up the lane to my drive. That was when I saw the R.E.D. truck. I came up the walk and there he was—Jake—dead on my doorstep."

"Channel Seven has been running a report all morning. They are saying there's facial damage, but no official cause of death."

Gloria Tewblu was well informed.

"That's good, isn't it? I mean, maybe he had a heart attack. If he died of natural causes, then I don't have anything to worry about. Do I?"

"We can hope. A lot will depend on the C.O.D. In the meantime, you decide if you wish to retain me. Your mother is a darling, and I would be happy to do her and you a favor. I will be tied to the West Coast in a high-profile trial, but since I am licensed to practice in New Mexico as well, I'm sure I can file motions and do what you need if the situation should arise. I advise you not to make any statements. Don't talk to any reporters. Keep a low profile. Call me when you have made a decision."

"Okay, and thanks."

Chill drove to the station feeling sated after a fantastic breakfast. It was barely eight in the morning and he was ready to get a jump on the day. He expected to see a few cars in the parking lot. What met his eye was a complete feeding frenzy of reporters and cameras. He got out of the car and elbowed his way to the head of the crowd.

"Sheriff, Sheriff. Are you the new sheriff?"

"I am."

"We have been trying to get an official statement from the Taos County sheriff's office for two weeks. Will you speak to us?"

"Two weeks? Why haven't you been able to speak to anyone?" Chill talked while he walked, wondering what had happened two weeks ago that the press was interested in, as well as what can of worms the commissioners had dumped him into.

"Maybe Jim Dunn put a gag order on all his deputies. All we know is that it has been impossible to get anyone from the office to go on camera. Will you talk to us?"

Chill halted. There was no escaping the press. He had learned that lesson in California. The less he had said about his ex-partner and her book, the more the press speculated.

"Fine, but just a few questions."

"Tell us about the scandal surrounding Sheriff Dunn." A female reported decked out like a snow-bunny in Gstaad shoved the microphone in Chill's face.

"I have no knowledge of any scandal in the Taos County sheriff's office."

"Are you saying you are unaware of the lawsuit that has been filed alleging sexual misconduct?"

"That is correct." Chill's spine tingled. His cop-radar was going off. This was a helluva thing to find out and a piss-poor way to find it.

About that time Jim Dunn appeared from the crowd of reporters. He elbowed his way through them. The guy was dressed in uniform, and only when he was about a yard from Chill did the reporters notice who he was.

For one frozen moment, Chill wondered if the county commissioners had neglected to tell the guy he had been fired. It would be damned awkward to have to tell him he had been replaced while they were both on live camera feed. Then Chill saw the flash of temper when their gazes locked. It was all the guy could do to keep from pushing the reporter out of the way and throwing a punch at Chill.

He had been fired all right, and he wasn't too happy about it.

"If you've got any questions, you ask me," Jim snapped. His pulse was pounding in a big vein in his forehead. "This guy can't tell you anything because there is nothing to tell. I'm being victimized by a pack of women looking for publicity and a cash settlement, as well as the stuffed shirts who call themselves the county commissioners. They are trying to screw me out of my retirement."

Dunn hitched up his pants and puffed out his chest. "The only scandal I know anything about is Carmen Pollini murdering Jake Harris."

"Is that an official statement?" Chill saw the glitter in her eyes. The reporter smelled blood in the water. "Are you going on record as the former sheriff of Taos County saying you feel Carmen Pollini is guilty?"

She played out the rope like a pro. Chill wondered if Jim would make a noose and slip it around his fat neck.

"No comment." Suddenly Jim Dunn started walking. He cut across the parking lot, trying to avoid the biggest clutch of reporters—mostly women. That struck Chill as odd.

"Tell us about the lawsuit, Sheriff."

"No comment."

"Will you at least give us your thoughts about your termination?" One of the reporters ran in front of Jim, forcing him to halt in his tracks. A freckle-faced kid who didn't have any neck skidded to a stop beside her. He stuck his camera in Jim's face.

Jim Dunn doubled up his fist. The kid grinned, just daring him to do it on camera.

"Mr. Dunn, tell us what you think about Hugh Blaines being brought in to serve as sheriff." Ski-bunny reporter went for the jugular with her shiny white teeth flashing for the camera.

"What do I think? I think the county is screwing me over, but I'm not going down without a fight. I know things. I know things certain people in this department would be wise to keep out of the public eye. And I also know Carmen Pollini had better sleep with one eye open from now on."

Chill read the M.E.'s report again. He rubbed his temples. Was the headache from tension or all the gum he had been masticating?

"It just doesn't make sense."

"I beg your pardon?"

Chill looked up to find Deputy Victoria Smith in his office. She had been very helpful all morning. Almost too helpful. He realized he was jaded beyond the norm, but anybody who spent that much time accommodating a new boss had something to hide—or was she just a natural brown-nose? He could of course simply go to the county commissioners and get their side of the story about Jim Dunn's history and what they knew, if anything, about the mysterious way his letter of interest had shown up right on time for their meeting. But that is just what it would be, one sided. Chill didn't work that way. He preferred to watch and listen and make his own deductions. Every time he looked at Deputy Smith, his cop-radar tingled.

"I was just thinking out loud." Chill popped another piece of gum in his mouth.

Deputy Smith—Chill didn't intend to get into the habit of using first names—loomed close enough to see what he was reading.

"Ah, Carmen." She smiled. "I suppose you have seen her arrest record?"

Of course he had, last night before he went to her house. "No, tell me about it."

"She's a bit of a hot-head. Her mother's family predates the *Mayflower* landing—a bit of a local celebrity. You know the type."

He knew the type intimately. "Can't say I do. I come from a dull little town."

Her eyes glittered for a moment, and the smile that almost touched her lips never quite materialized. She studied him like a sleazy agent studies a pretty young thing from Kansas who wants to be a star in Hollywood.

She knew about his past. He could smell it.

But how?

He hadn't applied for the job, so there was no long, drawn-out background check that could've come from inside this office. If it had, Dunn would've known what was coming and been spared the humiliation of being fired without notice. No, Chill was certain Jim Dunn had been blindsided by his sudden appearance as the new sheriff.

So just how had his information reached the county commissioners?

Someone had made sure his C.V. fell into the right hands at the right time.

He had to ask himself—were they doing him a favor or setting him for a long, hard fall?

CHAPTER TEN

Carmen stood in the crowd of people waiting at the Albuquerque International Airport, the Sun-Port to the natives. She stared at faces, some happy, some sad, and all connected in some way to someone on the plane coming in for a landing. A sea of people surged toward the gate when the plane taxied to the terminal.

According to her publisher's marketing department, the cover model on *A Hot Brand of Love* was the driving force behind her rising sales and appearance on several best-seller's lists.

"Marketing. You got to love 'em." Carmen tried to be stoic about their attitude, but it did rankle that her hard work, consistent self-promotion and ability to write a good book were dismissed in favor of a pretty face. Carmen blinked to find that pretty face coming toward her.

Her mouth went dry.

He was dressed in black leather pants and a vest—no shirt—just a vest, open, revealing a rock-hard, sculpted chest. A battered leather bag was carelessly slung over one shoulder.

He was the quintessential wanderer, a man with a past and no obvious destination, every woman's physical ideal. A man for all seasons, reasons and tantric positions.

The leather pants pulled, cupped and accentuated his crotch as he worked the cut in his strut and cruised across the industrial grade carpet toward her.

His glossy dark hair swung just at the top of those wide,

muscular shoulders. His eyes were icy blue, mysterious, enigmatic, and heavy lidded. His nose was slim and straight, with a sexy flare to the nostrils. When he walked he didn't lead with his chin or his chest, but what he did lead with got every female's attention.

Sex appeal oozed from his pores like nectar dripping from a ripe exotic bloom.

Carmen felt a little queasy. The last time she saw him, she had slapped his face and got them both ejected from a piano bar on Lexington and Fifth.

Now she had to work with him? Oh, dandy, just dandy. She made a mental note to give the marketing department a piece of her mind.

"Of all the models in all the world . . . Dax Des Planes." And the funniest part was that she hadn't even recognized him as the inspiration for the artist's rendition on her book cover.

"Hey." Eye-candy had stopped in front of her. His smile was lazy and seductive, friendly—until the moment he recognized her too.

"Carmen Sofia Pollini," he croaked. "Tell me this is some kind of joke. I'm being punked, right? Where are the hidden cameras?" He panned the crowd, anger and disappointment on his face when he came up dry.

More than one woman in the airport lurched to a stop. They stared at him in open-mouthed appreciation, or in furtive glances hidden from spouses, but all in homage of his male virility.

"I didn't know. Believe me, if I had I would've stopped them from sending you," Carmen said.

His nostrils flared, his eyes narrowed and then he shrugged. "Oh well, it's only for a couple of days, right? How bad can it be?"

"Right. How bad can it be?" She ignored the little voice in

her head that was screaming two days could be a very, very long time.

"So where do I go through customs?" he asked.

"What?" His question brought her to a painful stop. "I'm sorry. I thought you just asked me about customs—"

"Yes." He pulled a small blue booklet from his carry-on. "Got my passport. I hope we don't get held up too long. I'm starving."

"Passport?" Carmen repeated like a well-trained parrot.

"Yes, this is New Mexico right? Luckily I don't have anything to declare. We can zip right through customs and get across the border."

"You're confused. This is *New* Mexico. We are part of the forty-eight contiguous states."

"Contiguous?" His eyes widened, flashing their pale beauty like diamonds in the sun. "Do you mean I needed shots? I asked my agent about that, and she said no. Contiguous? Damn them. First I find you here, and now I'm going to catch something?"

All the loud throbbing in her temples must be affecting her hearing, because even he couldn't be so stupid as to think she had said contagious.

"You don't have to go through customs," she assured him.

"Are you sure? I gotta protect myself. I can't be arrested by Interpol or anything 'cause I didn't follow the rules when entering a foreign country. My agent says I could be big in Europe— maybe even France. Movie offers are coming in every day."

Okay, so Carmen was an intellectual snob. She might lust over his pecs, pack and package, but she could never have a conversation with him. She would take a brilliant homely guy over this hunk of beefcake any day.

The weak winter sun glinted off his dark hair when they stepped through the automatic doors of the airport terminal.

Tony pulled up to the curb. Dax Des Planes opened the door,

Carmen climbed into the front seat of the SUV.

"I guess this means I am supposed to sit in back?"

She realized with a little jolt that he hadn't been opening the door for her. Okay, dumb as a brick, stuck on himself, and no manners too. The marketing department was definitely off her Christmas card list.

Dax blinked at her for a moment, then he tossed in his bag and climbed into the backseat.

"Argh! There is some kind of animal—"

"Tyson!"

It was too late. Tyson was focused on Dax's earlobe. As daintily as if he was picking up a spicy canapé, his needle-sharp canines connected with Dax's perfectly shaped earlobe.

"Argh! Hey, what the hell?" Dax cringed into the seat, grabbing for his violated ear. "That dog rabid or what?"

"Of course he's not rabid. Bad dog, Tyson, bad dog. Sit!" Carmen twisted in her seat, being strangled by the seatbelt while Tony choked, snorted and tried not to chortle with laughter.

"Pop," she warned. He gave her a helpless look and swallowed his chuckle.

"Hey, is your driver laughing at me?" Dax frowned. It made his beautiful, vacant eyes lovelier.

Tony stopped laughing. "Driver? Hey, bud—"

"Cool, he speaks English. Is that great or what. I didn't expect to understand a thing they said here." Dax rubbed his ear.

Tony choked. "That's it. As soon as I pull this rig over, I'm going to bludgeon him to death with the tire iron I have in the back." Tony was glaring at Dax in the rearview mirror.

"This isn't my driver. This happens to be my father," Carmen informed Dax sharply before she turned back around, remembering exactly why she had slapped him and wishing she had done it harder. Her interest in chiding Tyson was gone; she hoped he violated Dax's other ear—or maybe acquired a taste for jugular veins between the airport and the hotel.

"Your dad? So you gave the old guy a job. I'm impressed. I guess you're not always a bitc—"

"Where is a parking place when you need one?" Tony snapped. "Tell you what, Carmen, I'll just throw this rig into park, you hit him over the head, and we'll open the door and dump him out. Just drive off and leave his ass bleeding in the street. What d'ya say?"

"Pop—" Carmen warned again, rubbing her pulsing temple.

Tyson smacked his lips and licked his chops. He was going for the gusto. Dax tried to push him off, but Tyson was built for this kind of hand-to-paw combat. Dax didn't have a chance when the little canine tank got rolling.

Dax screamed. Tony smiled at him in the rearview mirror. "Good dog, Tyson, take a nibble for me, will ya?"

By the time Tony dropped Carmen and Dax off at the hotel, the throb at Carmen's temples had turned into a full-fledged migraine complete with visual disturbances. She tried to ignore the little explosions of light as she gathered herself and plastered a smile on her face.

"So, where is my assistant?" Dax tapped his smoothly buffed nails on the counter while the front clerk checked the computer. Even with a Barney dinosaur Band-aid on each earlobe, Dax managed to look great.

"Assistant?" Since the airport, she had been repeating everything he said. She had begun to wonder if low IQ could be contagious.

"My agent always gets me an assistant. I can't work without an assistant."

"All I know is that you are supposed to be available at the book signing tonight, to pose with anybody who buys an autographed copy of my book."

Dax arched one elegant brow and Carmen felt like she had smuts on her face.

"I need someone to blow dry my hair and keep me supplied with bottled water and stuff. I have to have an assistant, Carmen."

"Of course you do. What was I thinking?" She smacked herself in the forehead with her palm while fireworks burst in front of her irises.

Carmen fussed with her hair, wrestling the dark strands back into the chignon that was no longer sleek or chic. Several stubborn locks refused to be tamed, falling down from her temples, brushing her shoulders.

"Well, damn." She made one last twist and poked in a hairpin. She gave herself a critical assessment in the mirror.

Nothing about her reflection pleased her. She didn't look any more like a successful author today than she had five years ago after her first sale.

She still saw a dark-eyed country girl staring back from the mirror. But, to be fair, her figure wasn't too bad. And Pop was right—her outfit did smack of *Dr. Zhivago.*

"This is as good as it gets."

She had ten minutes to get downstairs and set up for the seminar she was giving to aspiring writers and the book signing to follow.

She grabbed her tote bag, checking her supply of bookmarks and the tiny branding iron lapel pins she had brought for readers' gifts. The marketing department might believe that Dax was the definitive promotional gimmick, but she had a few ideas of her own for *A Hot Brand of Love.*

Taking a deep breath, standing tall in her high-heeled boots, she hurried to the elevator and punched the button.

The door swished open. The elevator was full of people, packed like sardines in a tin.

"I'll wait for the next one." She stared into the faces of the people waiting for the door to close again.

"Nonsense. I won't hear of it." A tall woman with a wide smile and bright red hair stepped back half a step, forcing everyone behind her to do the same. Carmen could swear she heard air being forced from lungs with an audible whoosh.

"Thanks." Carmen squeezed in, scrunching the tote to her side, trying not to mentally calculate the tonnage and the warning on the metal plate by the door. The sensation of movement vibrated through her feet. Someone's hot breath blasted rhythmically down the back of her collar. One by one the numbered lights blinked and then went dark until finally the control panel stopped on L.

Carmen started for the door. There was a hard yank on her bag. The entire thing dumped at her feet. Wallet, promotional lapel pins, checkbook, pens, tissues, lipstick and bookmarks fluttered to the carpet.

"Great." Carmen dropped to her knees, scraping her belongings back into the bag.

"Excuse me."

"Pardon me."

"Sorry."

A steady murmur of apologies drifted in the air while people stepped over and around her. She partially obstructed the door, but there was little she could do about it while she scrambled to retrieve her stuff. A big, callused hand appeared in front of her face, shoving bookmarks into the tote.

"Thank you, I appreciate your help." She looked up, but the man was striding away. She had the impression of height and pale hair and perhaps a long, dark coat before a figure melted into the crowd. Evidently there really were some gentlemen left in the world.

Then she saw Dax. He was dressed in chaps; the Levi's beneath were worn and soft in all the right places. A Stetson perched low over his eyes. A different leather vest was glove soft and wide open. His chest gleamed like a polished penny, all chiseled muscle. He reeked of rampant sex appeal and complete confidence in his lethal charms. Women were clustered around him in open adoration.

"Well, maybe the marketing department does know what they are talking about." Carmen admitted aloud.

CHAPTER ELEVEN

Carmen lingered by the elevator bank and watched women admire Dax's hard, tight backside, but her attention was drawn away when a silver-haired woman decked out in a black, mannish power suit appeared. Ethyl Gatz, wearing her thick, tinted glasses, was shod in designer running shoes and rummaging through her bag; she didn't see Carmen until she was inches from her.

"Hello, Ethyl." Carmen took great satisfaction when Ethyl's mouth turned down at the corners. Behind those dark shades, Carmen just knew she was goggle eyed.

"Carmen. What are you doing here?"

"Getting some answers, I hope. Why haven't you returned any of my calls or E-mails, Ethyl?" Carmen fell into step beside her agent when the woman veered off and kept walking—at a slightly faster pace than before. Ethyl threaded her way through the growing crowd of females. It was not easy for Carmen to keep up; her heels were high and the polished marble floor was slick as a sheet of black road ice.

Dax had worked his magic, and more than three dozen women were ogling him. In fact, Carmen thought one or two of them might swoon at any minute. She wasn't surprised when a woman nearby stumbled over her own feet as she stared at him. The surprise was that as she fell, she dropped her bag, Ethyl's wide, athletic shoe caught on it, flinging it in Carmen's path with Ethyl's next step. True to form, Carmen ended up tangled, and then, of course, she was unable to keep her balance on the slippery floor.

For a moment it was like a scene out of *Dancing with the Stars*—then the awkward waltz ended. Carmen reached out for something solid to steady herself. What she found was Ethyl's bony arm.

"Argh! Let me go. What are you doing?"

Instead of helping her, Ethyl swatted at her hand, making matters worse. She acted as if she were being attacked by an octopus. The more Ethyl threw her off, the more Carmen's instinct to hold on kicked in. It was silly slapstick. Grab, slap, shove, over and over again while Carmen did a fair imitation of Bambi on the frozen lake. She was dimly aware of the crowd of women clustered around Dax shifting their attention from his magnificence to her ungainly ballet. The more she flailed her arms and tried to regain her balance, the louder Ethyl screamed.

"Stop! Help! What are you doing?" Ethyl's screech got the attention of the hotel staff. "Help, get her off me." Carmen saw a flash of blue. A tall man in a hotel uniform was bearing down on her. He motioned to a couple of bellhops. Shoulder to shoulder they marched across the gleaming white marble floor toward Carmen, Ethyl and the crowd of women around Dax.

"Ethyl, stop screaming." Carmen tottered on her high-heeled boots. What kind of idiot polished these floors? Did they think hotel patrons had little suckers on their feet?

One last slide and they went down.

"You—you're trying to kill me!" Ethyl sat on her butt. Her dark glasses were crooked on her nose. Her power suit was askew. "Admit it, Carmen, you want to hurt me because of your money."

"What about my money?" At least Carmen was finally getting some answers. Her position on the floor wasn't exactly the greatest for tough negotiation, but at this point she would take what she could get.

"I spent it all." Ethyl said, whipping off her glasses. Her eyes were wide, white rimmed and wild. For a crazy moment Carmen thought maybe she was high.

"You did what?"

"I needed it. It is all gone. You can do what you like but your royalties are gone. So there."

"Then pay me back!" Carmen was stunned by Ethyl's confession and her attitude.

"Forget it, cookie. I'm not paying back a cent. I'm going to start bankruptcy proceedings and then take a long vacation on a sandy beach. Now get away from me. Security! Security! She tried to kill me!"

An hour later Ethyl had been taken to her room, under escort because she kept wailing that Carmen was trying to do her in, while Carmen tried to explain to a buttoned-down three-piece suit that she had not knocked Ms. Gatz down, or tried to bludgeon her with her laptop, as Ms. Gatz claimed.

"I tell you it was an accident. I stumbled."

"I think I had better call the authorities. Even though Ms. Gatz said she didn't want to press charges, I have the hotel's reputation to think of. We could be held liable if I don't take ordinary care. Surely you understand my position."

"Sure, I understand." Carmen flipped open her phone.

She was tired of trying to play nice with a bunch of crazies.

"Who are you calling?" the manager asked.

"My attorney—Gloria Tewblu."

"The feminist attorney? The one that handled the Doris Smith murder trial and defended those boys. The one who is a regular guest on CNN?"

Wow, did she really do all that? Carmen was impressed. Way to go, Mom!

"Mmm, that would be her, yes." Carmen covered her

surprise, allowing herself to give him what she hoped was a hard, flinty smile. "I'm sure she will wish to speak to you directly—"

"No, no, I'm sure we can work something out."

Later that afternoon, wearing flattering cowboy-cut jeans and low heeled ropers, with a nice floral arrangement from the hotel at her table, Carmen was signing books. This made the whole lousy day worth it. The fans were terrific.

"How do you spell that?" Carmen scrawled her fan's name on a custom bookplate and slapped it on the inside page of *A Hot Brand of Love*.

"I just love Monica Blaze. I wish I could be more like her," a young woman said, a blush rising to her hairline. She had purchased three books, one for herself and two for gifts.

"So do I," Carmen said with a wink. Her heroine was the perfect woman, a size one with one hundred seventy eight IQ and hot and cold running men. Who didn't want to be Monica Blaze?

"Thanks for writing such a great book." The pretty thirty-something smiled. "Now do I get a picture of me and Dax?"

Okay, so the marketing department was back on her Christmas card list. "Yes, just go stand in that line over there."

Carmen looked at the line. It wound around her table and out the big double doors. Dax was handsome, charming and a natural at working a room. Only she was aware of his shortcomings.

"Would you sign a book for me?" A tall blond man held out a copy of *A Hot Brand of Love*. Carmen had been surprised by how many men read her book. Several of them had told her how much they thought they were like her hero.

"Sure, what's your name?"

"It is a gift. Could you just write: 'to my biggest fan'?"

"Absolutely." Carmen glanced up. "Have you read the book?" She finished the plate and stuck it on the first page.

"Of course. I love Monica Blaze. I wonder, how much of you is in her."

Carmen held it out to the man. His fingertips brushed her hand when he took the book. She was ready to give him her pat answer, but there was something about the intensity of his gaze that halted her words. He was handsome in a stark, severe way—pale, serious, deep in his regard. He wore no hat, but the long, black denim duster gave him an old-west look. Carmen couldn't see his legs or feet, but she would've bet he was wearing nicely tailored Levi's and good boots.

"How's it going, baby-girl?" Tony leaned down and gave her a peck on the forehead. She turned toward her dad.

"Fine, Pop." When she looked back, the man was gone. Carmen glanced around, but it was as if he had just vanished.

"Don't tell me Sir Hunk-a-lot is actually drawing a crowd." Tony glared at Dax.

"He has been charming the pants off them," Carmen said. "Hopefully not in the literal sense." She grinned when several of the more mature women waiting on Dax gave Tony a sultry look of interest.

"Pop, I think you might give him a little competition. One or two of those women are giving you the come-hither look."

"Nope, I'm swearing off women. Tiff called me, she is filing for divorce."

"Alimony?"

"Lots."

"Property settlement?"

"As much as she can get."

"Ouch."

"I'm getting used to it. Your mother was the only ex-wife that didn't want cold, hard cash."

"No comment."

"Hey, you've only got two books left." Tony picked up a copy and turned it over to read the back blurb. "This sounds like a great read."

"Don't sound so surprised, Pop." Up until now Tony hadn't shown a lot of interest in Carmen's books. He said he didn't think they would be macho enough to interest him. And, of course, he had been chasing younger women, which didn't leave a lot of leisure time for reading.

"Sign those two for me so I can take you to dinner." Tony slapped the two copies down in front of Carmen.

"Pop—"

"I'm serious. I'll read one and give one to Aunt Theresa in New York. Hey, I saw a news truck outside. Any problems with the press?"

"No, but a reporter did come by earlier after the police finished with me." Carmen picked up a book, avoiding Tony's gaze.

"The police? What were the police doing here?" Tony blurted, drawing the attention of Dax and his bevy of women.

"I had this little, uhm, uh . . . altercation. But Mom was right, Gloria Tewblu is a powerhouse. After they talked to her, it was short and sweet."

"Carmen, what have you done?"

"I didn't do anything, Pop. And I don't want to talk about it."

"Tell me."

Carmen sighed. "It is too stupid to believe, but one of the reporters asked me a lot of questions. She wanted to know about Jim Dunn. She was asking about sexual discrimination and the sheriff's office. She kept insisting there was some sort of cover-up going on, said she kept getting stonewalled when she brought a camera crew to the police station. I got the feeling she was trying to dig up some dirt about something besides Jake Harris's death."

"What did you tell her?"

"I don't know anything to tell her. As far as Jake is concerned, I'm innocent. So that is what I said."

"Did that satisfy her?"

"Yes, until she saw these. Jim left a little calling card. Funny how the press picks right up on things like this." Carmen held up her hands and the long sleeve of her fluttery red silk shirt cuff fell back to reveal red marks and dark bruises coming up on both wrists where Jim Dunn had put the handcuffs on her.

"That son of a dog Jim Dunn is going to pay. Why didn't you tell me he manhandled you, Carmen?"

"I didn't realize they were so bad, honest. But the funny thing is the reporter didn't seem surprised. In fact it almost seemed like she was looking for them. Anyway, the conference chair overheard our conversation. In light of the awkward publicity and what happened today with Ethyl, she suggested it might be best if I go back home."

"What happened with Ethyl? Carmen, did you lose your temper again?" Tony's dark eyes were full of concern.

"No, I didn't lose my temper, just all my money. Evidently I'm flat broke." Carmen blinked back a sudden rush of hot tears.

"Carmen, you do not have to worry about money."

"I know, and I thank you for saying that, but the truth is, I do have to worry. I'm a grown woman and have my own obligations. I'm not a little girl anymore."

"You will always be my little girl. Now tell me what is going on with the conference. Are they running you off?"

"Allowing me to leave with dignity, I think. I just need to

leave a message for Ethyl Gatz and get my bill taken care of, and I'll be ready to go."

Carmen stepped outside into the clear, cold day. Tony was bringing around the SUV. She stood under the huge awning of the hotel breezeway, shielding her eyes from the sharp winter sun when she heard her name being called.

"Ms. Pollini. Here! Look this way, Miss Pollini."

"Tell us how you were acquainted with the victim, Jake Harris?"

"What is your side of the story?"

"Care to comment on the threats you made earlier, both to him and to your agent, Ethyl Gatz?"

"The Taos County sheriff's office has been rumored to be involved in an action of discrimination, sexual misconduct and brutality against women. Can you tell us your experiences? Were you victimized in any way by the sheriff's office?"

Carmen sucked in a breath. A half-dozen different voices were questioning her.

"Hey, what about this latest assault? We hear you tried to kill your former agent. Wanna comment on that?"

"I have nothing to say about Jake Harris. I did not try to kill anybody. And since I have not fired her, Ethyl is not my former agent—yet."

"Did you lose your control? Do you have anger issues? You have a police record that involves assault. True or false?"

Carmen bit her tongue. The accusation that she had a problem with her temper was making her crazy. Reporters from both Santa Fe and Albuquerque shoved microphones in her face while the bright lights of television cameras blinded her.

She turned away from the harsh light, shielding her eyes, and then she saw Ethyl. The reporters moved like bees in a swarm to surround the agent, but not before Carmen got a good, clear look at her being pushed in a wheelchair. Her neck was swathed in a white foam cervical brace, and an inflated arm brace encased her right arm. She looked like a Mack truck had run her down.

"It was an accident. The floor was slick. That's all. We slipped on the floor," Carmen yelled, but the reporters were no longer listening to her. They had better copy. Ethyl smiled weakly and spoke in a husky whisper.

"I'm screwed," Carmen moaned.

Then she looked up and saw Tony's SUV. He ignored the mob, the lights and the wheelchair, driving right up on the sidewalk, reaching across and opening the door for Carmen.

"Get in."

Carmen's heart swelled with affection for the two guys in her life as Tony gunned the SUV and Tyson leaned out the half-open window, snarling at one reporter who had decided he did want a comment and was loping beside the SUV.

"Thanks for springing me, Pop."

"*Por nada,* baby-girl. Listen, when I brought the SUV around, this was stuck under the windshield wiper." He held out a scrap of folded paper.

Carmen took it from his hand and unfolded it. The hotel logo was emblazoned across the top.

"You stole my book. Monica Blaze was my character! You are going to pay. I'm just getting started. You will regret ignoring me."

Her head swam and she felt a hard knot of tension twist in her gut. The person who wrote the E-mails had been right here! Maybe whoever it was had been at her signing. She tried to think back, to remember anybody who seemed threatening or odd in any way, but they all blurred together in her mind.

"Carmen? What is it? You have gone white as a sheet."

She folded the note and shoved it into the trash bag Tony had hanging from his dash.

"Nothing, Pop."

"Carmen, don't lie to me. Tell me what is going on."

She leaned back against the headrest and shut her eyes. She hadn't wanted to tell anybody, but if the person was actually following her, perhaps she should.

"I've been getting E-mails." Her voice had a quiver in it. She cleared her throat and tried again. "Somebody thinks I ripped off their book."

"E-mails are one thing, Carmen, but if some nut is leaving notes on my car, it means they were watching you."

Carmen nodded. "I know. I picked right up on that, Pop."

Somebody was following her. She had sort of adjusted to her secret admirer and the lingerie, but now she had to rethink everything. That last package had been left after Jake was murdered; she was sure of it. Now a note had been left on Tony's SUV. That meant someone had seen her go to Tony's, leave her car and ride with him. Was it all the same person? Was he or she twisted enough to exhibit two separate kinds of behavior—maybe have multi-personalities?

She glanced into the side mirror. "I must be getting paranoid."

"Why?" Tony flicked a glance at the mirror.

"I thought I saw that same black sports car in Santa Fe this morning."

"Lots of black sports cars in the City-Different. Still. . . ." Tony looked into the rearview mirror and frowned.

Carmen Sofia scooted down in the seat and closed her eyes. "Of course, you're right. Pop, I think I'm becoming paranoid."

"You're not paranoid if they really are out to get you, Carmen Sofia. Don't ever forget that."

CHAPTER TWELVE

Carmen Sofia sat in front of the stone fireplace in La Señora's lobby, sipping a glass of wine. The smooth plaster chimney-breast had absorbed heat and was releasing it slowly back into the room. The scent of her mother's cooking in the Coyote next door mingled with piñon wood smoke and filled the air with the attar of coming winter.

She tucked her stockinged feet up under the edge of the fleece throw Maria had given her and snuggled into it. It was nice—warm, cozy. She felt protected here. She cringed when the phone rang for the fiftieth time. She heard Tony pick it up and bark into the phone.

"No, Miss Pollini does not care to give a statement to the press. Don't call again."

It was the middle of the week, and La Señora del Destino was nearly empty, many of the tourists gone to other locales, the ski lodges closer to the slopes attracting them.

Carmen was glad.

Tony came into the room carrying a new bottle of wine; Tyson's nails clicked with each step while he followed. Tony splashed wine to fill up Carmen Sofia's glass, and then tipped up the bottle, taking a long swig.

Clearly this bottle had been designated a comfort beverage.

"No point in letting it go to waste." He flopped down in the chintz-covered easy chair beside her and used the remote to turn on the flat-screen TV mounted on the knotty pine wall.

Carmen loved books, but she was also an unabashed TV hound. She loved PBS mysteries, great love stories, *Monk* and *Prison Break*.

"Local romance author Carmen Pollini was released from jail pending further investigation. No comment was available from the Taos sheriff pending the autopsy report. At this time the victim's body is with the office of the medical investigator in Albuquerque."

"I see I managed to land right in the middle of the six o'clock news."

Tony turned the volume down but left the TV on.

"I wish they would hurry up and get the autopsy done. Jake just . . . died. I mean not everything has to be cloak and dagger, right?" Carmen Sofia slowly twirled the stem of her glass in her hands, watching the wave of wine swirl against the glass.

"I don't know, baby-girl. I keep wondering what the hell he was doing at your house. I think his death might be cloak and dagger after all. Especially now that you have told me about the E-mails and those gifts from somebody you don't even know."

Carmen Sofia took a big gulp of wine. "Pop, I need to go to my house."

"Why?"

"I'm going to get all those packages and—"

"Oh, I don't believe it! Look!" Tony grabbed the remote and turned up the sound.

The reporter's voice blasted through the quiet room. "Ethyl Gatz was injured today during a violent confrontation with Taos author Carmen Sofia Pollini today. Witnesses to the physical attack say threats were made by Ms. Pollini. There is speculation Ms. Pollini believes her agent has been stealing money from her."

"How do they find out about this stuff? If they were standing there listening then they wouldn't have to speculate about Ethyl stealing from me. She admitted it."

"I didn't know, Carmen, but I think you should get those parcels and take them to the new sheriff. Carmen, you have to trust somebody. You decide, but if you are planning to go home to get something, I'm going with you." Tony stood up just as his cell phone rang. Within moments he was having a heated argument with Tiffany about property settlements and spousal support.

Carmen grabbed her coat and Tony's keys. She slipped on a sweater that was hanging in the kitchen. She might or might not give the packages to the new sheriff, but she was going home. Now. And while Tony was distracted this was the best time to do it.

The drive to Carmen's house was quick; the SUV ate up the miles. Her mind was occupied with questions about what had happened. Her life had taken a dark turn, and things just kept getting worse. But Tony was right. She had to trust somebody; it might as well be Chill Blaines.

"I'm going to let the sheriff handle it." After all, he was new in town. He had no special agenda. If she was ever going to get a fair shake, it would be with him.

Carmen parked the SUV and ran to the backdoor. She used Tony's key to let herself in. She didn't turn on any lights as she hurried to the front closet to retrieve the packages.

But when she turned on the living-room lamp she gasped in surprise.

They were gone. Not one box, or a single bra and panty set, or even a scrap of tissue paper remained. For months Carmen had wished them all gone, but now that her closet floor was empty, she had a hollow void in her belly.

What did it all mean? Besides the fact that her home had been violated once again? The sensation of being watched clawed at her insides. Once again she had behaved impulsively, dashing off while Tony was occupied. Now she was alone, without even Tyson beside her.

"Idiot."

Carmen ran outside, jumped in the SUV and jammed it into gear. She sped all the way back to La Señora. The highway was nearly deserted, but she couldn't shake the feeling someone or something was right behind her.

Tony was pacing the floor with Maria on his heels when Carmen walked inside. She felt as if she was fourteen, had broken her curfew, and was sneaking in only to find her parents waiting to ground her for life.

"Carmen!" Maria rushed to her, stroking her hair, touching her face, gazing into her eyes as if she were searching for her deepest secrets. "Are you all right?"

"I'm fine."

"Good. Now what did you think you were doing?" Maria shrieked and spewed a string of harsh words in Spanish. "I'm too old—you are too old—for such behavior."

"We were worried sick." Tony pulled her into a painful hug. Then he shoved her away and looked hard at her while Maria continued her tirade in Spanish. Every now and then she would stop, stare at Carmen, shake her head and start again.

"Where did you go?"

"I went home."

"*Madre de Dios!* Why, Carmen?" Maria asked. "Your father told me what happened today—the note, the E-mails. Are you *loco?* Do you have some sort of death wish? Tell me, so I will know."

"I had to."

"I told you I would go with you, Carmen." Tony started to say more but Tyson sprang up from the floor, barking furiously at the front door of La Señora's lobby.

Chill entered and scanned the room with a quick gaze, one brow rising. Then, without a word, he went to stand in front of the roaring fireplace. Tony and Maria's lips were pinched into small, tight lines of disapproval.

Carmen could almost give the new sheriff a hug for rescuing her from her parents' wrath.

"Ah, that feels nice. Cold as a witch's—" He glanced at Carmen and halted what he was going to say. Was his action contrived to make her think he was concerned about her sensibilities? Then, when Tony and Maria weren't looking, he winked at her.

He was handling her! The knowledge set her teeth on edge. All right, more on edge. She was wary and cautious. Every nerve and muscle in her body went taut as she tried to figure out what he was thinking.

Maybe she was better off when Tony and Maria were grilling her.

"I hope you don't mind if I warm myself a moment." He was too polite, his manners at odds with the rough cut of his visage. "I should be used to the cold by now, but I'm not."

"Where did you say you were from?" Tony asked. His vague tone told Carmen he wasn't the least interested, but he was making polite conversation.

"California. Then I went to Nevada, then Arizona, Utah and now here. But I guess my blood is still thin, because I'm feeling the cold."

"Would you like a cup of hot tea? Cocoa?" Maria asked. Carmen wondered if her mother was trying to kill him with kindness. Would that be premeditated murder?

"Thank you, no."

"Something stronger?" Tony offered.

"No, no. I must be the only cop I know who can't stand hard

liquor. I do like an occasional beer, but I loathe distilled beverages. Can't handle the stuff."

"You might like margaritas," Carmen said.

He looked up at her and smiled. "I doubt it. Hard liquor doesn't agree with me, I wonder why that is?"

"I couldn't say," she snapped.

He was dressed in slacks, a western cut jacket and ostrich-hide boots, but his watch, the tasteful sterling cuff links on the silk shirt and the dudish bolo tie spoke of the city.

California, eh? She should've known.

"Not wearing a uniform, Sheriff?" Carmen goaded. "Or are you working undercover?"

His eyes riveted on Carmen's face. "Dressed like this I can go unnoticed—almost. I guess it is pointless to try and be inconspicuous here, though, isn't it?"

"Unless you are doing some sort of wolf in sheep's clothing thing," Carmen quipped, but her words lacked the sarcastic sting she had hoped for. She was still shaken from the incident at her house. She sat on the sofa, Tyson beside her. Tony sat on her opposite side.

Even with her loyal watchdog and Pop, she still felt stripped and vulnerable. She knew it was because of the break-in at her home, but knowing it intellectually and shrugging off the emotional effect were two different things.

She glanced at the sheriff, but Chill was staring at the television. Carmen realized with a sick lurch of her stomach that they were repeating the report on Ethyl's so-called assault.

"It wasn't like they said," she blurted.

One blunt, no-nonsense brow twitched. "Are you making a confession, Ms. Pollini?"

"Of course I'm not confessing. I didn't do what they are saying." She pointed at the television. "They said I assaulted Ethyl Gatz. I didn't, I just, uh, spoke to her, and then I left."

"Now that you bring it up, why did you leave so early? My understanding is that you were supposed to host a seminar. Is that the correct terminology? Host a seminar about novel writing?"

Slick. He was slick as bull snot.

Carmen clasped her hands together, but when those predatory eyes flicked over her white knuckles, she unclasped them and rested her hands on her thighs. The clamminess of her palms seeped right through her jeans.

"The conference chair thought it would be a good idea," Tony provided helpfully. Carmen shot him a warning glance, but it was too late. Chill was staring at him with those predatory eyes narrowed.

"And why was that?"

Carmen imagined a great cat, sitting, tail twitching, waiting for the moment when the mouse would break under the pressure of his gaze and run. Then he would spring upon her, devouring her with his sharp, savage teeth.

She wasn't going to break, and she sure as hell wasn't going to run.

"Look, Sheriff, you and I both know you have heard about what happened, probably from a dozen different people. Why don't you just drop the act and ask me whatever it is that is burning a hole in your tongue." Carmen balled her hands into fists and held them stiffly at her sides.

Tony coughed, but Carmen didn't know if he was shocked or amused at her flash of temper.

The atmosphere in the room altered slightly. Sheriff Chill Blaines continued to stare at Carmen, but there was something more in his gaze—an added little something that hadn't been there before.

Respect? Probably not. Satisfaction? Maybe.

Triumph? Yes! He thought he had just won. But what?

"Fine, we'll do it your way, Miss Pollini, with the gloves off. Tell me about the assault on Ms. Gatz at the Desert Dancer Hotel. And while you're at it, maybe you can tell me all about the death threats you made against her life."

CHAPTER THIRTEEN

"I didn't assault Ethyl or threaten her life." Carmen squirmed beneath his hard gaze, then mentally cursed herself for being so wimpy. She was innocent. She had nothing to worry about. "We had this silly accident. The floor was slick, and we fell down. Period. No drama, no threats." It wasn't precisely the truth; there had been a lot of drama, but he didn't need to know that.

He pulled a small notebook from his pocket and flipped it open. "I have accounts from at least two witnesses that she was screaming for help."

"Sure she was yelling for help. We fell."

"She wasn't yelling for help to get off the floor. I have witnesses who say she was yelling for help to get away from you."

"Well, yes, I suppose she was."

"And why was that?"

"Because she didn't want to talk to me." Carmen's temper was hitching up. She felt her control slipping and fought to maintain her calm façade.

"And why is that, Miss Pollini? Why didn't she want to talk to you?" He appeared to be reading his notes, but she knew it was all an act.

"Call me Carmen. If you are going to interrogate me, we should be on a first-name basis." She took a tiny bit of pleasure when he glanced up at her in surprise. For a moment those hard eyes lost their edge—but only for a moment. In less than a heartbeat, his steely focus returned.

"Fine. Carmen, then. Why was Miss Gatz trying to avoid having a conversation with you, Carmen? Wasn't she your literary agent?"

"Is."

"What?"

"Is. She is my literary agent. I haven't terminated our agreement."

His lips twitched. "Terminated. Interesting choice of words, but then I guess being a writer you would pick a strong descriptor. Tell me about your agent. It appears there was something causing friction between you. What was it?"

"She has been stealing money from me." Carmen wasn't going to lie. "I didn't want to believe that was why I hadn't received a check, but she admitted it."

If he was surprised, he hid it well. Carmen had the sinking sensation that he already knew the answer to all these questions—and more.

"And how much has she stolen?"

"I don't know. She didn't say."

"Can you make a guess?"

Carmen swallowed hard. Too much of her brain had been focused on showing him she was not intimidated. She should've paid more attention to what she was saying instead of trying to handle the hard-eyed cop. She realized way too late that she had walked down the wrong road. It was too late to turn back, but at least she hadn't lied—well, not exactly lied—about anything.

"The amount is probably somewhere in the low seven figures."

His lips twitched again. He looked Carmen in the eyes. "A strong motive for an assault. Or a murder."

"Murder?" Carmen repeated the word. She felt the blood

drain from her head. "That is a big leap from a scene at a hotel, isn't it?"

"Not as big a leap as you might think. Unlike my predecessor, I will wait for the autopsy results, but given where she was found and . . . uh, other details, it looks like murder."

"She? Who is dead?" She didn't really want to hear the answer.

"Didn't you know?" Chill bored a hole through her. "Surely the news is reporting on it, and I see your set is on."

"I don't know what you are talking about."

"Ethyl Gatz is dead. And the interesting thing is that she was found in exactly the same spot as Jake Harris—at your house. And there are a couple of other things but I can't release those details until my investigation is complete."

"But I was just there!" Carmen blurted.

"At your house? And did you see Ethyl Gatz while you were there?"

"I want to call my attorney," Carmen croaked.

"Good idea, I think you need one."

It was late, the coffee was bitter and Chill had a headache. Even though Gloria Tewblu, high-profile attorney, was in the middle of an equally high-profile divorce in California, she had done a conference call with Chill and Carmen.

So far Carmen was not in jail.

Chill read the autopsy report again. He rubbed his forehead with his rough index finger, but he just couldn't smooth out the wrinkles this report had caused.

Cause of death: extreme trauma to the zygomatic arch.

No trace of foreign matter, gun shot residue.

Traces of H_2O on the blown out eyeball.

Weapon: Unknown.

"How the hell could it be unknown?" Chill had seen a lot of

victims, had attended any number of post mortems. Traces of GSR, or dirt, or wood fibers or metal shavings, or something always remained.

"Until now, evidently."

A loud commotion outside drew his attention. He rose from his chair and went to the window. One of the county cruisers was careening around the building. He saw one of the deputies dash from the car with a coat over their head.

"What the hell?" He left his office and went into the hallway just in time to collide with Vicki Smith.

"Would you mind explaining to me what that was all about?"

She shook out the coat and looked up at him. Her white-blond hair was stylish, her makeup perfect. Underneath the mannish uniform he guessed she was a well-put-together woman; almost reminded him of a California trophy wife.

"Reporter," she said.

"So?"

"So, I am camera shy. I didn't want to talk to them."

"Judging by your makeshift hat you didn't want to be filmed either."

She stared at him for a moment. He had the strangest tug on his memory. For a split second she seemed familiar, like he had met her before.

"I guess you could say that. I hate reporters."

"Well, it would appear we have something in common. Have you made any headway tracking down more information on that nine-one-one call?"

"No, sir, not yet. But I'm still on it."

Chill watched her walk down the hall and enter a small office. She closed the door. He returned to his own office and did the same.

The autopsy report lay there like an ugly insult.

He put the paper aside, pulled the dusty, age darkened rolodex he had inherited from Jim Dunn toward him. He flipped through, some loose business cards falling out onto the desk. He dialed the Office of Medical Investigations in Albuquerque. It took a few minutes of routing, but finally he had the right guy. Chill explained who he was and what he wanted.

"I'm sorry, Sheriff, but what is in the report is all there is."

"The wound was clean?"

"Pristine. The only traces of anything on the victim were the victim's own skin and blood. The hole was neat, smooth edged, round and I don't have a clue what made it."

"Rubber bullet?"

"Possible, I suppose, though nothing at the scene supports that, and there was no rubber bullet. Unlikely the shooter would collect it. But I'm only the M.E. Listen, I used every test I know, I consulted with the crime-scene photos. There were no prints, no patterns, no traces of gun residue, no casings, *nada*, zip. This is a head-scratcher for sure."

"Okay, thanks for your time—and could you do me a favor and fax the results when you are done with the body of a female victim, name Ethyl Gatz?"

The sound of papers rustling and a few clicks on a keyboard. "Oh, yes, I see her here. Sure thing, Sheriff."

"Thanks."

Chill hung up the phone and leaned back in his chair. He laced his fingers behind his head and closed his eyes, trying to visualize the scene of Ethyl Gatz's murder. She had been face down in the mud, eyes open. The right eye was sunken, not blown out like Jake's, but traumatized in a very similar fashion. When they turned her over they found a neat little hole in her temple arch.

"Zygomatic arch shattered. But by what, we have no clue. And no casings," Chill said aloud, wishing Eloy was here so he could bounce ideas off him.

But there was nothing concrete to go on.

Chill knew, because he had processed the scene himself before the state police mobile forensic van had shown up. The only clue had been on the torn bit of paper in her hand: the signature area of a legal document. He was waiting to find out exactly what the document might have been.

What did it all mean? And where was Carmen Pollini when the woman died?

He picked up the cards that had fallen from the rolodex. One was for Maria's restaurant, the Blue Coyote, another for La Señora del Destino, the B&B. The third was a Santa Fe private eye.

Fred Brillstine, Discreet Investigations. Santa Fe, New Mexico. 505-311-5555.

Chill flipped it over. On the back in an untidy hand somebody had scrawled the two words "drug dealer" and the word "snitch."

It was like waving a red flag in front of a bull, or letting a dog get a whiff of a T-bone. Chill couldn't help himself. It was a damned compulsion with him, but he had to know, had to have answers, couldn't leave any loose thread dangling.

He punched in the number.

When Brillstine himself and not a secretary answered on the first ring, it told Chill volumes about the P.I.'s situation. He worked alone, and for whatever reason, didn't have an office staff.

"Mr. Brillstine, I'm the new Taos County sheriff. I wondered if we could meet for coffee sometime this week."

"And now for the latest coverage on the sensational double murder in Taos County." The too-cheerful morning news anchor announced.

Carmen choked on her chorizo and eggs. She had come to the Coyote's kitchen early, even before Maria was up. Now she was coughing, gagging and trying to listen all at the same time; she nearly had to use the stainless counter to perform a Heimlich on herself.

She had risen before the sun, written a couple of pages on her new novel, and then focused on the upcoming book signing at Buy the Book in Santa Fe.

Dax had called her yesterday evening, fuming over his lack of assistant, lack of limousine and having to work with Carmen at all. A headache had threatened all morning. Now it quit threatening and gave her a double-punch between the eyes.

"It must be a slow day in the world," she moaned, using a paper towel to clean up the mess she had made. The local media had made the murders their top story. Guilt by association, or for providing the crime scene twice, had made her name their favorite sound bite.

"The show must go on." She put her dishes in the big double sink and took Tyson out for his morning constitutional. He did his business, which she retrieved with a plastic baggie, and was happy to come back inside to loll around in the patio and keep watch through the doorway while Maria cooked the day's food for the Blue Coyote's customers.

Maria was at the counter chopping green chili, and Ramon was making flour tortillas when Carmen walked back in. The scents and the activity were a soothing balm to Carmen's nerves.

"Be careful today, Carmen. I have a bad feeling." Maria broke a dozen eggs into a round-bottomed stainless bowl. She used a whisk on them until they were a pale yellow froth, then she dumped them into the bowl containing the chopped chili.

Carmen smiled. Maria was a sophisticated, hardheaded, modern businesswoman one minute and superstitious, doting mother the next. How her father had ever wanted to find another woman, Carmen would never understand. From her point of view Maria was mercurial enough to be many women.

"I will, Mom, but honestly, after all that has already happened, what else could possibly go wrong?"

Dax had been flexing and posing all morning and sales were brisk. Ordinarily Carmen would've been overjoyed to see people approaching in a pack to buy her book. But today she didn't greet the large throng with enthusiasm, only dread.

"This is just all wrong." Carmen blinked at the group of people bearing down upon the table where she sat signing her books. This was the third wave, and they were all reporters.

As if to prove her right, a microphone swathed in what looked like a fuzzy condom was shoved into her face.

"Ms. Pollini, what can you tell us about the movie deal?"

"Movie deal?" Her heart did a happy little jig. Every author dreamed of having their book adapted into a movie. Trying to look cool and professional when she wanted to jump up and dance on the table she said, "Oh, I hadn't heard yet. Which of my books are they doing? Is it *Recipe for Murder* or *A Hot Brand of Love*? Maybe *A Twist in Time*? It is nice to see Hollywood interested in good old-fashioned romance again." She ran her fingers along the top of a book hoping she didn't look too much like a game-show hostess.

"Romance?" The reporter looked confused, glanced at the table, took in the photo on the dust jacket, looked back at Carmen and said, "No, the movie deal is going to be offered for a tell-all exposé of crime as you know it in Taos County."

Her heart and her smile were still falling when a different reporter shoved his way forward.

"We hear it is a seven-figure contract if you will name names."

"Names? What names?" Carmen was very confused.

"Come on, Carmen, give us a line. We can begin filming in six weeks if you will play ball. How much do you know about the lawsuit against ex-Sheriff Dunn? Did he try to sexually assault you? What about the bruises on your wrists? Is he into kinky sex?"

Her heart plummeted. Oh, so there was a book and movie deal; it just wasn't one of the books she had written. Hollywood was interested in one of those sleazy, so-called nonfiction exposés, which in reality were more fiction than truth. She didn't want to be one of those kinds of writers.

"Carmen. Look this way."

"Carmen, over here."

Carmen wished she could slink away, return to her little house, put on sweats and be an ordinary romance writer again. She twisted the end of the silk scarf looped around her neck and blinked into the bright lights, knowing she looked either like she was posing for a mug shot or, worse, a deer caught in the headlights. Her eyes burned with unshed tears of anger and frustration.

How had all this happened? How did she land in the middle of Jim Dunn's mess?

Chill stood behind a tall book dump at the end of the aisle and unwrapped two pieces of gum.

He had just stepped into a vortex of hell. Everything in life that bugged him was within his line of sight. First there was Carmen Pollini, writer-probably-murderer. Right next to her were aggressive reporters, only looking for a snappy line, not the truth. And then, the lowest of the low, the Hollywood types who had gathered like jackals on a fresh kill to offer a movie deal. His past flashed before his eyes like a theatrical trailer.

He and his female partner had worked well together. She'd had his back and he'd had hers. It was a great working relationship.

And then the book came out.

Hell, he hadn't even known she was writing a book. Each time she scribbled something in the little note pad she carried, he had naively thought she was taking notes on their current case. From the moment her book hit the stands, his life had never been the same. Between stress over the book and what had happened in the Jetne Sisco case, Chill had crumbled. He had quit a good job and left behind a nice life, and all in search of a little peace.

Now here he was again, staring into the void. He grabbed for more gum, but the pack was empty.

"Ms. Pollini, will you take the offer? Will you reveal the truth about the people found dead at your house?"

"Ms. Pollini."

"Ms. Pollini!"

It was Ontario all over again. Chill had come to this sleepy little town, not looking for a job, sure as hell not looking to stay. He was just killing time and passing through. Yet he was here now, and it felt as if his past followed him like a ghost.

Carmen was round-eyed, in shock, speechless. The reporters were closing in, inching nearer with each unanswered question.

And though he loathed her type, something deep inside him did a little jerk to see her surrounded by those bloodthirsty parasites. It took a minute for him to realize what he was experiencing.

It was pity.

He felt sorry for her.

Imagine that.

Okay, so maybe she wasn't the devil's handmaiden. She might be innocent—it could happen—although Chill had a hard time remembering the last time he met an innocent suspect. She looked good for both murders, for both motive and opportunity. She didn't have any alibi worth considering. Still, there were those E-mails and those packages. But if she was so innocent, then why didn't she come to him for help with those threats?

It didn't add up. And in spite of his dislike for the whole

ridiculous situation, he found himself moving toward the crowd of photogs and reporters. Right now they were focused on the pretty-boy, bright lights held up. The male model was milking it for all he was worth. Then, like a pack of hungry hyenas, they left him standing there and shifted back toward Carmen.

She blinked in the glare of the lights, leaning back to avoid the microphone being shoved up her nose.

At the very moment he was about to burst from the crowd and rescue the fair maiden, pretty-boy had a bona fide, ego-strutting meltdown.

"Hey, if you guys want a story that will sell, you should be talking to me." He jabbed himself in the chest with his thumb.

His high-pitched voice caught everyone's attention. Chill had to admire the guy; it took a lot of brass and ability to shut up a reporter, but he had managed to quell more than half a dozen of the cockroaches.

"And if there are any movie deals being offered, they should be coming to me. I can tell stories that will curl your hair about casting-couch auditions and other things that go on. I *know* things. I know things about Carmen Pollini, things she wouldn't want told. She's no different than any other writer. What do you think they really do at those conventions?"

"Why, you lousy rat!" Carmen exploded from her chair with her eyes snapping and her claws bared.

Chill melted back into the growing crowd just to watch unobserved. This was a once-in-a-lifetime opportunity to see just how bad her temper could be.

Carmen ignored the reporters, elbowing cameramen out of her way as she closed the distance between herself and Dax.

"How dare you?" She advanced on him until they were toe to toe. That in itself was a feat. She was so much shorter than the model, she had to stand on her toes and angle her neck, but she didn't seem to find the position in any way a hindrance to the tongue lashing she was providing.

"You smarmy creep. I'll tell you what goes on at those conventions. A lot of hardworking writers, editors and booksellers spend their time and energy trying to show the readers in this country how much we appreciate them."

"Uh-huh, yeah, but after dark—" Dax grinned at the reporters who were closing around them in a tightening circle.

"After dark, nothing happens except to those vulnerable women who are propositioned and seduced by the likes of you!"

There was a collective gasp from the few readers who had remained by the book table. It took half a second for everyone to digest what had been said; then comments and snickers rippled through the readers and the reporters. In a millisecond they processed the information and started shooting questions like Uzis.

"Ms. Pollini, are you saying you were seduced by Dax?"

"Ms. Pollini, were you and Dax lovers?"

"Ms. Pollini, did Dax seduce you, dump you and break your heart?"

"Carmen, are you sleeping with Dax now?"

"Of course not." Carmen gasped. "Where did you get such a ridiculous idea?"

Dax grinned and looped his arm around her shoulder. "We met at a conference. Yep, she was just a writer from the sticks. I could tell you things about Carmen—"

She shoved his arm off and stepped away, fury in her face. "Oh, I could—I could—"

"Just kill him?" Shouted a deep voice from the crowd.

Carmen turned to search the group. Chill watched her face. He couldn't deny it; there was murder in her eye.

CHAPTER FOURTEEN

Chill pulled into the parking lot and turned off the engine of the police cruiser. He got out of the car and started walking, charmed by the Spanish Colonial architecture. A light snow had been falling all morning, frosting the roofs and making the central plaza of Old Town Albuquerque look like something from a Currier and Ives print.

Brillstine had insisted they meet in the square in Albuquerque, not Santa Fe. He said he wanted to be out in the open with plenty of people around. Chill had assumed Brillstine would know the area, but the day was crisp and cold and not many tourists were enjoying the plaza.

He pulled up the collar of his shearling and turtled into the warmth. He was willing to tolerate a little cold if it meant getting some answers. Jim Dunn was not the run-of-the-mill cop. If he had a P.I.'s name in his rolodex, Chill's cop-radar said there was a damned good reason.

Brillstine had also told Chill to keep their meeting secret. No big hardship there. Chill hadn't decided who, if anybody, in his own department he could trust. The Taos sheriff's department wasn't that big. If Dunn was dirty, then somebody in the department knew it. Either they were on the take or they were being forced to remain silent.

Chill didn't like the prospect of either possibility, so he hadn't told anybody about this trip. His car radio started acting up just before he hit Albuquerque. It was a terrific quirk of fate. If anybody in Taos needed him, they were going to play hell getting him on the police radio.

Chill followed instructions and went to one of the wrought-iron benches surrounding the plaza. In summer it would offer a place to sit under the shade of the trees. Now it was cold, the view wintry and stark. Skeletal branches reached for the sky, reminding Chill that Old Town had seen the cowboy era come and go.

"Are you Sheriff Blaines?" A gruff whisper came from behind a bare, rough tree trunk.

"Who wants to know?" Chill thought this kind of thing only happened in old spy movies.

"I do."

"Sorry to be a hard-ass but I don't converse with trees. Who are you?"

A hat-covered head peeked around the trunk. A plaid muffler was wrapped over the bottom of the face, leaving only the eyes exposed—eyes that darted around like a mouse searching for a trap.

"I'm Fred Brillstine. Are you alone?"

Chill had worked with informants who burned drug lords and were not this paranoid. Something had surely spooked this fellow. "Yep. I did everything just like you asked. You want to search me?"

"No. I think I can trust you. Let's walk." Fred Brillstine stepped out from behind the tree. He was tall, thin, shrouded in a long, worn, brown trench coat. Chill felt like he had just entered the world of cheesy espionage and B movies.

"Tell me how you got my name and number," Brillstine demanded.

Chill could play by this guy's rules if it meant getting answers. "I found it in Jim Dunn's rolodex when I inherited it along with his job."

"I heard about Jim. Tough luck, eh?"

"Don't know the man. Was it luck or was it the truth?"

Fred Brillstine stopped walking. He looked into Chill's face for a long moment. "I don't know and I don't want to know. Jim Dunn has enemies. I wish I had never worked for him."

"What kind of work did you do for Jim Dunn?" Chill asked, trying to ignore the tingling tip of his half-frozen nose.

"Started out as a straight investigation. He wanted to see if he could find any dirt on a young woman."

The cop-radar was jingling now. Was Carmen in the middle of this? "Did you?"

"Not really. I kind of ran into a brick wall. What I did find looked good, almost too good."

"Too good?"

"Just a feeling. Anyway I got what he asked for, he paid me, then he contacted me again, wanting me to dig deeper. That's when they started coming." When what started coming?"

"The death threats. By E-mail. I get one a day, regular as clockwork. It upset my secretary so much she quit. Like I said, Jim Dunn has enemies."

"Tell me the name of the young woman he had you investigate."

Because of traffic and a new storm that brought snow, ice and blistering winds, it was late when Chill pulled back into the parking lot of the police station. The lot was empty and quiet, the white blanket muffling ordinary sound, making him edgy.

His cop-radar was still jangling in his head. He had turned over the information Brillstine had given him, turned it inside out, and studied every possibility.

He didn't like any of them. He jerked open the door and went inside the station.

He found Victoria Smith manning the phones and desk, only

one flickering fluorescent light burning overhead. The wind whipped around the building like a hungry bear on the prowl.

"Where have you been?" There was an edge to her voice that went right to Chill's last nerve.

"I was out. What's up?"

"The male model, what's his name? Dax?" She rummaged through some papers on her desk. "Yeah, that's him. He was kneecapped in the parking lot of Buy the Book."

Chill's skin felt too tight for his bones. He didn't like the pattern that was forming. Anybody who had a beef with Carmen Pollini seemed to have a bull's-eye on their back—or in this case, his knee.

"Any witnesses?"

"None."

"With all the press milling around nobody saw anything? Those bloodsuckers have a nose for news, and yet they are never of any use."

"The press had left shortly after Carmen Pollini. Evidently Dax had a few sweet-young-things hanging on his every word, so he stuck around charming them until nearly closing time."

"What is the victim saying?"

"He didn't see anything but he swears it was Carmen getting even for something he told the press. You were there today, weren't you?"

"Yeah, I was there. If you need me, call my cell phone." Chill turned on his heel.

"Where are you going?"

"To get some sleep."

Chill drove straight to La Señora del Destino, breaking the speed limit all the way.

He had waited long enough. Tonight he was getting answers from Ms. Carmen Pollini. "Or I'm locking her ass up," Chill snarled to nobody but himself.

Maybe Jim Dunn had been right on track to take her in. Perhaps he was dealing with a psycho. It did seem damned odd that anybody who crossed Carmen, from a deliveryman to a male model making sexual innuendos, got hurt. Dax was probably lucky he didn't have a smooth round hole in his head.

"Lucky the fool didn't go to Carmen's house," Chill muttered. But staying away from Carmen's house hadn't kept him from getting kneecapped.

Such was the state of Chill's mind when he strode into the B&B. The warmth from a roaring fire enveloped him as he entered the building. He heard voices and followed the sound. Tony, Maria, and Carmen were sitting in the snug wood-paneled front parlor-cum-lobby, their feet pointing toward the kiva style fireplace. They had their backs to him and he didn't announce his presence, preferring to listen.

"I'm telling you, Pop, Dax isn't worth the cost of a bullet!"

"Carmen! You don't mean that." Maria patted her daughter's shoulder.

"Yes, I do, Mom. He is low. You don't know what he has done. I could tell you stories—"

"Why don't you tell me instead, Miss Pollini?" Chill walked into the center of the room and slid into a leather armchair near Tony. He pulled out a stick of gum and chomped on it.

"Mr. Blaines, you go too far." Maria bristled. "This is a private conversation."

"Sorry, ma'am, but when I'm in the middle of investigating two murders, nothing is private."

Tony glared at Chill. "Then I think Carmen should call her attorney."

Chill had no intention of backing off. "Fine, you do that. Get her on the horn or get her here. I don't care which, but Carmen and I are going to have a talk, and if Gloria Tewblu wants to serve me with paper because of it, she can go for it. Any objections?"

"You know it is too late to reach anyone, Sheriff Blaines." Maria narrowed her eyes at him.

"Carmen, you can refuse. Then I will have to take you down to the station. You can sit in a cell until morning when your attorney can fly in. How about it, Carmen? You want to talk here or in your lawyer's presence at the jail?"

Carmen glared at him, but she didn't say a word. She also didn't reach for the cordless phone resting on the pine table beside the couch.

"Okay. I'll take that to mean you are volunteering to speak with me. Now Carmen, I want you to tell me what happened today between you and Dax Des Planes."

"He said something I didn't like."

"And?"

"And nothing. I finished signing my books and left. I went to see Millie Hyde, checked my house and then I came here. We all had dinner together after the rush."

"You didn't continue your little chat outside the bookstore later?"

"Of course not. Why? What has happened?" Carmen leaned toward Chill, her eyes wide. Either she didn't know, or this little gal deserved to win a Golden Globe for her acting.

"Dax got kneecapped. He's in the hospital in Santa Fe. Oh, and I hear he is threatening to sue you."

"Is he going to be all right?"

Chill shrugged, noticing she paid little attention to the threat of legal action.

"He may never be able to do *Swan Lake* again." Chill watched carefully, concentrating on her face and eyes for any tell, any little unguarded tick that might give him a clue. Everybody had a tell, Chill just had to figure out what Carmen's tell was.

Hot breath fanned across the side of his neck.

"Argh!" Chill swiped at his ear as a brown blur of solid weight rushed at him. He didn't know what to expect. Rats? Coyotes? Tony gone mad? What he didn't expect was a stout, well-fed canine. The same boxer Chill had seen in Carmen's photographs had taken a nibble of his ear.

"He bit me!" Chill exclaimed.

Tony laughed. "Good dog. Come." He patted the wide, wrinkled forehead and chucked the dog under his chin when Tyson trotted up beside him.

"Good dog? Are you crazy? He bites me and you tell him he is a good dog?" Chill's earlobe stung like fire. "What in hell do you mean, 'good dog'? I ought to shoot him."

Maria grinned. "You were not being nice to Carmen. He doesn't like it when people are nasty to Carmen."

"Yeah, well it looks like Carmen and her dog have a lot in common. Anybody who is nasty to Carmen gets hurt or dead. He bit me. He bit my ear, and you three are acting like he should be given the canine-of-the-year award."

"Hey, he wasn't named Tyson because he likes chicken." Carmen tried not to laugh as she told him.

Tyson hopped up on the loveseat and sat at Tony's side, leaning into the hand that scratched his ear. "Be happy he only went for the left one. He has been known to get them both."

"I should lock him up—and his master too." Chill touched his ear and felt something wet. Sure enough, it was blood. Chill had no trouble with blood, unless it was his own.

Tyson stared at him, his dark brown eyes watching Chill's every move. Then he started snarling, the hackles rising on his wide neck and shoulder. Chill realized the dog was staring past him at the big double doors that led to the private garden.

"Tyson? What is it boy?" Tony and the boxer left the loveseat at the same time. The dog started barking in earnest, the deep sound rumbling through the room, bouncing off the adobe walls.

"Someone is out there. I see a shadow," Maria said.

Chill reached the door in three long strides. He had his gun out, his eyes scanning the patio. There were tracks in the snow leading from the high wall and back again.

"Whoever it was jumped the wall."

"He left something behind." Tony stood near the fountain, Tyson was growling at a dark shape in the snow.

"It is a package. Addressed to Carmen."

CHAPTER FIFTEEN

Chill went outside and around the back of La Señora del Destino. The snow was falling harder, collecting in the nooks and crannies of the old adobe walls. The wind broomed white powder across the parking lot. He thought he saw faint footprints, but the weather was wiping away the evidence quicker than he could follow the trail. The prints.

There was no point in calling in a unit or giving chase. Whoever brought the package was long gone.

Unless the prints and the package had all been a plant. Tyson could've been barking for any number of reasons. Chill wasn't a green newbie at this. It would have been easy for Carmen to have planted the package at an earlier time and then call attention to it when she needed a diversion—just like now, when he was grilling her about Dax's injury.

Chill didn't like the direction of his thoughts, but Carmen's complicity was certainly something he would have to consider carefully. Right now he was freezing, and the answers were just as likely to be found in front of the fire as out in the storm.

When Chill reentered the building Tony, Maria and Tyson were still in the parlor. But Carmen was nowhere in sight. The nagging tingle of his cop-radar was binging again.

Carmen popped the lid on the acetaminophen and shook two into her palm. Then she shook out one more. Her headaches were getting worse, especially when she had to talk to that beady-eyed sheriff.

She tossed the pills into her mouth and ran a glass of water, when there came a sharp rap on her door. The pills got stuck, gagging her. She was coughing, trying not to strangle, when she heard the voice.

"Carmen?"

Eyes watering, trying to catch her breath, she whirled toward the door. Chill Blaines was knocking on her door. The man was like a bloodhound. No. He was a bloodsucker, an emotional vampire, a creature of the night. He was—

"I need to speak to you. Now."

"If I ignore you, it wouldn't do me any good, would it? You won't go away, will you?"

"No."

"What do you want to talk to me about?" She sagged onto the bed, glaring at the thick, locked door standing between her and the long-arm-of-the-law.

"I want you to open this package."

Carmen closed her eyes. She didn't even want to look at the package, because it only reminded her that someone was out there, stalking her, following her, sending her unwanted gifts that made her skin crawl. She dragged herself up and walked to the wooden door. She turned the key in the old wrought-iron lock and pulled the door open.

He stood there, all chiseled angles and condemning looks, holding a white box. It was tied up with a huge pink bow. How could such banal wrapping cover something so frightening?

"Why don't you open it, Sheriff? In fact, take it away and do whatever you want with it. I don't want to see it again."

"Aren't you curious about what's inside?"

"Not really."

"Could that be because you know what is in it?"

Carmen snatched the oversized box from his hands. She slammed it down on the mattress and ripped the bow off. Then she flung the lid off, tore through the scented tissue paper and jerked the Barbie pink lacy lingerie out.

"Surprise." Carmen thrust the slinky garment in his face. "Here, take it." A card fluttered to the floor.

Chill bent and picked it up. " 'Dearest Carmen. You've been on my mind. I hate to see you looking so sad—' "

"Stop! I don't want to hear it." Carmen clamped her hands over her ears, but couldn't block out the sheriff's deep voice.

" 'I hope you wear this tonight and have sweet dreams. Your number-one fan is on your side. I'm here to help.' "

Chill stopped reading. He pulled a tissue from the box near the bed and wrapped the card in it. Then he shoved it in his shirt pocket.

"Touching. Now, Carmen, I want to know why you haven't reported these gifts and the threats you've been getting."

"How do you know about that?" Carmen stared at Chill. "You read my E-mail that day, didn't you?"

"It's my job to be nosey. Have you received more?"

"I haven't checked," Carmen lied. She had checked every day, and every day there had been new threats. It was a childish thing to do, lying to the law, but Chill Blaines made her see red. She wasn't telling him anything.

Carmen's face was a study in stubborn determination. Chill knew the woman was digging in her heels. Obviously he wasn't getting through to her. Maybe it was time to try another tack.

"Carmen, what would it take for you to trust me?"

"Could you get your tongue notarized?"

He smiled. The broad had a mouth on her. Sharp tongue, sharp mind, soft curves. A powerful combination.

"Come on, stop trying to be so tough. Power up your laptop

and let's see what's there tonight. You know, I just might surprise you."

A short while later Chill and Carmen were at a table in the Blue Coyote with the laptop between them. The restaurant had been closed for hours, and they had the place to themselves. In an attempt to facilitate an atmosphere of peace between the two, Maria had insisted they have something to eat, but even her best leftover enchiladas, sopaipillas and rellenos had failed to smooth over the gulf of suspicion and distrust that stretched between them. Tony brought two blended margaritas to the table.

"Here. Maria told me to give you two these. She thinks you both could use some tequila."

Carmen tipped her glass up for a long drink. "You may need to bring me another one, Pop."

Chill raised a thick brow at the girly-looking drink.

Hard liquor was not his thing. He didn't like it or the way it affected him.

"What, no umbrella? That's kind of a frilly-looking drink. I'm more of a beer man."

"Ever hear the adage, When in Rome?" Carmen took a sip of her drink and licked the glass. "Of course, if you think you are too much of a pantywaist—"

Hey, it wasn't his style. He hated the hard stuff, but he wasn't about to let Carmen get his goat. Besides, this might be the perfect opportunity to interrogate an inebriated suspect. Besides, his earlobe was throbbing and he could use some oral anesthetic.

He would just sip at the stuff, then order a beer.

Right on cue Tyson padded toward the table.

"I bet the health department would take a dim view of your watchdog."

Tyson gave Chill a go-to-hell look as he padded by. He sat at Carmen's side, watching—probably waiting for a clear shot at the remaining, unblemished earlobe.

"You are really an unpleasant man. Has anybody ever told you that?"

"Once or twice." Chill suppressed a smile. That damned dog was something special. Chill had a soft spot for dogs, and especially gutty, quirky mutts with muggy faces that looked like puckered velvet. Tyson fit the bill on all three counts.

"Go on, try it. You might like it." Carmen indicated the salt-rimmed glass Chill still hadn't touched. She picked up a steaming sopaipilla and poked a hole in it with her index finger. Then she drizzled honey inside from a squeeze bottle Tony had provided.

She took a bite, licking at the honey that dripped. It was damned provocative.

"Will you answer a question?" Chill sipped the drink experimentally, tentatively. It was good; not sweet, not sour, some exotic blending that tingled on the back of his tongue. Not half bad, but he wasn't going to tell Carmen.

"So what do you want to know?" She forked a bit of enchilada into her mouth. She had a good appetite, not like those California waifs who lived on caffeine and the dream of becoming a Hollywood darling.

"Why didn't you report the E-mails?" He glanced at the screen of her laptop. There were at least a dozen E-mails with the same gobbledygook address.

"I didn't think it would be in my best interest." Carmen took another drink.

"In what way?" Chill took a sip of his margarita and studied her face. Was she on the level, or was she working her way to the top of the writing heap in another way? Could all this be some by-product of a publicity stunt gone bad? How in hell could a R.E.D. driver figure into that plan?

"Look, Jim Dunn didn't inspire a lot of confidence." Carmen set down her fork and looked Chill in the eye. "He has a reputation of being a good-ol'-boy, among other things. I didn't want to deal with him." She took another long sip of her drink.

"Okay, I can buy that. When did the threatening E-mails start coming?"

"It all started just before Jake . . . died."

"He was murdered. So was Ethyl. The same way." Chill bit out the words. "I want you to understand, Carmen. We have the autopsy reports now. It was murder, a double murder. The same method did them both. I will catch the person who did it. I always catch the bad guy—or girl."

She put her glass on the table, took a deep breath and looked him straight in the face. "Do you really think I did it?"

Did he?

She had a temper.

There was the mysterious incident that was so damning, nobody in town would actually mention the details.

He looked at her sparkling dark eyes and decided she was capable of hot emotions on several levels. He had no doubt Carmen could be moved to violence—passion—and deep affection.

"I haven't decided. I don't like to jump to conclusions until I see where the evidence leads me."

Okay, so maybe he had half-decided, but he wasn't going to admit it.

"Well, at least you are honest." She cut into her relleno and took a bite, clearly enjoying her food. Chill would bet this girl had never ordered California cuisine in her life. Yet she was trim, but not anorexic. Damn, it was a nice change to see a woman who didn't look like a freaking lollipop.

"Do I have chili on my chin?" she asked.

"What?"

"You were staring." Carmen sipped her drink, gazing at him over the salty rim.

The margarita was good. He had already sipped up half of it. Maybe that was why he kept thinking of Carmen as a woman instead of a possible suspect. He forced himself to focus on the murders, the clues, Carmen's motives and her failure to come clean.

"Now, tell me about the gifts from your secret admirer."

"Pop said you saw them at my house. I think there must be something unethical about that."

Chill suppressed a smile. She was a looker. Those dark brown eyes were deep and full of smarts. "There isn't. I didn't do a search. Your father found them and called my attention to them."

"He said you took a card with you. What did you do with it?"

"I'm having prints lifted and run against all the data bases if you must know."

"So, you don't think I'm guilty." Carmen sounded triumphant.

"One thing doesn't necessarily have anything to do with the other—does it?"

"You're the cop, you tell me." She grinned at him. This was the problem with questioning a suspect over dinner and drinks. It was tough as hell to keep it professional.

"Carmen, I'm not going to lie to you. Right now you are the most likely suspect. So unless you want to come clean with me and give me something else to go on, things don't look good for you, especially with the attack on Dax."

Carmen had come clean—or at least cleaner, she told herself. She let Chill copy down the address on the E-mails; she told him all she knew about the gifts from her secret admirer.

She did not tell him about the many arguments she had with Jake or the fact that Ethyl had told her she was going to file bankruptcy and thereby insure Carmen never got her royalty funds.

A girl couldn't give away all her secrets.

CHAPTER SIXTEEN

Chill took off his boots and skinned off his Pendleton shirt. There was something to be said for the cowboy-casual uniform he had adopted. He was aware he hadn't quite got it right— Carmen looked at his bolo tie and wrinkled her nose in distaste every time—but he was a work in progress.

Eventually he would have it down, and nobody would be able to tell him from a local.

He sat on the edge of the bed and poked the speed dial on his cell. Eloy's voice brought a smile to his face.

"This had better be good. It's late."

"What? No hello for an old friend?" Chill swiveled around and jammed a pillow under his head, wrestling with the thick bedspread he hadn't bothered to turn down.

"All right, let's start again. Hey, buddy! About time you called. Where are you?"

"New Mexico."

"Okay, you played the odds in Nevada and became nature-boy in Colorado. So what the hell does somebody do in the winter in New Mexico?" Eloy chuckled.

"Solve crimes?"

"Yeah, right. It must be nice to be on one long vacation. So you got nothing better to do than wake up old friends who have to be at the salt mine in three hours?"

"Vacation is over. I took a job as sheriff of Taos County."
Silence.

"Eloy?"

"Dammit to hell, Chill, if you wanted to go back to work, why not work for me?" The tone blistered Chill's sore ear, so he switched the phone to the other side.

"I didn't want to. It sort of just fell into my lap."

"Right. Uh-huh. So, I guess congratulations are in order. Congratulations. Thanks for calling."

Eloy was pissed, Chill knew that tone from way back.

"Eloy, I also called for a favor."

A snort. "You always had more brass than a marching band. First you tell me you are working for someone else and you want a favor. Not too smart, Chill. You should have asked for the favor first."

"I thought about that, but the minute I did you would've known." Chill couldn't help but laugh at his old friend.

"What do you need?"

"I'm going to give you an ISP address. I want you to track any messages incoming or outgoing over the last couple of months to two different E-mail addresses."

"Hey, doesn't New Mexico have this capability?"

"Probably, but I know I can trust you."

"That doesn't sound good. What have you got yourself into?"

"I'm not sure, but I've got two vics, and at least one person in my department has a past they are trying to hide."

Chill gave Eloy the E-mail addresses and hung up the phone. A white piece of paper was peeking out of the front pocket of the shirt he had tossed on the carpet. He picked it up, staring at the neat numbers.

He wasn't sure why he hadn't confronted Carmen about it. This little piece of paper would have caught her in a lie—the first real proof that she had not come clean. A part of Chill's brain—the hard-boiled cop part, nagged at him. It wasn't like him to hesitate when he had hard proof. And yet . . . there was something nagging at the back of his mind, something he had to analyze and digest before he confronted Carmen Pollini.

Carmen opened the drapes of room number three and looked down on a perfect winter morning.

She opened the old-fashioned window and leaned out. The air was clear; tiny sparkling jewels lay in the fluffy new fall of snow and in the frozen mist stirred by the breeze.

"You know, Tyson, I've been a coward lately, and I don't like it." Carmen had never let herself just roll along with the flow, but lately she had been off-kilter. Finding Jake's body had turned her into a victim, and she was sick of it. She filled her lungs with air and made a resolution.

"I'm going to find out who is stalking me and take charge of my life, Tyson." And as she said those words, it seemed a huge weight lifted from her shoulders. She was smiling, inside and out, about to turn away from the lovely view when a sleek, black sports car roared out of the La Señora del Destino parking lot, spraying up a rooster tail of snow.

Chill had left the B&B early. Whether it was because he wanted to get a jump on the day or because he wanted to avoid Carmen Pollini, he couldn't decide. It was hard to be objective when he looked into those dark eyes.

"Not all the bad girls look like dirt bags," he reminded himself.

The police station was buzzing with activity when he walked in. Victoria Smith jumped up out of her chair and brought him an envelope and a cup of coffee.

"Sir, this came by FedEx. Looks like it is from a bank in Taos." The strip on the envelope was intact, but Chill would bet his bottom dollar Victoria wished she had X-ray vision.

"Mmm, it is." He took the envelope and the cup and went

into his office, leaving her standing there, salivating with curiosity. Chill was beginning to like his office. Nice thing about small towns; they rarely went for all that glass-window crap. There wasn't a single window in his office. Once he closed the door he was alone, away from prying eyes.

He ripped the strip and dumped the papers out onto his desk.

Carmen Pollini's financial life lay before him in neat columns of numbers on several sheets of computer printouts. Chill's eye found the bottom line and read each column.

He slammed the cup of hot brew down on the desk, sloshing some, burning his hand.

"I'll be a son of—she's done it again." He exploded from his chair and headed for the door.

"Sir?" Victoria Smith called out.

He didn't even slow down as he headed to the Crown Vic. This time she was going to jail, and if he had his way, she was going to stay there.

"Tyson, calm down. We aren't going home to stay, just long enough to meet the glaziers and get them started." Carmen drove carefully, under the speed limit, hands at two and ten, checking her rearview mirror often. The last thing she wanted was to attract the attention of a sharp-eyed sheriff.

The day was glorious. Sparkling diamonds winked in the deep blanket of untouched snow in the fields on either side of the highway.

She turned on to her lane and slammed on the brakes so hard, Tyson lost his footing and ended up on the floorboard.

He glared up at her.

"Sorry," Carmen said, never taking her eyes off the scene before her. Once again her road looked like a parking lot. There were vans, cars, pickups.

"What gives? It's not time for Penny's party."

A group of wild-looking people with futuristic weaponry in their hands was milling around in the street. She eased up to a small group and put her window down.

"What's going on?"

"Penny sold a painting to a gallery in New York!" one dread-head said.

"She is giving out free food and booze until it runs out." Another guy brandished a neon blue phazer that would've done any Trekkie proud.

"What are those, stun guns?" Carmen asked.

"Nah, we're paintballers, dude," the dread-head said.

"Ahh, I see," Carmen lied. She didn't know crap about paint-ballers. "Thanks." She rolled up her window and drove down the lane, the sense of déjà vu chilling her.

"I'm not a victim. I'm not a victim." She rolled her shoulders as if she could shrug off the memory of the last time she did this. Finally a space appeared and she drove into it.

"Come on, Tyson." She was glad he was with her.

The boxer jumped out of the car. He plunged into a deep drift, finding virgin snow. He plowed through it, coming up with a little clump of white on his nose.

Carmen checked her watch. The glaziers were due in less than half an hour.

"Half an hour. What could possibly happen in half an hour?"

She had decided to get her house in order and move back in. Staying at La Señora was a wimpy, immature decision. She was a grown woman and should be back in her own home.

She told herself that having Sheriff Blaines next door had nothing to do with changing her address.

The house had that awful, abandoned feel when she let herself inside, but she ignored it and grabbed a broom, turned on the furnace and started sweeping up the glass. Each step crunched more glass under the soles of her fur-lined boots, grating on her nerves like nails dragged over a chalkboard.

"Too quiet." Carmen flipped on her CD player. Tyson was still outside, playing snow-plow. She swept in time to the music, dumping the shards into a trash bag as she went.

It broke her heart to see her gingham curtains, made by her own two hands, ripped and torn by the glass. She grabbed a chair and pulled it near the broken window. The rod was over her head so she had to stretch to reach it. Her fingers closed over the end and she was able to take it down and slide the ruined curtains off and into the pile of glass.

The last song on the CD ended. For a brief moment there was silence—or there should've been. Carmen could hear the mournful strains of music coming from the direction of her bedroom. She listened hard, but then her own CD player selected another tune, blaring it out and filling the kitchen with music.

Carmen jumped from the chair and jammed down the stop button. The CD was silent, but music was still playing somewhere else in the house.

No matter what was in that room, she wasn't going to cut and run. Not again. Uh-huh, no way. She was not a victim.

She grabbed up the broom, holding it like a weapon, and crept to the living room, down the hall until she could see the doorway to her bedroom.

She screamed and ran.

Chill spat out his old gum and dug for a new pack in the inside pocket of the down vest he was wearing over his shoulder holster. He unwrapped a stick and popped it into his mouth. He wasn't happy.

He'd rushed from the P.D. to La Señora del Destino only to discover that Carmen had flown the coop. He pushed the accelerator to the floor, his lights flashing, his temper rising. He should've known.

"After all, she is a writer. That should've been all I needed to know. Can't reason with them, can't trust them. When will I ever learn?"

He was convinced now. She was guilty as sin. He still didn't have a reasonable motive for Jake's murder but Ethyl was classic.

"Sheesh. Stealing from her client. There couldn't be a better reason for a hot-head like Carmen to do her in."

He was still bothered by the lack of forensics or any clue to the murder weapon, but that would come. When he had Carmen in custody, he was going to sweat her old-school until he got some answers.

He turned on his siren. The car fishtailed a bit when he swung on to the road. He braked sharply, stunned to see the collection of vehicles parked along the lane. Crowds of people were dancing and laughing in the snowy street, their voices carrying on the crisp, cold air.

"Dammit all to hell," Chill cursed as he threw the car into park. He barreled out of the car and did a quick jog toward Carmen's house. The police tape was still across the front door area, so he headed to the backyard. Tyson met him, snow crusted on his nose, his tongue lolling out of his mouth like a red Christmas ribbon. He was in a frisky mood, leaping and barking. But suddenly the air was filled with a woman's high-pitched scream. Tyson started growling.

"What the hell?" Chill put his hand on the butt of his gun, but he was hit hard in the chest before he could pull it out. He landed on his keister in the snow.

"He's here! He's here!" Carmen was beside him. She tried to crawl away, but he grabbed her by the elbow, dragging her to her feet when he stood up, and then spun her around to face him.

"Who is here?"

"My secret admirer! The stalker." Her face was whiter than the snow clinging to her clothes.

"Where?"

"My bedroom."

Chill let go of her elbow. "Stay put. And keep Tyson here too, I don't want him getting shot." He drew his gun and slipped in through the open kitchen door. Moving as quietly as he could, he went room to room, checking each one before he moved on, working his way toward Carmen's bedroom. He remembered the layout of the house from his tour with Tony.

The doorway of her room yawned before him. He saw it all before he was even in the room. A hard knot formed in his gut, and his assurance that Carmen was guilty quaked a little.

Stacked neatly in the middle of the bed, each one tied with a pretty pink bow, were all the boxes he had seen in the hall closet the night he and Tony checked Carmen's house. Burning candles were everywhere: on the dresser, the nightstand, the bookshelf, filling the room with a cloying, sweet scent. A vase of pink roses with a balloon card sat on a plant stand.

But there was no stalker.

Chill checked the closet, the bathroom and moved to the broken bedroom window. The glass had been carefully removed, the curtain fluttered out the tall opening.

He stuck his head out and looked into the snow beneath the window. Deep footprints caught his eye.

Whirling on his heel, Chill headed to the front of the house. He flung open the door and peered out. Footprints came from the back of the house, ran along the side, toward the cluster of cars parked along the road.

"Son of a—" With this many cars and people coming and going into Penny Black's house, Chill knew he had little chance of catching the perp, but he wasn't giving up.

He holstered his gun and ran toward the road, following the tracks until they blended into the slush created by the dancing party-goers. One girl grabbed Chill's arm, doing a little jig, laughing. If the stalker were among this group, then he was blending in well. It might be any of them—or none of them.

Chill untangled himself from the group and returned to Carmen's house. He entered the house through the front door and closed it behind him, throwing the dead bolt. It was way past time for Carmen and him to have a talk.

CHAPTER SEVENTEEN

Carmen was shaking, and no matter how she tried to control the tremors, her body would not obey. The scene in her bedroom flashed through her mind. Even now, the sweet smell of the roses made her stomach roll, and the flicker of the candles still burned the back of her eyelids.

"Here, drink this." Chill shoved a Styrofoam cup into her hands. She took it and obediently sipped. Something hot, strong and bitter slid down her throat. Coffee? Maybe.

"Now tell me again, from the top," Chill ordered.

Carmen blinked and tried to focus. She was sitting in the sheriff's office, the door shut, Tyson beside her. Funny, she didn't quite remember how she got here.

"Carmen?"

"Oh, okay. I—I called the glaziers. They were coming to replace the glass so I could move back home. I heard a noise, it was . . . music." Her voice cracked. Embarrassment at her weakness sent heat flooding her cheeks.

So much for not being a victim.

"Go on." Chill stared at her, not a whit of sympathy in his gaze. Okay, fine. She could hold up to anything this hard-ass tossed at her.

"I went into the bedroom. The packages were on my bed, I saw—something. A shadow. A movement from the corner of my eye. Now that I think back, it was his reflection in my mirror, I screamed and ran. Then I bumped into you. The rest you know."

"Could you identify him?"

"No, I don't think so. It was just a flash, and mostly his back and the side of his head. He was fair. That's about all I can tell you."

Chill leaned back in his chair and watched her.

"You know, I was coming to arrest you. I had my siren wailing and lights going—"

"He . . . he must've heard you and left." She shivered again.

"Possible. Or maybe you staged the whole thing, huh?"

"How dare you?" She put the cup on the edge of his desk and leaned forward. "What kind of sicko do you think I am?"

"I'm not quite sure, but I know you are a liar."

The word hit her like a slap to the face. Carmen did a lot of stupid things, okay. Maybe. From time to time she might even bend the truth some, but she had never been called a liar.

She stood up, closed the space between her and the man leaning back in his chair. She slapped Sheriff Chill Blaines across the cheek.

Carmen expected him to cuff her and take her to a cell. Instead he growled—or rumbled. And that rumble turned into a deep belly laugh.

"I wouldn't advise you to make a habit of that, but you just saved yourself a night in the lockup."

"You are crazy. Has anybody ever told you that?"

"More than once."

"I don't understand," Carmen whispered.

"Yeah, I know you don't, but I do. I understand liars, cheats, con artists and the genuine act of an innocent person. This might be the first time I have seen you act spontaneously without thinking it over and deciding on the pros and cons." Chill rubbed his cheek. "You've got one hell of a temper."

"So everyone keeps telling me." Carmen sagged back into her chair, weary and confused.

A knock on the door, and the door opened. Victoria Smith stepped inside.

"I'm headed over to Carmen's place like you wanted."

"Good. I want the house processed top to bottom, and I don't want to call in the Staters on this. Can you handle it alone?"

"Sure." Her face was a calm picture of confidence. As usual, she was neat as a pin, her pale hair up off her slender neck. The mannish uniform actually looked good on her slender form.

"Glad to hear it. I want prints, pictures, and I want the place sealed tight."

"Got it."

Chill started to turn away, but paused. "Hey, Smith, where did you train?"

"Cal—" She bit off her words. "All officers go through the New Mexico Academy to get certified here."

"Oh, I didn't know that," Chill lied. "Then I won't have to worry that you will screw it up."

"No, sir."

When the door was closed, Chill once again observed Carmen, sitting stiff as a cadaver in a gray metal chair that had probably been here since Carter was in office.

Tyson nudged Carmen's arm until she gave him a pat on the head. Then he rested his wide, wrinkled head in her lap.

Chill smiled. That was one cute mutt.

The drive from the police station to La Señora del Destino was slow, due to the influx of elk hunters. Chill had never seen so many weapons openly displayed. Right now it was only the black-powder enthusiasts and the bow hunters, but Tony had warned him that soon the town would swell with trophy hunters wanting to bag one of the monsters New Mexico was famous for producing. It tickled Chill that the tree-hugging Hollywood types would be cheek by jowl with testosterone-overloaded predators for the next few months. Evidently, shooting was a hobby in this area. He cast a sidelong glance at his passenger.

"Carmen, do you hunt?" he asked.

"I beg your pardon?"

"Do you hunt? Elk, deer or other things?"

"If by other things you mean humans, no, Sheriff, I do not hunt. When I was younger my dad taught me how to use a gun, if that is what you are getting at, but I haven't gone out on a hunt in years. How about you? Are you a Bambi-killer?"

He smiled. "Is that what you call them here?"

"It's not what I call them, but some of the more recent additions to the area certainly use that term."

"So I guess it would be no hardship to find lots of crack shots in the area."

"None whatsoever. Nine out ten people in Taos County could hit a bull's-eye most of the time. We have gun enthusiasts, bow-hunters, and there is even a paintball club in Red River. La Señora will be packed by this weekend, and it won't let up until around Christmas." Carmen thought about the room she was occupying. Her mother was losing money by having her there.

She should go home, but the image of those pink bows wouldn't leave her head. She sat and stared out the passenger window. The sheriff insisted he drive her home, and truth to tell, she was glad he did.

"It's starting to snow again," Carmen said softly.

Chill silently cursed, wondering what that would do to his crime scene. He glanced in the rearview mirror.

Tyson evidently didn't mind the expanded metal barrier separating him from Carmen, because he had curled up and was snoring.

"Doesn't that dog ever bark just for the sake of noise?"

Carmen stirred and turned to look at him. "Not much. Only

when something is really bothering him."

"What about that ear thing?"

Carmen shrugged. "Who knows? It started when he was just a puppy. He only does it to people who yell at me or do something he thinks is threatening."

"Most guard dogs go for the throat." Chill glanced at her, and for a split second they locked gazes. It was like touching a live wire.

"Tyson doesn't think he needs to be a guard dog."

"After what happened today, maybe he better reevaluate his position."

Tony and Maria ushered them into the parlor as soon as they opened the front door of La Señora. Tony had built a roaring fire to warm the room. He shoved a cup of something dark into Chill and Carmen's hands. Evidently Chill had called ahead. Carmen wondered how much he had told them.

"What is this?" Chill asked, peering into the cup.

"Irish coffee. Good for warming the insides."

Carmen took a sip. "Rather generous with the Irish part, weren't you, Pop?" The drink blazed a trail all the way down. She marveled that Chill still had a heavy down jacket on. Of course, he probably had ice-water running in his veins.

"Carmen, you are forbidden to return to your house until this is over," Tony roared.

"You know, she is just like you—hot-headed, impulsive. I try. *Madre de Dios,* how I try! But it does no good." Maria said a prayer in Spanish, gesturing with her hands. "Can't you do anything with her?"

"Me? What do you mean, she is just like me? She has your hot Latin temper and your stubborn streak."

Chill set the cup aside. Seemed like every time he turned around, they were trying to get him to drink hard liquor. "Who does she get the habit of withholding information from?"

"Him."

"Her."

They spoke simultaneously.

Chill had grown up in a foster home, and although it had been stable, it had lacked this kind of reckless, affectionate communication. He glanced at Carmen, who was sipping her coffee, her fingers clutched tightly around the cup. He wondered how she felt, being discussed like she was a teenager instead of a grown and capable woman.

And it wasn't difficult to see that Carmen's temper—the temper she got from both her parents—was simmering just below the surface. So when Chill said, "Well, I'm going to help you both out. I'm making it a legal order. Carmen is not to go near her house without a police escort. It is being taped off as a multiple-homicide and crime scene," he wasn't surprised to see her eyes flash and her cheeks turn rosy.

She was ticked off.

"Damn you!" She surged to her feet, startling Tyson awake. He growled low in his chest. "Damn you." Carmen walked toward the fire, drawn by the glow that matched her mood. "I'm the victim here. Somebody—who, I would like to point out, is still free—murdered two people on my front step. My house has been violated. It is like rape, you know, having some person going through my stuff, sending me intimate presents, lewd clothing, thinking God knows what. Now you want to rake me over the coals while you pussyfoot around an investigation. What are you actually doing to find my stalker?"

Tyson was still growling, patrolling around the room, circling Chill who was the object of Carmen's fury. He made a lunge for the earlobe, but Chill was ready. He bounded from the chair and dropped down on one knee and playfully cuffed the dog.

He grasped the thick, muscled neck and gave Tyson a friendly shake.

"Not today, pooch, but nice try." He roughed him around a bit, grabbed up the loose skin on the scruff of the neck. Then he stood up and turned to Carmen.

"So what are you saying, Carmen? Are you implying I'm not doing my job?"

"I'm saying I want to know what is going on. I want to be treated with respect and not have you looking at me like I'm a suspect."

"You are a suspect," Chill said dryly.

"Pullleeeze." Carmen put her hands on her hips and silently dared him to accuse her of anything.

"Okay, I admit I have a few doubts about your guilt, but I still have a lot of unanswered questions."

Carmen sagged into a chair, her hot-fast temper already burned out. "Make you a deal?"

"I don't make deals."

She ignored him and continued. "I will answer all of your questions, not call my attorney anymore, and be cooperative to the nth degree if you will include me in what is going on. I think that is little enough to ask."

Chill narrowed his eyes and stared at her for a long, silent moment. "Deal. Now tell me about your bank account."

She sighed when she thought about her anorexic finances. "I have about five hundred dollars in my account that I borrowed from my dad. He will confirm the loan, just in case you don't believe me."

"I did make Carmen a loan." Tony was sitting next to Maria on the couch and. . . . Were they holding hands?

The world had turned upside down!

"Lie number one, Carmen." Chill pulled a fat envelope from the pocket inside his jacket. She saw the gun strapped to his body and shivered. He might act like a laid-back, gum-chewing guy, but she realized with a jolt that underneath the façade he was a hard-honed professional. Except for now—while he was calling her a liar.

"What are you talking about?" She thought they had reached an accord, but within five seconds he had turned on her again.

He opened the envelope and handed her the papers from inside. They were printouts from her bank. Her eye traveled from her name at the top to the balance column.

"But this is not possible." She read it again. "This is either a very bad joke, or the accounting error of the century, but either way, it is not correct."

"Sorry, but numbers don't lie. Oldest rule of police work, follow the money."

"I'm telling you this is a mistake. I do not have a quarter of a million dollars in my checking account."

CHAPTER EIGHTEEN

"A quarter of a mil?" Tony whistled a long, low sound that made Carmen's temples throb.

"No way." She looked at the papers again.

"It's in black and white," Chill challenged, raising one blunt brow.

"Where did it come from?" Carmen asked, her mind reeling. "I was bouncing checks."

"Yes, I know. That's all there too. You were bouncing twenty-dollar checks at the gas pump. Then the money appeared."

"So where did it come from?" she repeated.

"I was kind of hoping you were going to tell me that, Carmen." Chill sat down, keeping a sharp eye on Tyson. The dog was sitting nearby, his stubby tail bumping on the wood floor each time he wagged it. Chill could swear the dog was grinning. Was he happy or just contemplating a little lobe *du jour?* Chill made himself a promise to get a dog—just like Tyson. Even if he was just passing through, when summer came he could find a dog like Tyson before he moved on.

"I don't know." Carmen's voice was spiced with fatigue and defeat. "I can't imagine."

"All right. Tell me about this." From his jacket, Chill pulled a plastic bag with a bright red label.

Just how big were the pockets in that thing?

Carmen took the bag and looked at the torn piece of water-stained paper inside. "What is it?"

"It is the corner of a bankruptcy document. It was found in Ethyl Gatz's hand."

Carmen felt her cheeks start to burn. She had hoped nobody knew about the bankruptcy. She hadn't lied, but she had certainly edited that part out of her statement to the police in Albuquerque and when she spoke to Chill.

"You knew about her plan to file bankruptcy, didn't you? You knew if she did that, any chance you had to recover your money was just about nil. You knew all about it and decided to kill her before she could execute the documents and screw you out of all your money."

"No! Yes, I knew about the bankruptcy. She taunted me with it in Albuquerque. You think I murdered her and then somehow got my money? How? How did I do that?"

"It plays, Carmen. I haven't figured that out yet. Maybe she was carrying around the cash. But you got the money and deposited it to your account. She couldn't file bankruptcy if she was dead."

Carmen raised a brow. "What kind of cop are you?"

"I beg your pardon?"

"Did you ask the tellers?"

"Ask the tellers what?"

"Sheriff." She emphasized the title. "This is not the big city. Everyone knows everyone and they also know everyone's business. The Taos Telegraph is faster than the speed of light. I can assure you that whoever put this in my account would be remembered. If I had made that substantial deposit, the teller I dealt with would be able to tell you the time and the date. Or was it done by wire transfer?"

Chill pulled a little notebook from his shirt pocket. He flipped a couple of pages. "No. It was a deposit made in-house." He felt a little sheepish, but hell, he *had* been raised in the big city. He hadn't thought about the lack of anonymity of a small town.

Carmen was right. Everyone knew everyone else, and since friends and neighbors worked at banks, loan companies, doctor and dentist's office, they knew all there was to know about each other. He hated to make mistakes—hated it even more that Carmen had caught it. But she was right. In fact, it made him look at the crime from a different perspective.

"Point taken. I will get on that."

Carmen felt better already. She noticed Chill wasn't half-bad-looking when he was not in iron-jawed-interrogator mode. They were sitting there, both of them digesting all the new information that had been revealed, when someone knocked on the front door of La Señora. Nobody ever knocked. They simply stepped inside and registered.

Chill was at the door in four long strides. He flung it open and found a R.E.D. delivery man standing there in the cold, snow collecting on his hat and the shoulders of his jacket.

"I have a package for Carmen Pollini. Is she here?"

"Yes." Chill took the package, which was about the size of a pizza, holding it by one corner, trying to touch as little surface area as possible. "Where did you get this?"

The driver looked at Chill suspiciously. "It was loaded on my truck with the rest of my deliveries. Is there a problem?"

"No, no problem." Chill signed the bill of lading, shut the door and brought the package to Carmen.

She stared at it. "I don't want to open it. You do it."

"Do you have some rubber gloves?" Chill asked Maria.

"Sure. In the kitchen of the Coyote."

Chill followed her outside and through the central courtyard, where Tyson chose to remain while they went into the Blue Coyote.

The kitchen was bustling as usual. He noted the relief on the faces of the staff when Maria appeared, and their crestfallen expression when she ignored them and pulled a pair of gloves from a box on a high stainless shelf over the deep, industrial sink.

"We use these when we handle meat for the tacos."

"They'll do." Chill pulled the gloves on and took the package to a back counter, Maria, Carmen and Tony following.

The box had no return address, only the R.E.D. label. "I'll go to the office later and question anyone who might have handled this," he told no one in particular. The staff was trying to cook and watch Chill at the same time. Carmen couldn't blame them. It was like a scene out of a movie as he peeled back the tape, doing his best not to disturb any more of the wrapping than necessary. It took long minutes.

Tension rolled off Carmen in waves.

Finally he lifted an edge of the brown paper and revealed a bright scarlet box of name brand chocolates. He lifted the lid with a pen. Beneath the thick white paper, rows of chocolate, light, dark and creamy glistened. There was no card.

"Have you got a sweet tooth?" he asked Carmen.

"Not anymore," she croaked.

"Good, because I'm sending this to a lab to be tested. I don't want you to end up being my third victim."

CHAPTER NINETEEN

"Hello?"

"Hey, Chill, I got your information on that ISP." Eloy sounded a lot friendlier than the last time they had talked.

"That was fast." Chill chewed on his gum.

"Hey, I run a tight ship. And besides, what are friends for?" There was humor in Eloy's question.

"To take advantage of?"

"Dick head," Eloy growled.

"So what have you got?" Chill glared at the stack of evidence and papers that so far had not yielded the epiphany he needed to solve the murders. He had found an old, battered briefcase in the closet and had appropriated it, taking the stuff with him everywhere he went. He didn't like to work this way, but under the circumstances he felt it was necessary.

"The ISP you gave me was set up by someone with a fair bit of knowledge, I would say. The E-mails are being routed all over the place, but I finally nailed them down to some cybercafés in Albuquerque, Salt Lake City and Phoenix."

"Okay."

"The first address you gave me, the one for the writer there in Taos, had something else kind of interesting."

"Oh?"

"Yeah. Whoever has been sending these had tried to get them through to her before, but had a wrong digit in the E-mail. The first three, sent weeks ahead of the ones that finally got through, had bounced back to the ISP. Some time later the messages had been resent with the correction."

"So that means the unsub had been cyberstalking long before the victim thought."

"That plays for me. The other thing is that I didn't find any E-mails from the ISP to the private dick's address."

"I was afraid of that." Chill scrubbed his hand down his face. "I had hoped I was wrong."

"Do you need any more help? I always knew you couldn't get along without me."

"You know what you can do with specific body parts and specific places, old buddy. But yeah, now that you mention it, I need you to check one more thing, and I need it kept quiet."

"Shoot."

"Check and see if the P.I. has been getting any mail from Taos.nm.gov."

"But isn't that your E-mail address, marshal? Taos County Sheriff?" Eloy was smiling; Chill heard it in his voice.

"Yep."

"Whoa. Listen, you better watch your back there, buddy." Eloy sounded less amused now.

"Believe me, I'm sleeping with one eye open."

Carmen sat in her room in La Señora and pounded on the keyboard, using her nervous energy to get ahead of her looming deadline. The last couple of weeks had been relatively quiet—if having a cop sleeping next door and Tony slipping on the ice in the Blue Coyote parking lot could be considered peaceful.

Carmen paused with her fingers on the home keys. Funny how quickly Maria had offered Tony a room at La Señora. Now the whole family was under the tiled red roof. Carmen would've suspected it was all a setup to watch her, except Tony's foot was twice its normal size and the parts that protruded from the heavy walking cast were bruised in shades of designer mauve and purple. Maria and Tony were getting along well—as well as gas and an open flame ever did, anyway.

Still, things were not too bad if you were a glass-half-full kind of gal. Sales on *A Hot Brand of Love* had gone through the roof. Jake and Ethyl's murders were still the hot topic. Every time the news channel flashed Carmen's name and image across the screen, somebody bought a book, or so it seemed. She thought there was some sort of moral lesson in all of it, but she wasn't sure what it could be. A part of her was elated with the sales figures. Another part of her, the pragmatic, small-town girl from New Mexico, was sickened by the fact that the old saw about there being no such thing as bad publicity was evidently true. Ex-Sheriff Jim Dunn was receiving the same treatment, as more evidence about his alleged abuse was uncovered. Every time he poked his head out of his house, somebody was there with a camera.

Carmen wondered if maybe the county commissioners had known and anticipated the whole thing. It would be impossible for any of the deputies to do their job if that mob of paparazzi were at the police station. Maybe Chill being hired was not such a bad thing.

She was so busy wool-gathering, the ringing phone startled her. She picked it up. "Carmen Pollini."

"Hey, it's Dax."

She leaned back in her chair and put her sock-covered feet up on the desk. They hadn't done any signings together since his kneecapping, for obvious reasons. It was hard to be a sexy hunk with a huge bandage on one knee. She'd heard he was still in the hospital—through the Taos Telegraph—milking his injury for all it was worth.

"Aren't you breaking some rule by calling me? I heard you were going to sue me. I'm sure there must be a truly sick person who could use the bed you are lounging in, Dax."

"Carmen, that's all publicity. You know that. None of it is true. I wouldn't sue you, babe. We're friends."

"Friends?"

Her head started to throb as his honeyed words dripped through the phone. Dax was the embodiment of all that was wrong with the country. He said and did whatever made the news and took no responsibility for his actions or lack of truth. His life was one big sound bite.

"What do you want, Dax?"

"I just wanted to tell you I'm leaving tomorrow, headed back to New York."

"Have a nice trip."

"Don't be that way. Hey, you should be nice to me. I called to do you a favor."

"What kind of favor? I thought you learned I'm not interested in what you are peddling."

"Look, I just called to let you know that somebody came by here today and left something for you."

Carmen sat up, her feet thudding on the thick carpet. "For me?"

"Yeah. I thought it was kind of strange, but somebody left a letter for you here at the hospital."

She could hear the sound of rustling paper.

"Good grief! Did you open it?" Just when she thought he couldn't get any lower.

"Nah, of course not. I was just smelling it."

"Smelling it?" Once again she found herself repeating everything he said. What was it about Dax that sucked the intelligence out of the room?

"Yeah. The envelope is scented."

"Scented?"

"Yeah, something flowery. It's nice. Hey, Carmen, do you

swing both ways?"

"Dax, watch your mouth."

"Just joking."

"I'll be there to pick up the letter in half an hour—and this better not be some sort of prank, or you will be sorry."

It had taken way too long, but Chill finally had the tox report on the box of chocolates, along with the final toxicology reports on both Jake and Ethyl.

"And I'm still coming up empty." He ran his hand through his hair, noting that he needed a haircut. He glanced out his office window to see that it was snowing again. He leaned back in his chair and watched the flakes drift by. He felt like one of those tiny figures inside a snow-globe.

This was a crazy damned place, but it was getting under his skin. The New Mexico landscape was truly enchanted, even though it attracted some screwy types. He couldn't step outside the B&B without seeing a dozen hunters decked out in winter camo and armed to the teeth, as well as nubile ski bunnies enjoying both Red River and Santa Fe slopes. There were also Buddhists and people who looked like they were stuck in the sixties, cowboys and millionaires.

And then there was Carmen.

"Ah, Carmen." He couldn't help but grin. She was getting under his skin too.

A dangerous thing.

"She could be guilty," he told himself.

She could be, but his gut told him she wasn't. Since the chocolates had arrived, she had been downright obedient. She still had that smart mouth on her, but without that she just wouldn't be Carmen. Tony and Maria had been thanking him daily, giving him special food, taking care of his laundry and anything else he might require, just to show their gratitude.

It was some family.

Chill's smile slipped. He hadn't known anything like this kind of family life since his parents died. That single event had shaped his life, both because of the foster care system and the fact their murders remained unsolved.

He had sworn to make a difference, to get the bad guy, and he'd been content to do it alone. But staying at La Señora had given him a taste of something he didn't know he had missed.

When he fled California on some vague mission to travel the old Route 66, he sure hadn't expected to be living in a crazy hotel that doubled as a home, with a mother, a father, a mouthy daughter, two unsolved murders, a dog with an ear fetish, and bits and pieces of evidence that refused to congeal.

"Damn." Chill picked up the report again. The chocolates had been tainted, but only with enough laxative to make someone sick, not a fatal amount. Very different from the other gifts. Almost like a taunt or a warning.

"I'm missing something."

Chill gathered the papers and tucked them into the briefcase. Then he laced his fingers behind his head and stared out the window some more. Perhaps it was a Zen thing. Maybe if he watched the snowflakes. . . .

The buzzer on his desk sounded.

"Sir, you have a call." Victoria Smith's voice crackled over the intercom.

Chill picked up the phone. "Blaines."

"Hey, buddy, are you sitting down?" Eloy's voice brought him up straight in the chair.

"Tell me."

"I have the information on your P.I. Just as you suspected. The threatening E-mails are coming straight out of your own office."

★ ★ ★ ★ ★

Carmen walked down the shiny, antiseptic hall, nodding and smiling at a blur of people in scrubs. She paused at the desk only long enough to get Dax's room number, then she hurried on.

If Dax could tell her what the person looked like, maybe she could figure out who her stalker was.

She turned the corner and nearly ran headlong into a tall man. He reached out and grabbed her shoulders to steady her.

"Ooops." He grinned at her. His face was lean, craggy, his gaze intense.

He looked familiar. She was certain she had seen him before. Someone from a signing?

"Sorry, my fault. I was looking for a room." She smiled awkwardly and looked at her shoulder. His hand was still on her, his grip firm. She wasn't sure why, but the gesture seemed oddly intimate.

He followed the line of her gaze. "Oh, sorry." He released her. "What room are you looking for? I'd be more than happy to help you find it."

"One-A." Carmen knew she had heard this man's voice before—but where? Since she sold her first book, she had done dozens of signings. After a while everyone looked and sounded familiar. She shrugged off the thought. She needed to find Dax.

"Carmen?" Dax called her name. She glanced around and saw him just inside a doorway. She turned back to thank the man, but he was gone. He had disappeared completely and silently.

"Hey, you made good time. I thought I heard your voice in the hallway." Dax motioned to her. "Were you talking to yourself?"

"Didn't you see him?"

"I didn't see anybody but you. Come in." Dax acted like he

was playing host at his home instead of a hospital room.

She looked down the hallway again, but there was no sign of the man she had been talking to.

"So, do you receive mysterious scented mail often, Carmen?" Dax was holding a long envelope in his hand.

"Who brought it?"

He sniffed the envelope, paying no attention to her.

"Dax?"

"What?"

"Who brought the letter for me?"

"Uh, I dunno. I woke up from a little nap. You know, after lunch and a sponge bath, it is great to take a nap—"

"The letter, Dax, the letter?"

"Oh, all right. I woke up. It was on the table there. The nurse said some guy had dropped it off and asked for me to get it to you."

"So you never saw him?"

"Nah."

"Which nurse was it? Do you remember her name?"

"Lopez or Sanchez or Ramirez, they all kind of sound the same to me."

Carmen held out her hand, palm up. Dax put the letter into it after one last sniff.

"Carmen Pollini." Chill strode into the room, his face dark as a western thunderstorm. "What am I going to do with you? Tony called half out of his mind. What do you mean, going off and scaring him to death like that?"

Okay, now this was weird. Her father had sent the sheriff, who was a lodger at his ex-wife's B&B, to track down his daughter, who was still the top suspect in a double homicide. Carmen shook her head at the absurdity of it all.

"Well?" Chill lifted a dark brow, gave Dax a dirty look and focused back on her, acting as if he were her older brother.

"I left a note." She did not just say that!

"A note?"

"Why am I answering to you, Sheriff? You are the law, not my big brother and not my nanny. I'm over twenty-one. If I want to visit Dax in the hospital, I most certainly do not need your permission."

Her words hit Chill like a slap in the face. He was acting like a fool. She was right. He was the law, not her guardian angel. But when Tony called, he hadn't hesitated. It wasn't like Chill. One failed marriage in his youth had taught him to use caution and restraint, two things he lacked whenever he was around any of the Pollini-Alvarez family.

"You're right. You don't answer to me, but your father was worried. He doesn't like being laid up and feeling helpless. You should call him." He offered her his cell phone, feeling a little sheepish.

She frowned at it.

"You forgot yours in your room. Maria found it when Tony kept calling."

"Oh." Carmen took the phone. She could imagine how concerned they were when she didn't answer. It wasn't like her to forget her phone. She punched in the number.

"Pop? Yes, I'm fine. Yes, Chill is here. Yes, yes, I will. Sorry. Yes. Soon." She shut the phone feeling like a schoolgirl who had disappointed her parents.

"So, Sheriff, how is the murder investigation going?" Dax asked with a cheery smile. He hopped up on his bed and laced his fingers behind his head.

Chill swiveled his head to stare at the lounging model. The sheriff's eyes were narrowed, his face chiseled, lean, pensive. His hair had darkened, and Carmen was struck by how intimidating he could appear when he put on that tough-cop persona. Yet over the last few weeks she had come to trust him.

"I can't discuss that," Chill said flatly. "In Carmen's note she said you had something to give her."

Chill took a step toward the bed. Dax pushed into it as if he were trying to retreat into the firm elevated mattress.

"So what did you give her?" His tone was harsh.

Dax swallowed so hard, his manly Adam's apple bobbed. His eyes were round. His lips moved, but no sound came out. Carmen took pity on him.

"He gave me this." Carmen waved the envelope in the air, letting Chill get a good look at it. A faint, sweet perfume wafted off it.

"Who's it from?" Chill's nostrils flared for a moment. He was a better bloodhound than Tyson.

"Don't know. Haven't opened it."

"What are you waiting for?"

"You." She grinned. "I wouldn't dream of contaminating evidence that you might want, Sheriff."

Chill was stunned by her words, but he did his best to hide his surprise. "Oh?"

"Uh-huh. I told you I would cooperate." She turned to Dax. "Have a nice trip back to New York, Dax, and thanks for not suing me."

"No problem, Carmen."

Chill and Carmen fell into step beside each other. Neither one of them saw the tall man watching them from the elevator bank with hard-eyed jealousy.

CHAPTER TWENTY

"So, were you really waiting for me, or was that all a bunch of double-talk?"

"I didn't know you were going to track me to the hospital, but I did think you might want to find a pair of rubber gloves and use tweezers and a magnifying glass on this sucker." She tapped the envelope against her hand as they stepped outside into a fresh flurry of snow.

"Carmen, are you laughing at me?"

"Me? Laugh at you? Never. But I have to tell you, Chill, there is a warmth in your voice. What gives?"

"Warmth. That is an oxymoron isn't it? Chill—warmth. Get it?"

What he said struck both of them as funny and they laughed. It was nice, a way to release the tension Carmen hadn't even realized was gripping her. She wasn't about to admit it, but she was glad Chill showed up.

"A little afraid to open it?"

His face was solemn. She was surprised by his empathy. "Uh-huh. Lately packages, letters and gifts haven't exactly been warm fuzzies."

"Let's go to the station. I'm sure the envelope has been handled too much already, but you are correct in thinking I would like to keep whatever is inside pristine until we can take some prints."

Carmen nodded. Sometimes it was nice to have a big, burly cop at one's side.

The traffic was bumper to bumper on the highway. Signs had sprouted overnight announcing that the annual Cowboy-Snowdown would hit town in just a couple of weeks—scheduled to coincide with the Thanksgiving holidays.

"What is a cowboy-snowdown anyway?" Chill drummed his fingers impatiently on the steering wheel. Carmen had agreed to let him drive, but now she was uncomfortable in the passenger seat. She couldn't shake the sensation of being watched. Chill was glaring straight ahead at the car in front of him, but she could feel the burn of somebody's gaze on her neck.

"It is a cross between a rodeo and normal skiing. It is wild, crazy and I suppose a little on the dangerous side. Cowboys get towed on snowboards behind horses—"

"They what?" His head swiveled around.

She smiled. "It loses something in the translation, I guess. Basically, anything you can do on the snow is done with horses added. You just have to see it."

"Sounds wacky. What else goes on?"

"Vendors and artists will be out in force. Some of the local clubs usually have booths. Taxidermists, food vendors, that type of thing."

"Damn, I hate sitting in traffic." He heaved a sigh, puffing out his cheeks as he expelled the breath. Carmen watched him pat his pockets until he located a pack of gum.

"You used to be a smoker," she stated.

He looked at her, puzzled. "You can tell?"

"The gum." She nodded at his hand, where he was deftly unwrapping a piece with one hand. "And the classic, impatient type A personality traits."

Chill lifted a brow, popped the gum in and chomped down,

showing his front teeth in what might have been a grin or a snarl; she wasn't sure. "I recognized I needed to change some things in my life. I used to smoke. I used to be married. I used to do a lot of things that were bad for me."

"Ouch. You consider marriage bad for your health?"

"Toxic—at least mine was. What's the story with your parents, if you don't mind sharing?"

It was Carmen's turn to raise a brow. "Is this on the record, Sheriff?"

"Not at all. I like your parents, and you know how curious we type A's are."

The traffic was thinning a bit and Chill gave more attention to his driving, but she knew his ears were pricked and alert as a fox's.

"Fine. If this is not some sneaky line of questioning to see if they produced a serial killer, I don't mind sharing." She grinned when his brows furrowed together in a frown. He chewed the gum with robust abandon.

"My parents met in New York City—a college trip for her. My dad is a former-Brooklynite. It was love at first sight. Mom wouldn't live in New York if you gave her the keys to the city. Pop came out here to continue courting her and fell in love with New Mexico as well."

"Very pretty story, but I was thinking more about their marital discord."

"Ah, the divorce with a capital D." Carmen sighed. "It was awful. Pop made a lot of money almost overnight. He wanted to travel, but Mom is more grounded to the soil, so to speak. La Señora and the Blue Coyote don't make a ton of money, but the property and the recipes have been in the Alvarez family for many generations. She wouldn't budge, and Pop did the one thing she would divorce him for—he strayed."

Chill regarded her with a fleeting glance. "And you, Carmen?

Any men in your life?"

"That's kind of personal, but no."

"Why?"

Carmen blinked. Why? That was a loaded question. "I kind of intimidate men."

Chill glanced at her in disbelief. "You? You intimidate men? I admit you have a mouth on you, but a secure guy could find a witty, smart, mouthy woman pretty damned sexy. What kind of cream puffs have you been hanging around? They must be real wimps if they find a feisty woman like you intimidating."

She tried not to smile at the left-handed compliment. It was nice to hear Chill say something positive—okay, semi-positive—about her.

"You see there was this incident. . . ."

"I keep hearing people mention that. Why don't you tell me what happened? There are usually three sides to any story: yours, theirs and the truth."

"Uh-huh, just as I suspected. This is turning out to be an interrogation. You just want details about my past brush with the law."

"Come on, Carmen, tell me what happened." He grinned.

"Maybe someday, if and when I decide you can be trusted with sensitive information."

He chuckled but didn't say more. She realized they were at the police station. She hadn't even noticed the trip. Carmen was grateful he had engaged her in conversation, because it had kept her mind off the letter. Now it all came flooding back. Her stomach knotted and a hard lump formed in her throat.

"Scared?" Chill asked what she had been denying.

"Yes."

"Well, let's go open this puppy and see what it says."

Chill got out of the car and strode to the door, glancing back to see if Carmen was following him. He was no gallant, that was for sure, but there was something about him. He had a rough-edged charm that was sort of comforting—kind of like a nice heavy quilt that had been done up in some scratchy material. It kept you warm and safe, but you couldn't get too cozy with it.

Carmen walked into the station behind Chill, ignoring the grins and smirks of the male deputies. Victoria Smith was on duty as well. She gave an almost imperceptible nod that Carmen chose to think was friendly encouragement and not some sort of acknowledgement that the sheriff had his suspect in tow.

"At least this time you don't have to be fingerprinted," Chill announced cheerfully, casting a withering glance at the other officers. Carmen had to smile when they ducked their heads and found ways to be busy. Okay, so he wasn't all bad.

"You are a bit intimidating, Sheriff."

"I try. Believe me, I do try."

They walked into his office and he closed the door behind them. She was surprised when he also locked it.

"Are you planning on having your wicked way with me?" she quipped.

"Hardly, but I do want privacy. I don't like people looking over my shoulder."

Carmen hated to acknowledge that his blunt rebuff deflated her ego, kind of like a sharp pin to a balloon. But her bruised feelings were shoved aside when she thought about his remark, considering the other people in the building were his fellow officers and subordinates. She sensed there was something going on, but her own problems blotted out her curiosity about Chill's supervisory techniques.

"Now, let's take a look." Chill had gloved up with the speed and efficiency of a surgeon. He slid the tip of his pocketknife blade down the edge of the envelope and oh-so-carefully tipped out the contents. One slender page, folded in thirds, lay on the blotter of his desk. He used the knife tip to open it up, holding down the edges with one gloved digit.

"What? What does it say?" Carmen couldn't look.

"You aren't going to believe it."

"Is it bad? Is it worse than the others?"

"Depends on your point of view. It is completely blank."

"Blank? How can it be blank?" She moved nearer to get a look. She leaned over the desk, her shoulder brushing against the hard bulk of Chill's body.

"What does this mean?"

"It means you are going under twenty-four-hour guard starting right now."

"What? Why?"

"Because this letter was meant for one purpose, Carmen. It was bait—to bring you to the hospital. And the only reason someone would want to get you there is because he was waiting for you to arrive."

CHAPTER TWENTY-ONE

"Waiting—for me?" Carmen's knees were rubbery. Chill eased her into his chair. "But . . . that means, I can't believe what you are implying."

"Come on, Carmen, you're a smart lady. There is only one reason to lure you to the hospital, and we both know what it must be."

"Abduction."

"Bingo. Give the lady a prize." Chill frowned at the envelope. "I'm going to dust this of course, but I'll bet you dinner at the Coyote tonight that the paper is clean. Our guy is no slouch. He left the envelope in such a manner as to be anonymous, knowing it would be handled by dozens of people: nurses, the patient, maybe an aide or cleaning staff. Clever, very clever. He knew Dax would call you, and he knew you would come."

"Are you saying he was there?"

"I'm sure he was. Our guy doesn't leave much to chance. He was probably right there, and I hate to think what might've happened if Tony hadn't called me."

Chill glanced up from his musing. Carmen's face was whiter than the sheet of blank paper. She was scared—terrified—and he had been rambling on about how close she had come to being kidnapped.

"You poor kid. I didn't think. . . ."

"You really believe that?"

"Yeah, probably watching us the entire time. Carmen, I know

you're tired of hearing this over and over again, but you can't go anywhere alone. I know how easy it is for the bad guys to rig a car, or orchestrate a hit-and-run. I've seen people killed before. Your parents are right to be worried. I'm worried too. I have two corpses, and I consider this envelope an attempt to kidnap."

"So what do you want me to do?"

Chill opened a drawer. "Write down your calendar for the next month. Until we get this thing solved, I'm your new shadow."

Chill was as good as his word. He followed Carmen back to the hospital to pick up her car and then tailed her, nearly driving up her tailpipe, all the way to La Señora. He parked quickly and stood by her car while she did the same. Then he opened her car door, supported her elbow, escorted her inside the building and shut the door behind her.

None of which would have been too unusual except Chill had never opened a door for her in the past.

Tyson was happy to see her, jumping up and doing a little twisty-flip in the air.

"Where did you find that dog?" Chill was grinning.

Carmen guessed he wasn't mad about his ear.

"His entire litter was being sold in a park in Santa Fe."

"He's some dog." Chill bent down and chucked Tyson under the chin. Tyson's wrinkled face wrinkled a bit more when he panted, his tongue lolling out in a canine expression of sheer joy. Chill rubbed his scruff vigorously. Tyson leaned into it, his hind leg scratching nothing but air.

"I think he's decided he likes you."

"Good, 'cause I like him too."

A thump and swish announced Tony hobbling on one crutch. His foot was still swollen and mottled in bruises.

"Pop. You should stay off that foot."

"Yeah, I know. But this came for Chill, and I thought it might be important." He had a flat Priority Mail envelope tucked under one arm. He fished it out and handed it to Chill.

"I've been waiting for this." He pulled the strip.

"What is it, or is that classified?" Carmen helped Tony to the sofa, where he collapsed with a lot of relief and no grace whatsoever. "I wouldn't want you to have to kill me if you tell me."

Chill paused long enough to give her a look. "It is the fingerprint report on all the prints we took from your house and the gift boxes. We also dusted the note that was left under Tony's windshield wiper in Albuquerque."

"Come, sit." Tony patted the sofa beside him. Tyson hopped right up and snuggled close. "Not you, big mutt. I was talking to Carmen."

Tyson turned around twice and settled his butt in Tony's direction.

"That's okay, Pop. I'm fine right here." *Here* was near the fire, because Carmen couldn't shake the frost from her bones. She savored the heat flowing over her skin, but it didn't dispel the coldness.

Chill removed the papers and scanned them, flipping through them one by one. "Interesting."

"Any good news?" Tony asked.

"We have the same prints in Carmen's bedroom, on the gifts, but a different set on the chocolates. They, however, are not on file with any agency. Whoever our guy is, he has no record."

"Two sets of prints?"

"Not so unusual. Our guy could've worn gloves when he dosed the candy. Those prints could be someone from the factory."

"I suppose that should make me feel better, right? I mean at least I'm not being stalked by some serial rapist or murderer who has a record a mile long." Carmen's voice cracked, so she turned to the fire and pretended to warm her hands while she swallowed the hard, thick lump in her throat. She didn't think she would ever be warm again.

"And the note from Albuquerque?" Tony asked.

"That was clean. No prints at all."

"What does it mean?" Carmen blinked to keep tears from coming.

Chill was suddenly beside her. He didn't try to touch her; she was very grateful for that.

"It will be all right, Carmen. We'll get this guy, and I promise nobody is going to get to you as long as your mutt and I'm around."

"I made a promise to myself that I wasn't going to be a passive victim. This feels an awful lot like I'm allowing myself to be victimized."

"Carmen, you are an intelligent woman. Never be mistaken. There is a huge difference between being a victim and being cautious. Besides, it is a damned sight better to be a live victim than a dead heroine."

That afternoon the television news flashed ex-Taos County Sheriff Jim Dunn's face across the screen. It was not a flattering photo. In fact, it looked a lot like a mug shot.

"Would you look at that?" Tony was mesmerized as the reporter updated everyone on the latest news.

"More than a dozen women have come forward to give testimony to the grand jury. Inside sources say Jim Dunn will be prosecuted for sexual misconduct, sexual harassment of suspects, and five counts of police harassment and sexual assault. There is rumored to be a female deputy who was sexually harassed, but both the sheriff's office and the Taos County commissioners refuse to comment. An anonymous source has told this reporter that Dunn used blackmail tactics to keep his victims silent."

"Could that be the reason she did it . . . ?" Chill murmured. He might not be getting very far with Carmen's case, but he was almost ready to close the other open file on his desk.

"Can you cook like this?" Chill was eating flan, wondering how he had managed to live thirty-five years and never have tasted it before. It was strange. Flan and margaritas were a California thing but he hadn't found them in California. Maybe it was growing up in foster care, or maybe he hadn't been very adventurous until lately.

Carmen's dark, slender brows arched. "Me? Cook? I can do enough to keep from starving, but I'm not an artist like my mother."

"Hey, is it my imagination or do your parents seem to be getting along?"

Carmen watched her dad balancing on his crutches near Maria. They were talking to each other, smiling. "Yep, it does look like they are getting along."

"Say, do you want your flan?" Chill asked.

"What? No, it's full of calories. You can have it."

Chill dragged the dessert dish to his side of the table. He scooped up a spoonful. It melted on his tongue. If heaven had a flavor, he was certain it must be flan.

Suddenly a chorus of car alarms filled the air outside. People in the Blue Coyote dining room dropped forks, set their glasses aside and ran out to the parking lot in a herd to see if it was their car.

Carmen didn't know why, but when the crowd flowed to the parking lot, Chill pulled Carmen aside, and trailed along behind them. Once outside, he veered off from the throng, heading to the B&B lot where his SUV and Carmen's car were parked.

"What are we doing?" Carmen whispered.

"Following a hunch. Stay nearby." Chill pulled his gun and held it close to his body. They hadn't bothered to grab coats, and Carmen's teeth were already chattering. It was cold, clear, with more than six inches of new snow on the ground.

She followed Chill, her ears straining for any sound as they went to their cars. She saw his SUV. It looked fine. Then she followed Chill to her vehicle.

A little squeak of anguish escaped her lips.

All the windows were shattered. A white piece of paper fluttered underneath the bent windshield wiper against the shattered glass. Chill circled the car, checking the shadows and underneath. Then he snatched up the paper and hurried Carmen back to the Blue Coyote, holstering his gun discreetly at the door so he wouldn't frighten the patrons.

Once again seated at their table Chill spread out the paper on the table. Carmen stared at the words written in dark marker while her stomach knotted into a painful ball.

"How many more people will die before you tell the world you stole my book?"

"Carmen, you have really pissed somebody off."

"Why do you sound so cheerful about it?"

"Because this little stunt told me something—something very important." He scooped up the last spoonful of flan and popped it in his mouth.

"What?"

"I have a theory."

"Want to share?"

"Okay, I will. My theory is that the person who wrote this is definitely not your secret admirer. I am almost certain we are dealing with two entirely different stalkers. One of them appears to admire you and the other. . . ."

"Hates me."

CHAPTER TWENTY-TWO

Carmen woke early. The gray dawn was streaky, the sky leaden with the threat of more snow. She had slept badly, dreading the phone call she knew she had to make.

"Coward." She slammed her fist into the pillow and repositioned it behind her head. It might as well have been a brick, for all the comfort it was giving her. Tyson lifted his head and gave her a dire look from his spot at the foot of the bed.

"Sorry, *Jefe,* I'm getting up." She threw back the comforter, most of it landing on Tyson. He sighed in satisfaction, burrowed deeper and was snoring in minutes.

"Rat." She slid her feet into her fur-lined mules and pulled on a robe. There was only one drawback to living at La Señora, and that was the need to go downstairs for coffee. Maria refused to have coffeemakers in the rooms, determined to keep the antiques from water marks and spills. And she liked to see her lodgers at the Blue Coyote.

Maria would be up soon, but for now the place was silent as a tomb. Even Carmen's breathing seemed overly loud, intrusive. One tread squeaked under her foot as she left the stairs and stepped into the front lobby of La Señora.

She paused, listening hard. For a moment she thought she heard something, but now it was quiet again. She released the breath she had been holding and picked up the telephone. It was early; if she was lucky she could simply leave a message on her insurance agent's phone and avoid all conversation with him.

Then again, she hadn't been too lucky lately.

"Taos County Insurance," Mr. Hardwick answered on the first ring.

"Mr. Hardwick, this is Carmen Pollini." Was that a groan she heard on the other end of the line?

"Yes?"

"I—that is, my car was vandalized," Carmen blurted in a rush. It was early. She hadn't had caffeine and she was having a conversation with Mr. Hardass. Clearly she stood in the seventh circle of hell.

"Was there a full moon last night?"

"I'm sorry, I don't understand." Okay, now he was just playing with her. Her head was full of cotton, unfocused. She would kill for a cup of coffee. Then, as if in answer to her wish, she smelled the aroma of a pot brewing. Hardwick's voice pulled her back from the olfactory hallucination.

"We have done some demographics and found that kind of destruction of property happens more often during a full moon, which is odd, because one would think light from a full moon would increase the chance of being seen. Of course, since it is your car that was hit, it could've been done for any number of reasons."

"Mr. Hardwick, I would rather not have you analyze me this early in the morning. I just want to report the damage to my car so you can come out and take pictures."

"Why can't you drive it in?"

"Because my tires were slashed. Didn't I say that?"

A heavy, long-suffering sigh hissed through the phone lines. "No, you didn't. Fine. I'll take the photograph, but it will have to be after my Rotary breakfast."

"That'll be fine. I'm sure not going anywhere."

"Where is the car parked, Ms. Pollini?"

"In the parking lot between the Blue Coyote and La Señora del Destino, I'm staying here indefinitely."

"Trouble at home?" Suddenly he sounded interested.

"No more than usual," Carmen snapped. She sure wasn't going to tell the biggest gossip in Taos any secrets.

"Ms. Pollini, I suppose you know your rates will be going up again?" He sounded cheerful.

"Of course. I wouldn't expect anything less."

Carmen hung up the phone. It was a longer route to go through the front hall and dining room, but her mules and robe were no match for the snow in the courtyard. She had just stepped into the dim dining room when she got another whiff of coffee.

Somebody was definitely in the kitchen. But it wasn't Maria or Tony, because they would've switched on the dining-room lights. Her mouth went dry.

Could the stalker be here? She snatched up a heavy red glass candle from one of the tables. Its cold weight was reassuring as she crept through the dining room toward the kitchen, with the candle raised to coldcock somebody.

Carmen slowly pushed the door open. The smell of the fresh coffee filled her nose. Her caffeine-starved brain was being bewitched, but she clenched her jaw and ignored it.

"Morning." Chill's voice was like a shot in the silence. She jumped and swung at the same instant, the candle connecting soundly with the side of his head, clipping his ear.

"Ouch! Damn! First Tyson and now you. Is there something about my ears you don't like, Carmen?" He rubbed the side of his head with one hand and took the candleholder away from her with the other. "I've known some grouchy women in the morning, but you take the cake. Have a cup of coffee before you hurt someone."

"I thought everyone was asleep." Carmen grabbed a mug and filled it to the top. She was grumpy, but it was damned rude of him to point it out.

"I've been up for quite some time."

She turned around and leaned against the cold, hard stainless counter. A fat accordion file was spread out nearby. Her gaze was drawn to an official-looking document with a clinical drawing of a human.

"Autopsy reports," he said in answer to her silent question.

"And?"

"I'm still not sure what the murder weapon was."

She leaned a little closer and inspected the report.

There was a notation near the temple area where a circle had been drawn.

"I just don't get it. Something hit both victims hard enough to shatter bone, and yet left absolutely no residue. We have to find another way to flush this creep out. And I think I may have figured out a way. Have another cup of coffee, Carmen. You are going to need it. I want you wide awake when I tell you my plan."

"Chill, I don't want to insult you, but have you lost your freaking mind?"

Carmen stared at Chill over the rim of her third cup of coffee. They had finished breakfast at what had become their customary table and were now well into a second carafe of coffee. They had watched the morning rush come and go. Now the Blue Coyote had cleared out, the diners headed for the ski lifts, shopping for the upcoming holidays, or getting ready for the Red River–Taos Cowboy-Snowdown.

"Ms. Pollini, if I weren't a secure type, I could be wounded by your lack of confidence in me. I'm a professional. You can trust me."

Carmen barely suppressed the urge to smile. Their relationship had morphed into a prickly sort of friendship. She hated to admit it, but Chill Blaines was good company. He talked a lot more than Tyson, and sometimes had a whole lot less hot air. But not today. His plan was nothing short of *loco*.

"Carmen? What are you thinking?" He frowned at her across the small table.

"I was thinking I'm not a suspect anymore."

"Don't go putting words in my mouth," Chill said with a straight face.

She was about to lay into him with the sharp side of her tongue when his phone rang. He flipped it open, his attention focused on the call.

"Blaines." There was a long pause, and Carmen could hear the tinny voice on the other end before Chill said, "Now, isn't that interesting? Fine, you go take the report. No, I don't want Frank to do it. I want you to go." Chill closed the phone and set it aside. He was grinning like a hungry fox.

"What?" Carmen leaned toward him, hoping it was a break in the case.

"Jim Dunn just called the station to report vandalism to his car."

"But if his car was hit then it probably wasn't my stalker."

"Carmen, Carmen. How many times do I have to tell you not to make assumptions? There are vandalisms and then there are vandalisms." Chill arched a brow.

"What does that mean?"

"I can't say just yet. If I turned out to be wrong, it would shake your confidence in me—not to mention making me look foolish, and I try to never look foolish. I'll wait until I get the report from Victoria Smith before I make any assumptions."

The wintry sun blazed through the front window of La Señora's parlor, shining on the keyboard while Carmen typed. All this confinement had been hard on her, but great for her deadline. She was on the last chapter of her book, way ahead of deadline. Tyson was curled up by the fireplace, his shiny brown coat glistening in the sunshine.

She glanced at the old clock on the registration desk. Chill had been gone for more than an hour. Curiosity was nibbling at the edges of her mind, sapping off her concentration.

"Oh, shoot." She gave in and saved the file, powered down and closed the laptop. The front door opened and Chill came in with a gust of snowy wind a minute later. He stamped his feet on the rug at the door to dislodge the rim of snow on his boots.

"Really coming down out there."

"Good. Red River needs all the fresh powder they can get for Snowdown. What did you find out?"

Chill peeled off his shearling coat and hung it on the wooden hall tree. "What? No offer of coffee? Just straight to what I found out? Carmen, you need to learn how to butter up a man or you'll turn out to be an old maid."

"That is a ridiculous and archaic term." She bristled.

"Archaic or not, it is the truth." Chill rubbed Tyson's ears when he came over to sniff his boots. "Come on, I'll buy you a cup. Maybe Maria has some leftover flan."

"Far be it from me to say anything, Sheriff, being a pre-old-maid, but if you keep hitting the flan, you are going to get fat and then no woman will want you."

"Men don't get fat, they get beefy."

Carmen shook her head as she followed him through the corridor and out into the central courtyard. Tyson was snowplowing through the new white powder when they entered the Blue Coyote's kitchen. Tony was on his crutches at the counter, chopping onions. Carmen had never seen her father so domestic. He had definitely left that to Maria before. It was kind of nice to see him sharing her passion for cooking.

A few moments later, Chill and Carmen were seated at their small corner table, steaming cups of strong coffee in front of them. Chill also had a serving of flan, the caramel dripping down the side like flat-topped volcano about to erupt.

"Carmen, you should learn how to make this flan." Chill was licking caramel off the back of his spoon.

"No, I shouldn't. I told you it is loaded with calories."

"Hey, that is hitting way below the belt. First you besmirch my sanity and now you are hinting that I'm putting on weight. I think I should be offended."

"I doubt you offend that easily." Carmen took her coffee spoon and dipped up a dollop of flan. It melted on her tongue.

"That is a very intimate thing to do. Careful, Carmen, or the local gossips will have us as an item."

"What do you know about the local gossips?" She found herself oddly intrigued by the idea. Chill was a man's man, not the type of guy Carmen usually liked, and yet he had a certain rough appeal.

"Oh, I know a lot. For instance, I know that Jim Dunn reported a vandalism after he had a Rotary breakfast. I know he had a conversation with a certain insurance agent at that breakfast. I know that he reported his car had been egged and his tires had the valve stems opened and all the air let out." He waggled his brows.

Carmen stared at him with her spoon hovering just above the creamy flan. His words sizzled through her brain and back again. Comprehension dawned as her temper began to flare.

"That lousy rat."

"Which one? The gossiping insurance agent or the ex-sheriff?" Chill asked mildly, reaching out to take hold of fingers over the spoon and dip it into the flan so she could have another bite.

"Both. What happened to confidentiality? Isn't Hardwick

supposed to keep my claims private?"

"I dunno. It isn't like surgery, but he obviously did talk about it to Jim, though he must've left out some details or Jim couldn't bring himself to break the windows of his own car. But look at the bright side."

"There's a bright side?"

"Sure."

"What is it?" Carmen ate the flan that Chill directed toward her mouth. She wasn't about to tell him, but flan was one of her favorite foods. She struggled through junior high to keep her weight down, and it was all because of flan.

"We are back on track. Jim's vandal is not your stalker. Well, it could be a stalker, but I have an idea that Jim did his own car, and I don't think your stalker is Jim."

"Stop! You're giving me a headache. What does all this mean?"

"It means we are going to bait your stalker. This Cowboy-Snowdown thing fascinates me. I want you to be my escort. Show me the sights."

"And . . . ?"

"And you will be visible, tempting and out there for your stalker to see so I can bust the rotten S.O.B."

CHAPTER TWENTY-THREE

Carmen blinked at the fury in Chill's words. His nickname fit him. He was a cool customer. Only now did she realize, with a considerable jolt, that he was really ticked off because the stalker was still loose. Funny, she had considered herself to be quite a good judge of character, but in his case she kept being surprised.

"What?" Chill asked. "You're looking at me like I have flan on my upper lip."

"I just realized you're a nice guy." Carmen was a bit annoyed with herself for being so dim around this man. She had thought he was a bit of a jughead, all bloodhound nose and no brain or passion. There was more to Chill than met the eye.

"Bite your tongue. Cops can't be nice guys. The good guys, possibly, but not nice guys. Besides, you don't know anything about me. I could have a past."

"Somehow I doubt it."

"I have the vague notion I should be offended by that."

"Oh, and why is that?"

"Hmmm, let me see. Good guys finish last comes to mind. But how about you, Carmen? Are you ready to tell me the deepest, darkest secret of your past?"

She looked at him as if he had sprouted two heads, both of them ugly. "If you are talking about my arrest . . . no." She had no intention of revealing the details of her past—at least not yet. She trusted Chill, but not enough to share that with him.

"So, nice guy—good cop, tell me about your great plan to

use me as bait."

"Don't think for a minute I'm unaware of you changing the subject. I'll let it drop for now, but I'm getting the entire story out of you eventually."

"Mmm, I hate to shake your confidence, Chill, but it may be a tougher job than you think."

"A gauntlet being dropped, Carmen? I love a challenge."

They stared at each other over the dining table, but what had started out as a friendly challenge morphed into something else entirely. Carmen's clothes felt tight and too hot. She watched a strange alertness enter Chill's eyes.

Were they attracted to each other?

No, they couldn't be. Could they?

Chill shook his head as if he had heard her mental question. "Hey, put on your snow boots and heavy coat."

"Because?"

"There is a Millionaire Car Show in Santa Fe today and we're going."

"Taos County paying you that big a salary, are they? Or do you really have a past—a trust fund, maybe, and you are independently wealthy?" Carmen waggled her brows. They were back to normal. Whatever normal was for them.

"Hardly. Besides you're the one who's going to be looking at all that power with a critical eye."

Carmen glared at him over the last bite of flan. "I told you I don't know anything about the money that was deposited into my account, and I'm sure not going to spend any of it, because it is a mistake and I'm not going to be arrested for fraud by spending any of it."

"Easy, Carmen. You're not going to really buy." Chill sat back and grinned like a well fed tabby—or was it a sleek mountain lion?

"Then what are we going for?"

"To give you a crash course in vehicle I.D. I figure there will be a fair amount of sleek, low-slung sports cars there. Maybe one of them will be black."

Carmen shoved herself away from the table, nearly knocking the chair over in her eagerness. "I'll meet you out front."

CHAPTER TWENTY-FOUR

A hard, tight ball of anxiety had settled in Carmen's stomach the moment Chill maneuvered the SUV into the parking lot. Flashy red and flashy blue sports cars were everywhere. And then her eye drifted over an entire row of ebony cars. If her stalker was here, he was hiding in plain sight.

"I feel like I have a big bull's-eye painted on my forehead," Carmen said.

Chill shut off the engine and gave her his full attention. He was good at that, focusing on her like she was the only other being on the planet.

"Carmen, you're safe. If I didn't think I could protect you, I wouldn't bring you out. Have a little confidence." He grinned, but there was a tightness at the corners of his mouth that hadn't been there earlier in the morning. It did nothing to boost her belief in him.

"Have a little faith, kiddo." He lightly cuffed Carmen on the shoulder. It bothered her in some elemental way, the gesture oddly suggesting that she was just one of the guys.

"I wouldn't want to put too much of my hope in a leaky vessel." She opened the door and climbed down. There was a rounded mound of snow around the entire perimeter of the parking lot where it had been shoveled, like a glittering bumper pad of white. She had to admit the sports cars looked fabulous against the backdrop of winter. She came around the front of the SUV. Chill looped his arm around her shoulder.

"Hey, what's up?" She stiffened and leaned away, but he didn't let her go.

He was good, no denying it.

Without any trouble at all, he pulled her closer to his hip. "Relax. Smile." He was showing enough white enamel to do a toothpaste ad. "We're supposed to be having fun, Carmen."

"Look, if you—" Carmen began.

"Carmen, we're out here to kill two birds with one stone—so to speak. First, I want you to really look at all these cars. If you find one that looks like the black sports car you saw from your window, tell me. But we have another opportunity here. If your stalker is among the rich car owners—you know, stalking you today—it can't hurt to shake him up a little."

His words hit her like a fist. "Oh, Chill, you don't think he is here? You don't think he followed us?"

"Why not? He followed you to Albuquerque. I want him to think there is a new man in your life. I want that possessive bastard's blood to boil. If he gets careless, he will start to make mistakes."

The bright sun reflecting off the snow and the chrome of the cars blinded Carmen. She could only chalk it up to nerves that she had forgotten how brilliant the New Mexican winter sun could be.

"Here, take these." Chill shoved a pair of reflective wrap-around shades into her hand without ever lifting his possessive grip from her shoulders.

Yep, definitely good and slick.

The glasses were too big of course. She managed to balance them on the top of her ears. Now instead of painful blue-white, everything was comfortably shaded; dim, orange and expensive.

"Wow. That's a lot of moolah sitting out there," she whispered.

"Uh-huh. You know I asked Victoria Smith about doing a

DMV check on black sports cars in New Mexico, and she laughed. Evidently Los Alamos has more millionaires per capita than any other place in the United States. She seemed to think that without at least a model, the list would be in the hundreds— possibly the thousands."

"Taos County has quite a few fat cats now too. New Mexico, especially around Santa Fe and Taos, has become a movie Mecca, and Governor Richardson has been doing all he can to promote the industry, including tax incentives. Lots of old-ranchers have sold out or been crowded out by people in the movie biz with deep pockets who don't mind the commute."

"Try as I might, I can't think of any way I could twist that around and tie it to your problem. The way I see it, Mr. Poisoned Pen really believes you stole his book and he is trying to frame you for the murders." Chill was scanning the crowd; his eyes never stopped moving.

"Ha. So you finally admit you think I'm innocent." Carmen felt safe beside him with the heavy weight of his arm across her shoulders.

"I don't think you are innocent by a long shot, but I doubt you shot Jake or Ethyl."

Without thinking, she looped her free arm around his waist. When he glanced down at her, she snatched it away, embarrassed.

"Leave it. It looks natural."

She put it back, hyper-aware of how natural it felt to do so.

"You were telling me about the ranchers," he prompted.

"I don't know a lot, but my neighbor Millie Hyde could tell you all about the old-timers. Her family has been here for generations, and she has a big place in Red River. I think her nephew actually lives up there and does something with the property. Maybe they still run cattle. I could have her call you."

"Yeah, do that."

Carmen lurched to a halt.

"What is it?"

"That car. There." It was low and cat-like. The general shape and design seemed familiar, even though the paint job was a sophisticated creamy pearl.

"Is this like the car you saw outside La Señora?"

"Yes. Yes, it is. I remember the little horse."

"Bingo, Carmen. We now at least know we are looking for a Ferrari."

"So now we have a place to start to look for my stalker?"

"And by Snowdown, with a little luck and some good police work, we may have a description of the creep. Now come and look at this car and tell me if you think driving this thing would improve my image."

CHAPTER TWENTY-FIVE

Over the next two days Carmen received more than twenty threatening E-mails. Chill and Eloy thought they were going to catch up to the perp, but each time they isolated the message as coming from a cybercafé, he was long gone.

Chill was getting damned tired of being jerked around. He was pissed off and frustrated. He had about given up on technology as a police weapon, but Eloy was still confident.

"We'll get the bastard. It is just taking time. He is no idiot. Listen, let me prove it to you. Let me set up a trap in your office software."

"How is that going to help?" Chill growled into the phone.

"You have a dirty cop. Or at least you have hinted that you do. Let me flush the bad apple out of the barrel."

"Fine, Eloy. Dazzle me." Chill hung up the phone and leaned back in his chair. He had the sniffles. His throat was sore, and he was coming down with a cold. "Serves me right for going outside barefoot."

He hadn't told Carmen about her late-night visitor. Chill had heard a noise and gone downstairs to investigate. A man's silhouette vaulted over the patio wall. With his service revolver drawn, Chill had given chase, barefoot, through the deep snow.

"The S.O.B. is like a cat." He disappeared into the neighborhood, leaving Chill out in the cold.

Literally.

Of course, he didn't know if it was Lover Boy, Carmen's

stalker, or Poison Pen, the guy trying to destroy her, but whoever this guy was, he was in top shape: strong, agile and fast.

Chill didn't have time to be sick. Snowdown was upon them. He shoved himself up out of his chair and went to the break room. Vicki Smith was there, making herself a cup of tea.

"You look like hell," she said. "That red nose from too much nightlife, or are you getting sick?"

"Nosey, aren't you?" He grabbed a mug and filled it with hot water from the dispenser. Then he grabbed a teabag, stripped it open and dunked it.

"Sick. No doubt about it."

He looked up at her, and she nodded toward the cup of tea.

"You aren't a tea kind of guy."

"You are very perceptive about men, Vicki."

"Yeah, sometimes." She frowned at the cup while she poured in liquid creamer.

"Want a little coffee with that creamer?"

"What? Oh." She halted the pale stream, clearly flustered.

"Something on your mind?" Chill found several packets of lemon juice and poured them into his tea. His foster mother was a big believer in hot tea with lemon.

"I. . . . Yeah, there is."

"Shoot." Chill leaned against the counter. She couldn't look him in the eye, something that made Chill very nervous.

"I want you to know . . . that is, I need to come clean. . . ."

One of the other deputies stuck his head in the door. "Chill, you have a call from Millie Hyde."

"Can we do this later?" Chill hated to leave Smith hanging. "I've been playing phone tag with her for days."

"No problem." Vicki Smith left the room, and Chill had the sinking feeling he had just blown off something important.

By the time Chill drove to the lane leading to Millie Hyde's house, he was coughing. He glanced at Carmen's house as he drove by. The yard was a soft, deep mound of untouched snow.

"That's a good sign," he muttered to himself. When he was passing Penny Black's house, he saw a flash of color and slowed down. It was a realtor's sign, red, blue and orange, a sharp contrast with the white snow.

When he pulled up to Millie's gate, a stock dog appeared, barking as if he were guarding the gates of hell.

"What is it with these people and their dogs?" He turned off the cruiser, coughing. Millie Hyde came out of her house, striding down the snow-packed lane like a woman half her age.

"Annie, heel." She unlatched the gate and gestured Chill inside.

"Thanks for returning my call," Chill said as he walked beside her.

"I only did it so you would stop phoning me ten times a day."

The dog kept a weather eye on him even after they went inside. Chill was staring at the western décor, complete with vintage paintings, antique guns, and mounted heads of deer and elk displayed on the rustic, knotty pine walls, when Millie spoke again.

"You look rough. Coming down with something?"

"A head cold."

"I've got just the thing. Follow me."

He did follow her through the old-west time capsule of the living room, into the dining room and finally the kitchen. An old cast-iron cookstove with gleaming nickel plating was giving off waves of welcoming heat.

"Is that a wood burner?" He was fascinated to see one in use.

"Yep, only way to cook. Now take a load off while I fix you an old-fashioned cure."

The dog positioned herself between the hot stove and Chill,

her wary eyes following Millie around the room.

"What's on your mind? Why have you been burning up the phone lines trying to reach me?"

"Carmen said your family has been here a long time." Chill's voice was becoming thick and nasally.

"More than a hundred years on my paternal side. Longer on the other." Millie was pouring something into a saucepan, but her back was to Chill and he couldn't see what the secret ingredients were.

"So you know all the old-timers and the newcomers."

"Mostly. What is it you want to know? Who all the long-haired arty types are who come to Penny's parties? Did they get out of hand a couple of nights ago?"

"I'm not sure. I didn't get any complaints. I was more interested in finding out if you know of anybody who got nudged off their land—somebody who might hold a grudge. Someone who might have an ax to grind with Carmen Pollini."

Millie was stirring whatever was in the saucepan.

"Lots of folks got nudged out, and lots of folks hold grudges. I don't know of any connection to Carmen. Look, Sheriff, when all the Californians came in here and started building mansions next to working ranches, the die was cast. Taxes were raised, whole families were displaced, but that was just the beginning. A struggling rancher could sell off a couple of fallow acres to a Hollywood producer and make more money than he could in a couple of good years with his beeves. Yeah, I know a lot of locals with heartburn. Why? As I say, how could any of that possibly connect with the bodies on Carmen's doorstep?"

Chill was getting that foggy, unfocused feeling of illness. It hurt to swallow. He was having a tough time connecting the dots. If he had some reason for asking the question, the fever had dried up the thought.

"It probably doesn't. Just part of my investigation. I've been following leads in more than one direction."

"How is Carmen doing?" Millie poured the warm mixture into a mug and placed it in front of Chill.

"She's holding up."

"Don't let that get cold. Chug it as soon as you can stand the heat." Millie watched him with unblinking concentration.

Chill picked up the cup with both hands. The ceramic felt good, solid and hot in his palms. He took an experimental sniff.

There was no scent that made it beyond his stuffed-up nose.

He sipped.

It wasn't too hot.

"What's in this?"

"A bunch of organic stuff. An old family recipe. Don't be a sissy. I have a nephew who is a pantywaist. Won't even hunt like a real man. Plays with fake guns. I don't know, maybe he's gay—he never misses one of Penny's parties—but he can chug the cure when he has a cold. Now tip it up and drink it."

Chill tipped up the cup and gulped it down. The heat felt good on his sore throat. His belly warmed, and he got a head-rush.

"What was that?"

"Old-fashioned cure. Never fails. You'll start feeling the effects within half an hour."

Chill was already feeling the effects of the hot home remedy when he left Millie's house. He backed out of her drive, determined to go straight to La Señora, hit the mattress and stay there until Snowdown. But when he saw the realtor's sign again, he stopped in front of Penny Black's house.

It was quiet as a tomb when he walked up the steps and knocked on the door. He found it hard to reconcile all the stories he had heard about the artist's wild parties and the utter solitude of the morning.

After a short wait, the door was opened by a man. The guy

was huge but not lumpy, steroid-induced big. He had long, strong, corded worked-his-ass-off-to-get-them muscles. He had six inches and fifty pounds on Chill.

In his present condition Chill hoped the guy was a friendly.

"Vhat you vant?" His accent was pure Scandinavian. Chill had a mental image of the guy decked out in skins, holding Thor's hammer while a Wagner opera played in the background.

Chill fumbled out his badge and showed it to the guy. "I want to speak with Ms. Black." A peculiar tingle was moving across his scalp, and he had the sensation of his skin shrinking around his skull.

Millie's cure must be working.

"Come in." The man moved aside and there was a small female, looking wan and small in contrast, behind him. She was wearing a black silk kimono embroidered with golden dragons.

"Ms. Black?"

"Yes." She certainly didn't fit Chill's first impression of her as a bold, Bohemian artist. This woman was skittish, pale and had dark circles under her eyes as if she been unable to sleep from worry, not partying. Something had sure taken the wind out of her sails.

"Remember me? Sheriff Blaines?"

"Yes. We talked when Jake was killed. This is Lars, my bodyguard."

Chill extended his hand. It was quickly engulfed by Lars's giant paw.

"Bodyguard. Good career choice." Chill winked at Lars. It took his eyes a long time to refocus. He cast an eye around the open room. A skylight overhead provided a bright bar of sunlight that reflected off the stark, bare white walls. Canvases of all sizes were stacked up against the walls. There were some stunning landscapes, bright with green and golden hues. And there were some abstract paintings as well. Chill saw some color photos clamped to the tops of identical, but larger, paintings. He was no art expert, but he recognized them as old masters. He meandered closer, and although it took a moment to focus, he made out Penny's signature in the lower right hand corner of them all.

"They are copies, and clearly marked as such. I'm not a forger."

"I never implied you were."

Lars folded his arms across his massive chest and stood silently, observing. Chill decided he liked Annie and Tyson better when it came to watchdogs, although this guy looked like he could take off an ear if he wanted to.

"You have a lot of talent. I assume you are making a nice living off your art." Chill meant it; she was good. "I'm kind of surprised to see you do copies."

"People want real oils for their houses, but they don't have real money to buy good paintings. I offer another option. They are getting a copy that is well executed, and I make a little money. But I will probably be doing less of that now. I have had a few works sell recently in New York, at New York prices." Penny fidgeted with her hands, picking at her nails.

"I see you're selling your house. Moving to a bigger place?"

She glanced at Lars and then toward the French doors that Chill had just now noticed were swathed in dark sheets.

"Hardly. I love this place, and I really can't afford anything as nice at today's prices."

"Then why are you selling out?"

"I'm getting the hell out of this place before another dead body turns up—or something worse happens."

CHAPTER TWENTY-SIX

"Define something worse." Chill's shrunken scalp had begun to feel hot, and the tip of his nose was tingling.

"Bad karma! I don't know what is going on with Carmen, but I think she has a big karmic debt to pay off. I just don't want those bad vibes touching me." Penny was pacing back and forth under the skylight like a trapped animal.

"Is there some reason why you think she has bad karma?"

"The lights, the shadows. Maybe her place is haunted. Both of those murders. I think it is haunted." Penny Black shivered, the silk kimono shimmering in the overhead light. "I can't take it anymore. I'm taking the first offer I get on this house, and I'm heading east. Lars has agreed to come with me until I get settled and put all this behind me."

"*Ja.*"

"Tell me about the lights and the shadows." Chill was having a tough time following the conversation. Could Millie Hyde have poisoned him?

"At night lights flicker and then vanish. Then at the French doors a couple of nights ago I saw the shadow of . . . I don't know what it was, but it spooked me good. Thank goodness Lars was still here after the party. I phoned the realtor the next morning."

"Mind if I have a look?" Chill was headed for the doors. His hand was almost on the sheeting.

"No!" Penny squeaked. "You can look, but go out the front

door. Those stay locked and covered until I'm gone."

Chill went outside. The change in temperature urged him to tug his collar up. He tried to blink away the fogginess in his head. It was starting to snow as he made his way around Penny's house toward the back. Even in his present condition, he could see there was a regular path worn from the back of Penny's house, going toward Carmen's backyard. The snow had been trampled down, and even the fresh fall had not fluffed it back up.

"Somebody's been beating a path between Penny and Carmen's doors. Now if I knew who and why, it would be great."

Chill drove to La Señora, feeling weirdly numb and disoriented. He parked the cruiser, locked it and tottered toward the B&B. He opened the door—did it just bounce back against the wall?—and staggered in. The warmth of the reception area hit him like a fist. He fumbled with the door before he finally got it closed.

"I would never criticize the law, but you look like you have a snoot full," Tony quipped.

"Uh-uh, not me. I don't drink anything but beer . . . and margaritas." Chill thought he might be slurring his words, but he wasn't sure.

"Yeah, right. Lemme help you." Tony thumped his way to Chill and supported them both on his crutch and one good foot. They made it to the oversized chair beside the registration desk just in time for Chill to fall into it.

"Sheriff, don't take this personally but you are plastered."

"Nonschense. I haven't had a drop." He couldn't be drunk, but something was seriously wrong with his body. "Maybe I have the Hanta virus."

"Wrong season."

"Maybe it's the bird flu."

"That would be the wrong continent. Face it, Chill, you're wasted."

Carmen came downstairs. Chill looked up at her through the fog. When had there been fog in the B&B registration lobby?

"What happened to Chill?" She stepped forward and peered up at him. He felt like a science experiment gone wrong.

"I think he's three sheets to the wind. He says he hasn't touched a drop, but the evidence strongly supports my theory."

"You sound like a cop, Pop. Where have you been, Chill?"

Carmen leaned over and touched his head. It was a little warm. She sniffed at him. Tyson soon joined her and did a little sniffing of his own.

"I went to schpeek to Millie Hyde."

Carmen stood up. "Did she happen to fix you one of her old-fashioned cold remedies?"

"Uh-huh." Chill felt like he was swimming through molasses. "Sschomething hot."

"Oh, man. You poor, poor thing." Carmen smiled sympathetically at him. "I feel for you."

He kind of liked that for some goofy reason he couldn't figure out. Chill hated motherly women, detested pity parties, and shunned weak, wimpy men who didn't have the balls to take care of themselves. But he liked Carmen's tone of concern.

"Whatsch's the matter witch me?" He told himself he wasn't whining.

"Millie's cold cure is made of ten shots of well-aged bourbon, four shots of gin and two shots of vodka. She cuts it with a little sugar and lemon juice."

"Unfortunate devil," Tony said.

"Whatsch ya talking about? Whatsch the matter? Am I dying?" Chill managed to croak.

"You will wish you were dead by tomorrow," Carmen said. "Come on, Pop. Help me put him to bed before he goes toes up right here in Mom's reception area."

Chill had nightmares. Not boogey-man dreams, but disjointed, teenage-horror dreams. He saw dead bodies with one eye blown out, mingled with the mounted trophies on Millie's walls that morphed into spectral shapes in snow, and ice—jagged, lethal.

And at the center of them all was Carmen.

In one scenario, she was innocent as Snow White with bluebirds and woodland animals skipping around her. The next moment she was dark, with sharp fangs and claws.

He woke up because someone was yelling.

It took him a minute to realize it was him making all the noise.

He sat up in bed, but a bomb went off inside his head.

"Oh" was all he could say, for the act of speech was more painful than breathing, and that was about 10.1 on the Richter scale of agony.

He'd been poisoned. There was no doubt about it, Millie Hyde had tried to kill him.

"I'm going to go arrest her." Yeah. Right after the sledgehammer inside his skull quit torturing him.

He was lying there, contemplating the satisfaction he would get out of charging Millie with attempted murder, when someone banged on his door.

"Go away. I'm dying."

He heard the unmistakable sound of a key being inserted into a lock, and the latch clicking. The door eased open, sending a shaft of painfully bright light arcing across his face.

"Argh! Get out!" Chill pulled the pillow over his head, trying to muffle the sound of stomping feet and his own gasps for oxygen.

"Chill, you better drink this. Come on, it will make you feel better." Carmen's voice was loud—too loud.

"I can't feel better. I've been poisoned. Millie tried to kill me. She must be the killer."

The sound of a giggle made his temples hurt.

"Come on, Chill, suck it up. Be the big, tough cop I know you are."

He pulled the pillow off his head and squinted experimentally at Carmen. She was holding a tall glass and a bottle of aspirin.

"That won't help. I need IV painkillers at the very least. Probably a blood transfusion too. Maybe a liver transplant."

She laughed.

"Stop it. That hurts."

"So Millie fixed you her cold remedy, huh? Believe me, I sympathize. I couldn't look at my computer screen without wearing sunglasses for almost two weeks. I think the booze damaged my retinas permanently."

"Booze? Not poison?"

"Nope, just a few shots of her favorite hooch. Amazing what happens when she combines them, huh?"

Chill sat up—slowly, very slowly. He was mortified. So this was a hangover; just a hangover. How could he have been so stupid? He was embarrassed.

"Hey, grab that comforter. You are about to reveal all your secrets to me." Carmen turned her back and giggled again.

Chill grabbed for the comforter, just barely saving himself from further embarrassment.

"Drink this." Carmen turned around and shoved the glass into his hand. Then she tipped out four aspirin.

"Four?"

"You'll thank me in an hour."

He tossed them back. Carmen went to the window and opened the heavy drapes. Snow was falling outside, making the world brighter and more painful, but Chill clamped his back teeth together and ignored it.

He was tough. He could take it.

"When you feel up to it, come down and have some coffee. The caffeine also helps."

Carmen shut the door and Chill moaned. Okay, so he was acting like a pantywaist, but a guy could suffer in private—couldn't he?

Carmen was sitting at her usual table finishing her breakfast burrito when Chill appeared, coming through the front lobby entrance. He was wearing dark sunglasses and moved as if his head was in one of those halos that people have to wear when they have broken their necks. He crossed the room, and she tried not to laugh when he squatted and eased himself into the chair opposite her as if he had a book balanced on top of his head.

"Coffee," he croaked.

She poured him a cup from the carafe and watched as he picked it up with a shaky hand. The brew was steaming, but he seemed not to notice when he took a long sip.

"Thank God." He finished it off and put the empty cup back into the saucer. Carmen filled it again.

"You're an angel."

Those dark glasses were a little unnerving, but she knew how his eyes felt.

"Why are you all dressed up?" he asked.

"Hey, you noticed. The damage to your retinas is not permanent. That's great."

"Stop hedging. What's with the glad-rags?"

"One of the television stations in Albuquerque is doing a live feed interview with me this morning."

"I don't want you going anywhere."

"No *problema, mon* General." Carmen grinned. "We are doing it from La Señora's courtyard. The cameraman and his whole crew are out there right now setting up."

"Oh, terrific. You pick a day when I can't even focus to open up La Señora to whatever freak may be out there trying to get at you. Carmen, don't you have a single chromosome devoted to self-preservation?"

Half an hour later, Chill had made it outside. Carmen was right; the coffee and aspirins had helped.

"This is a bloody security nightmare." Even through his sunglasses, the glare of snow lying like a fluffy blanket over the courtyard was brutal. At least the cold, crisp air cleared his head a bit more. Chill popped gum into his mouth and chewed like it was two-inch-thick bull hide. Damn, but a cigarette would be good right about now.

"Watch it, buddy!" A big guy with a loop of thick, black cable and a wild set of dreadlocks, barreled past Chill. "We are behind schedule. Nobody is allowed in here but crew."

"Consider me your security chief." Chill dug out his badge and showed it to the guy.

"Taos County sheriff? Are you kidding, man? Where is your ten-gallon hat and six-shooter." White teeth flashed when he smiled. He looked like he should be playing in a reggae band.

"Casual Friday," Chill growled.

The toothy smile slipped. "Okay, okay. Look, just stay out of the way will ya? I don't want to have Sarah the Shark yelling at me 'cause you are getting in her shot."

"Sarah the Shark?"

"Yea, the anchorwoman. She can smell blood in the water a mile away. She is really jazzed about this interview. Says it is going to make her career."

Chapter Twenty-Seven

"Just relax, smile and let me do all the work." Sarah the Shark had seen to Carmen's microphone, running it up her long sleeve, then clipping it to her turtleneck, making it almost invisible.

Chill stood against the plastered wall with his hands in his shearling jacket pockets. His headache had subsided to a dull thrum behind his eyes. He ignored it and focused on the scene in front of him.

"What kinds of questions will you be asking?" Carmen shuffled some cards in her hands. "I have some sales figures, quotes from *Publishers Weekly* and a blurb from my publisher."

"That sounds fine, just fine." Sharky-Sarah flashed a row of sharp teeth. Definitely a carnivore at the top of the food chain.

Chill's bad-guy radar started binging. Or was it just a by-product of his hangover that had his stomach knotting up?

"Okay, Sarah, we go live in three, two, one. . . ."

"Good morning. I am Sarah Shellman, and welcome to *Focus on the Facts*. This morning we are coming to you live from Taos, New Mexico. My guest today is the best-selling novelist, Carmen Pollini."

Chill watched the cameraman swivel slightly in Carmen's direction. Her smile was a bit stiff, but she looked great against the wintry background. Her dark hair and eyes were spectacular.

"So tell us about yourself, Carmen. I can call you Carmen, can't I?"

215

"Yes, of course."

"Good. Now Carmen, your books, which have been set in and around Taos, have been gaining popularity lately."

"Yes, I'm pleased to say that *A Hot Brand of Love* is still holding steady on several top best-seller's lists." Carmen smiled like a proud parent.

"Yes, it has. Now what do you think is responsible for that rise?"

That radar kicked up again. Chill shifted on his feet, kicking a small pile of snow out of his way.

"I have the readers to thank—"

"The readers? Or would it be the notoriety surrounding the double murder?"

"I don't think—"

"Or perhaps it has something to do with the charges being filed against Sheriff Jim Dunn. You have a character like him in your book, don't you, Ms. Pollini? A crooked cop, on the take, blackmailing local citizens? Could it be your book is based in fact? Could it be the rise in sales is because of your involvement in the murders? Or the blackmail? Or both?"

Carmen's dark eyes grew round. She retreated back into her chair as the Shark leaned forward, shoving a big, ugly microphone with some sort of padded cover in Carmen's face.

"I—I. . . ."

"Do something, Chill." Tony had hobbled outside.

"Hey, I'm not a boxer. I can't very well go up and bite her earlobe, can I?"

"You are the law, aren't you? Do something."

Chill walked in front of the cameraman and positioned himself in front of Carmen.

"I'm Sheriff Blaines. If you have any questions about an ongoing investigation, they should be directed to my office."

Sharky glared up at him, then she rose to her feet. She leveled a gaze at Chill that told him the gloves were off and she was getting ready to take a swing.

"Fine, Sheriff. Tell us what is being done to solve the double homicide. And then would you explain to the public why the charges against Jim Dunn are coming out of Bernalillo County and not Taos County? Could it be there was some graft or corruption that prevented you from doing your job?"

"No comment."

"Well, then, perhaps Ms. Pollini would care to comment on the E-mail I received this morning. In this E-mail a witness claims to have solid proof that Ms. Pollini murdered both victims and that it is a direct result of the fact that she plagiarized *A Hot Brand of Love*. So, tell me, Ms. Pollini, did you steal the book, *A Hot Brand of Love*? Were Jake and your agent going to go public with proof? Are you a murderer? And are you only still free because you and Sheriff Blaines are sleeping under the same roof?"

Chill's headache returned, right along with the bitter memory of all the gossip, innuendo and crap he'd endured in California. Carmen's face was nearly as pale as the snow behind the ruthless reporter. So the perp had gone to the press, huh? And he was going to sink her with unsubstantiated rumors, was he? And this reporter was going to try and smear them both by hinting there was something improper in their living arrangements, was she?

Chill's jaw tensed and then, even though he knew it was a mistake, he opened his mouth. He wasn't going to stand by and watch it happen. Not again. Not to Carmen, and not to him.

"I have a few things to say, Ms. Shellman." He snatched the microphone from her hand, and looked straight at the woolly dreadlocks sticking out on either side of the camera. Then Chill took a deep breath and let it fly.

★ ★ ★ ★ ★

Five minutes later the cameraman had packed away his gear, amid a few deep chuckles. Sharky had dried her tears and had been escorted from the courtyard, and Carmen had been bustled inside for Maria and Tony to comfort.

"Man, I got to give you props." The cameraman was still grinning. "I mean, man, I did a stint in the service, but you had some words and phrases there that were truly inspired. I didn't even know a person could do that kind of kinky thing with a microphone, but with the explicit instructions you gave the Shark, she might be able to pull it off." He laughed again.

Chill popped another piece of gum in his mouth. He hadn't intended to go so blue, but Sharky brought out the worst in him. She was the embodiment of all the Internal Affairs investigators and yellow journalism he had been subjected to when that sorry, tell-all book came out. In California he had felt powerless to stop the barrage.

This time he had the power, and even if it all ended up with him out of a job, he was going to put his badge to use now. Besides, he was only passing through anyway. Come spring, he was pointing his SUV in the direction of old Route 66.

"I had a few things to get off my chest," he said as much to himself as to the cameraman. "Unfortunately, your boss got in the way."

"Hey, no problem. I enjoyed it. And she isn't my boss. If she was, I would be looking for another job. I got the short straw and had to come today, but now I'm glad I did. Keep the faith, man." The cameraman gave Chill a complicated handshake that ended with a knuckle-to-knuckle bump.

Then he was gone.

Chill was left alone in the cold. The formerly pristine courtyard looked like a centipede wearing jackboots had been through it. He kicked at a pile of half-melted snow with his boot.

This crime was driving him crazy. The suspect was a crafty son of a buck. He had evaded Eloy's attempts to catch him at the cybercafés, he had been able to come and go around Taos without causing so much as a ripple, and now he had sent propaganda to the press.

"And I still don't have a solid lead." Chill put together another colorful phrase that would have impressed the cameraman.

"Focus, Chill, focus," he muttered. Damn, he needed a smoke.

He did have one small satisfaction; he knew that Carmen was being stalked by two entirely different creeps. But that thought made him feel impotent and hollow inside.

"I need a cigarette, and I need it soon." He left the courtyard and went into La Señora. The lobby was empty when he stomped through and went out to his rig in the parking lot.

"There has got to be one cigarette somewhere in here." He checked the door panels, the glove box and the pocket in his sun visor.

Nothing.

"The console." He opened the hard vinyl console and pulled out a handful of napkins, papers and two books of matches from a casino in Nevada. He found the traffic ticket he had got the first day he arrived. That, he shoved into his Levi's pocket and continued to dig.

"Ah."

There at the bottom was one bent, dried-up cigarette. He picked it up like he would a wounded bird, not squeezing too tightly.

He put the unfiltered end to his lip and struck a match. He put the flame to the end and puffed. He was just about to inhale, savoring the feel of the paper in his hand.

"Chill! Come quick. Carmen's stalker is on the phone!"

He dropped the cigarette. It landed in a half-frozen puddle of dirty water.

"Some days a guy just can't get a break."

CHAPTER TWENTY-EIGHT

"What did he say?" Chill ran to the door where Tony was trying to balance on his crutch and hold it open at the same time.

"I answered. He said he had been sending Carmen gifts. Called himself her number-one fan. He wanted to speak to her."

"Why did you give the phone to Carmen?" Chill barreled through the door, nearly knocking Tony off his feet.

"Give me a little credit. I didn't. She had answered the extension in the Blue Coyote at the same time. She was already on the line. He said he had seen the live news this morning and was going to help."

"Crap."

Chill jogged through the lobby of La Señora, through the courtyard, and took the shortcut through the kitchen, dodging hot plates and surprised kitchen staff. He entered the Blue Coyote and saw Maria patting Carmen's arm. She was holding the wireless phone.

"I want you to leave me alone," Carmen said.

Chill wrenched the phone from her tight grip, punched the speaker button on the phone and pushed down the receiver in one quick motion. A smooth male voice filled the room.

"Carmen, I want you to know I'm your number-one fan. I have come to realize that you are not the kind of woman who appreciates chocolates or lingerie. And of course, I should have realized a soul as pure as yours would not be impressed by the vulgarity of money. So I have called to let you know that I will now offer you something else. Something you need."

Chill leaned close enough to whisper into Carmen's ear. "Play him. Keep him talking. Don't lose your temper."

Her dark eyes flashed, but she nodded. Chill flipped open his cell phone and stepped away. "Vicki, this is Chill. Is there any way we can trace a call?"

"No, Chill. This is not L.A. The only way we could trace a call is if we were already set up with a tap."

"Damn."

He closed the phone. It was all up to Carmen and him.

"Wouldn't it just be easier to meet me face to face and ask me what I like or don't like?" Carmen asked.

"Ah, but we have met before. You just didn't realize I was different from your other fans. And I tried again, once. At your house, remember? The meeting was less than satisfactory. I had to leave early when I heard the police sirens."

"I was startled. You ambushed me. I'm talking about a real meeting, over a cup of cappuccino, like normal people."

A rich, throaty laugh brought the hairs on Chill's neck to attention.

"Normal? What is normal, Carmen? You know, I should be offended. You are indicating in your own charming way that you don't think I am normal. You might be surprised."

"I didn't mean to offend you, I—"

"No, don't apologize. We will meet again, Carmen, soon. But for now, just know I'm your number-one fan. I know you didn't plagiarize. You couldn't. It's not in your character. Rest easy. I will find the liar who is making you unhappy, and I'll take care of it. It is obvious that bumbling cop can't keep you safe. But I can, and I will."

The line went dead.

Carmen looked up at Chill, and for the first time since he

first met her, there was abject terror in her eyes.

"He is so . . . sure of himself," she said softly.

"Charming, smooth, confident. If it wasn't for the evidence to the contrary, I would say he sounds perfectly normal, except he has a hard-on-crush for you." Chill wanted to hit something, but that was a childish idea. He needed to keep a cool head; do the work and find this guy.

Before Mr. Charm and Personality found Carmen's other stalker and another corpse turned up.

Chill felt as though someone had flipped a light switch.

"That's it! Why didn't I think of it before? That is it!"

"What?"

"I know who killed Jake and Ethyl, and I know why!"

Chill sat at his desk at the station making notes. It was the only answer. It all came together. Every person who had a beef with Carmen met an untimely end.

"Gotcha." Chill drew a dark circle on the pad where he had written *suspect/stalker number one—Lover Boy.*

Yep, he had the bastard now.

He leaned back in his chair and clasped his fingers behind his head. Millie's cure had worked. Maybe the old adage about things not killing you making you stronger was true. His throat didn't hurt, his sniffles were gone and his mind was clear. He was firing on all cylinders now.

"Sheriff?" Vicki Smith stuck her head in the door. "Do you have the keys to your cruiser? It's time to get it serviced."

"Sure." Chill dug into his pocket, yanking out a few crumpled bills, a piece of paper and finally the keys. He tossed them to her. She caught them and left.

Victoria Smith was a good cop, one of the best. In spite of what he had found out. He was going to have to deal with that problem, and soon.

His gaze fell on the yellow paper, his copy of the traffic citation he had received. He tilted his head and looked at it. Then he smoothed it out and read it line by line.

"Son of a—so that is how my previous employment record turned up at the county commissioners' office." Chill's temper flared. Pieces fell into place. All it had taken was running his California license when he was stopped. That would bring up his information. The rest would have been a piece of cake for anyone able to use a computer.

"So I was maneuvered into this job."

The only question that was still a little cloudy was why—and what benefit was there in having Chill in office instead of Jim Dunn?

Carmen stared at the blank screen. Not a single spark of dialogue or an idea for action popped into her head.

She had writer's block for the first time since she started writing.

"And it is all because of some liar."

Her editor had called her, giving her reassurance that the publishing house would support her, even though the cost of attorney's fees, should it come to court, would be Carmen's responsibility.

So far she hadn't touched any of the money sitting in her account, but things were getting tight. If only she knew where that money came from. Suddenly the light dawned. She became rigid as knowledge ripped through her.

"Of course. My number-one fan. He drives an expensive black sports car, and what did he say? I wouldn't be impressed by something as vulgar as money? So he was the one who made the anonymous deposit into my account."

It was all so confusing. Carmen felt like a deer in the crosshairs. It was only a matter of time until one or both of her stalkers tracked her down, found her alone, and then what?

"Unless I take the bull by the horns." Carmen shut down her laptop. She put on her coat and gloves, put a leash on Tyson and headed for the door.

Posters for Snowdown were taped, tacked and glued to every surface imaginable. Carmen's boots crunched on the thin crust of ice that had formed on the light dusting of morning snow. She had ignored Maria and Tony's pleas and threats as she put on her sunglasses and left La Señora. The bright glare of the wintry day was invigorating.

"No wonder I can't write," she muttered to Tyson while they walked. No writer could create in a vacuum, and since this nightmare started that was exactly what her world had become.

She was suffocating.

Chill and her parents meant well, but nobody could keep her safe. The key was to flush out the bad guys, and that was exactly what she was going to do. Her plan wasn't any crazier than Chill's.

She was getting ready to cross the street when the squall of a high-powered engine drew her attention. She expected to see a black sports car. Instead, a police cruiser slung snow at her feet as it careened to a stop, cutting off her path.

Chill exploded from the car, his face a study in controlled fury while he stood in the V of the open car door. "What in Sam-damn-hell do you think you are doing?"

"I'm taking Tyson out for a stroll and baiting one or both of my stalkers. What are you doing, Chill? Setting a good example for crazy drivers?"

"Get in."

"No."

"Damn it, Carmen, get in."

"No."

"You leave me no choice." He stomped around the car, pulling a pair of shiny cuffs from behind his back. "Carmen, you are under arrest."

"What's the charge?"

"I don't know. Jaywalking. I'll think of something. Now watch your head and get in the damned car."

Tyson hopped in, glad to be out of the snow. Carmen glared at Chill, but she had no choice but to obey when he put his palm on the top of her head and guided her into the car.

As he was pulling away, Chill glanced in his rearview mirror. A tall man in a long duster was leaning against a building, watching.

"That was the sneakiest, most low-down, vile, high-handed trick. Unlock these things." Carmen had finally lost the temper everyone claimed she possessed. Chill's hand at the small of her back was like salt in an open wound. He opened the door of the police station and ushered her inside like a protective uncle.

"It was for your own good." He unlocked the cuffs and led her into his office. Vicki Smith tried not to smile when they walked past her, but Carmen could tell it was a struggle.

"Bull. You are just throwing your weight around. Well, I'm tired of it. I'm not going to hide at La Señora while two men have complete freedom to make me miserable. I want to flush out the creep who claims I stole his book, because right after you arrest him, I'm going to sue the bastard."

"Carmen, you don't understand. This is serious. I know what can happen when police let down their guard. One of the finest women I ever knew was murdered because the Feds let down their guard. You are not going to become a good-looking corpse—not on my watch."

Carmen studied Chill's face. It was stark with emotion. Her temper deflated like a punctured balloon.

"Tell me about it."

"First let me buy you a cup of lousy coffee." He opened his office door. "Maybe there is even a stale donut in the break room."

"Wow, you really know how to show a girl a good time. Now quit stalling and tell me."

"I was on the force in California in an area that has a real bad meth problem. We had been after a major player for a long time, but he was slippery as an eel. Then we caught a break."

"Somebody turn state's evidence?" Carmen took a sip of the brew Chill had poured into a Styrofoam cup. It was bitter on her tongue.

"You have written way too many mystery novels. Somebody rarely turns. No, our break was a witness to a double homicide. One of the victims was an undercover cop."

"Stop taking cheap shots at what I do for a living and tell me the story."

"The witness was a young college student. She was smart and brave. She came forward, volunteered testimony. It didn't hurt that she was taking classes in criminal justice. She was the perfect witness. I will never forget the look in her eyes. She had terrific eyes—the eyes of a lioness. She took the stand and buried that bastard with the truth."

Vicki Smith came into the break room and poured the old coffee into the sink. She went about building a fresh pot while Chill talked.

"I will never forget her eyes. Never."

"So the story had a happy ending?" Carmen took another sip. She could handle strong coffee, but this stuff was caustic. She poured her own coffee down the sink.

"Oh, yeah, until Sisco's people put a hit on her. The Feds had relaxed their protection when he went to Vacaville. She died in a burning car. That is never going to happen to someone on my watch. Never."

Carmen noticed Vicki Smith's hands were shaking. All the color had drained from her face. She fumbled the coffee filter, spilled grounds on the counter, swiped them into the trash and refilled a new filter.

"Are you all right?" Carmen touched her shoulder lightly.

"Yeah, fine." Vicki turned and looked at Chill.

He focused on her face, his eyes skimming over her features and back to her wide eyes in less than a second. Then the color leached from his face as well.

"What the devil is wrong with you two? I swear, you both look like you have seen a ghost."

CHAPTER TWENTY-NINE

Chill had driven Carmen and Tyson back to La Señora on autopilot. He couldn't believe it, but there was no doubt in his mind.

It *was* her.

"Chill, what is the matter?" Carmen's voice cut through the fog of shock in his head. "I feel like I missed out on the punch line to a joke or something. You and Vicki were definitely communicating on some level that was non-verbal. What's up?"

"Nothing."

For one brief sizzling moment Carmen wondered if Chill and Vicki were an item, but she discounted it for a couple of reasons. One: he was too professional to indulge in an office romance. Two: Since he lived at La Señora she knew his comings and goings, and Vicki didn't see him off-hours. So what had happened in that break room?

She glanced at his stony profile and crossed her arms, feeling cranky that she was left out.

"Fine, do the guy thing. Keep it all to yourself. Your business and I don't want to know anyway. But nothing has changed. I'm tired of hiding. Snowdown starts tomorrow and I'm ready to implement your plan. I don't care how crazy it seems. I'm going to be there, live and in your face."

It was a carnival on snow. Cowboys on sleek muscled horses towed empty sleds, sending rooster tails of snow over the gathering crowds. Men and women in sleek bibs, stylish ski attire, or any combination of jeans and down vests whooped, and hollered, waving poles draped with bandanas in the air like medieval heralds.

Buddhists, tree-huggers, trust-fund babies, cowboys and snow-bunnies in expensive sunglasses jostled for a better view of the festivities, clustering along the rope barriers like Romans at the coliseum. Farther down the roped-off area booths had been erected to form a food court. Hungry dreadlock-coiffed doggers could buy roasted turkey legs, steins of beer, funnel cakes, burritos and corn dogs. There was even a tattoo artist with an airbrush creating temporary artwork of the wild-eyed cowboy-snowdown logo on bulging biceps or any other body part shoved in his face, while a local artist was sketching zany caricatures.

"This is a security nightmare." Chill had a moment of doubt. What had he been thinking? He put his arm around Carmen's waist and yanked her from the path of a stilt-walker, who unbelievably had a set of snowshoes attached to the bottoms of the long sticks. Tyson growled as the webbed contraptions swept by, but he kept pace with Carmen, dodging hooves, chunky stacked heels and designer ski boots.

"My life has been a security nightmare. I'm sick of what these two jerks have done to my life. I don't know if I'm going to get shot in the head, taken to dinner or sued in the next five minutes. Enough is enough. When your buddy from the television station arrives and starts filming, I hope the live feed will be more than either of the stalkers can resist. So here I am, bait on the hoof." Carmen pulled out of his grip and did a little dancing pirouette in the snow.

"You actually believe that is a good thing, don't you?"

"Look at me, Chill."

She didn't need to tell him to do that. He had watched her

walk down the stairs this morning, decked out in winter white, the ski duds tight in all the right places. His eyes had skimmed over her body and sent red-hot information to his brain and his loins at the same time when she put on an outrageously expensive white wool coat. She was a looker and had a quick mind, smart mouth and guts. If he wasn't careful, he could get very attached to her.

Carmen took off her shades and stared at Chill. "I haven't had sun in weeks. I'm white as this snow, out of shape from sitting on my butt, and I have writer's block. Things have got to change."

Some of the light had gone out of her eyes. It reminded him of Lily Platero. She had been afraid and rightly so, but she had done what she believed was right. Carmen was not going to end up like Lily.

"Fine, let's get to it." Chill grabbed Carmen's hand and crabbed his way through the throng of people, pulling her with him. He stumbled into a young man with winter camo duds on.

"Hey man, want a schedule?" The guy thrust a paper at Chill.

"Of what?"

"Paintball Melee. It is the bomb, man. We do the same circuit every year. Phoenix is coming up. It rocks, man."

Chill took the flyer and elbowed his way to the booth where cameras were being set up. He put his back to the crowd and shielded Carmen with his body.

"Chill! Buddy." Dreadlocks and a black camera lens greeted Chill and Carmen.

"I appreciate this." Chill executed the complicated handshake.

"No problem, man. My boss was thrilled to get the exclusive. I've got the mikes set up and the cameras you wanted facing the crowd. Come on, let's get you miked up."

"Good, good." Chill was still carrying the flyer. While Carmen was preparing for the interview, he glanced down at it.

Something about the dates caught his attention. He frowned and read the list of dates and locations again, trying to loosen a pebble of memory. Something about the list seemed familiar.

"Chill?" Carmen's voice ripped away his concentration.

"Yeah, what?"

"I'm ready."

He looked up to see Carmen pull a hot pink boa from the pocket of her pale coat. She wrapped it around her neck. That bright flash of color made her stick out like a bull's-eye was painted on her chest. Thank God she had so many layers on that nobody would notice the bulk of the bulletproof vest. Only problem was, the killer had made two flawless head shots. That thought ripped through Chill's gut with painful clarity.

He spun around, scanning the crowd, seeing the faces of his deputies here and there. They were all in plain clothes, some dressed as skiers, some as cowboys. Only their steely gazes and the lumps of their shoulder holsters made them stand out in a crowd.

"Okay, Carmen baby, we are going live in five, four, three, two, one—" The camera man pointed his finger at Carmen the instant a red light flashed on the front of the camera. She stared at the light, serious and focused.

"Hello, I'm Carmen Sofia Pollini. Recently a cowardly liar has made an anonymous claim that I stole his book idea. I wanted to take this opportunity to defend myself."

Tyson sat obediently beside Carmen's chair. Chill glanced around at the gathering crowd. Some people appeared to be truly interested; others were just eager to be in the vicinity of a television camera. That was fine with him. They could mug it up all they wanted. The other cameras set up in plain sight, pointing here and there, would record things he and his officers might miss. The plan was to get as much footage as possible and then review it all frame by frame.

He glanced down at the paper in his hand.

What was it about those dates and locations? They were so familiar. Like bees buzzing in his head, they flitted around, but he just couldn't quite get the bees to land.

A group of rowdy types, some of them in winter camo, walked by. The sun glinted on a weapon that any bony-headed Klingon warrior would be proud to carry.

The memory of Millie Hyde's house flashed in his mind. Chill remembered the same kind of space-age-looking gun had been in her den along with all the vintage firearms. At the time he had been half-sick, and then he had been dosed with her old-fashioned cure, so he hadn't picked up on it.

"A paintball gun," he whispered.

"—and so, as you can easily see by the date on this cancelled stamp on this sealed envelope, I mailed this to myself more than eighteen months ago." Carmen held up a Tyvek shipping envelope. With a certain amount of flourish, she ripped it open and withdrew the thick, rubber-banded papers. "This is the raw manuscript of *A Hot Brand of Love*. My editor also has a copy mailed the same day. She has sent a notarized statement, by the way, that clearly states I sent her a proposal on this very book more than a year before I mailed this completed book to myself."

Chill smiled at her. She gave him an almost imperceptible nod, took a deep breath and continued.

"So if the cowardly liar who has made these accusations against me would like to show up with his proof, we can compare the manuscripts live on television. KALA television has offered to keep their cameras rolling throughout the day. I challenge you, whoever you are, to come forward and see if your proof is as solid as mine."

Chill pulled a piece of gum out of the new pack. He ran his hand over his service revolver and scanned the crowd.

"Hey, Carmen, what about the dead literary agent? Would

she have backed you up, or would she have proved you are a thief?" A disembodied voice called out.

Chill whirled around. He couldn't tell where the voice came from. He made his way to the cameraman.

Carmen never skipped a beat. She kept to her agenda, calmly outlining her proof. Then she flashed a million-dollar smile at the crowd. The red light went out on the front of the camera. She sighed and unclipped the mike.

"Where did that voice come from? Do you think one of the crowd cameras might have pointed in that direction?" Chill asked.

"I couldn't tell. We will just have to look at the tape later and see."

Chill scrubbed his palm down his face and unwrapped the fresh stick of gum. If he was right, then both perps would be here or would see the live feed. The one Chill had dubbed the Poisoned Pen would be trying to prove his claim of having his novel stolen, and the other, Lover Boy, a cold-blooded murderer, would be trying to remove the threat from Carmen's life just as he had done with Jake, Ethyl, and by kneecapping Gorgeous-George, the model, when he had a beef with Carmen.

Still, something kept pinging around inside Chill's head like a pebble in a jar. Something wouldn't fall into place. There was a piece of the puzzle that just didn't want to fit. And that question only made his cop-radar ping louder, because the inference was that Ethyl could confirm or deny the plagiarism claim.

What if the killer had eliminated her because she could prove Carmen was innocent of that charge?

But if that was the case, then Lover Boy stalker wasn't the killer. . . .

It had something to do with those dates on the paintballer's flyer. Paintballers . . . dates . . . locations.

Data played over and over in Chill's head.

"Come on, handsome, buy a girl a drink?" Carmen smiled up at Chill. She was a pistol. He hated writers, but this girl—this romance writer with the loose-cannon attitude—was not typical. He liked her, and he had to admit some of the attraction was her refusal to come clean with him about her police record. He had seen the record, but that was the official side, written by Jim Dunn. He was sure there was much more to the story. Half the fun was needling Carmen to tell him about it. It had become a game with them—his asking and her refusing to tell.

"How about it?" she said.

"Sure, hot chocolate would be good." Chill looped his arm around her shoulder. Not because it would drive her admirer crazy, which it would, but because it felt good and natural to do it. She must've not minded too much, because she didn't shrug his arm off.

They fell into step, Tyson scampering at Carmen's side. Snowdown had attracted every personality type Chill could imagine. It was almost as big a circus as a California beach event.

"So, what did you think of my interview?" she asked as they crunched through the snow.

"I think you tried really hard to piss off whoever it is who claims you stole the book. And I bet Lover Boy was watching too."

"I was going for obvious."

"Oh, yeah. Pissy, superior, righteous. . . ."

"Good. That's the tone I was going for—pissy, I mean. Now let's just hope he—they—had a television on."

"I doubt he did." Chill maneuvered her toward a booth serving coffee, cocoa and cappuccino.

"Really?" Disappointment rang in her question.

"Yep. I imagine he was standing right out here in the crowd, looking you straight in the face while you spoke."

"You think he was the guy who yelled a question from the crowd?"

"Could be, but I think our Poisoned-Pen is a coward. Standing a few feet away and yelling is a gutsy thing to do. What if we saw him?"

"So we didn't see him?"

"I'm hoping we got him on tape. Barry is going to get us all the film. I'm hoping that someone is going to look familiar—Lover Boy said you met him. You are a sharp woman, Carmen. I bet you will remember him. And if we can do posters of a face, he will lose his anonymity."

Carmen swallowed hard. She had been serious about not being a victim anymore, but the idea that one or both of her stalkers was watching her right now was a little unnerving.

Chill ordered their cocoa and paid for it. He put a tall, paper-wrapped disposable cup into her hand. He was scanning the crowd when his lips curled up at the edge. Not a smile, but he was amused about something.

"The cavalry is here."

She followed his line of vision and saw Tony, struggling to walk with a cane, his fat walking cast getting wet in the deep snow, Maria at his side.

"We came to keep an eye on Carmen." Tony's balance was shaky, but Carmen was grateful Chill didn't mention it.

"Anything happen yet?" Maria was swathed in gray wool with a furry hat that any Russian Czarina would be proud to own.

"Not a thing, except for Carmen throwing down the gauntlet."

"We watched it. You did good, kid." Tony winked.

"So, what do you want to do while I'm dangling myself as live bait in front of a couple of sharks?" Carmen's smile was all bravado; her knees were shaking.

"Let's go watch the paintballers. They have a small course set up and some bull's-eyes," Tony said. "I saw a flyer near the front entrance."

That brought Chill's mind back to the schedule of the paint-balling club's melees. Something was nagging at the edge of his consciousness, giving him a headache. It was as if he were chasing a scrap of paper in the wind: just when he thought he could grab it, it flittered away.

"Sure, why not? It'll be great to see a target on something other than me." Carmen dropped back to walk with Tony, while Maria fell into step beside Chill. Tyson split his time between both couples, pausing for the slower couple to catch up, or sprinting back and forth.

Up ahead a rough racetrack had been snowplowed. Cowboys in outrageous garb rode horses whose hot, steaming breath created wispy clouds. One big roan pawed the snow, pulled at the bit between his teeth.

"That's Millie's nephew, Cay," Maria said. "Only man around who can ride Widowmaker."

"Widowmaker? Quite a name." Chill watched the young man flick the reins, expertly controlling the big brute.

"In this case a literal truth. Millie's brother, Wes, was breaking that colt when he died."

Carmen heard what her mother said, and for one moment she was transported back in time. She could almost hear Millie's voice . . . "Some people need killing."

Had Millie mourned her brother's passing?

A loud western whoop made Carmen jump. She looked back at the flat track, padded on either side by a thick bumper of snow and bales of straw stacked haphazardly. Tyson jumped up on a bale and sat down, holding his hind-end just above the prickly straw.

"What are they going to do?" Chill lingered by the edge of the course. Tony hobbled up, trying to adjust his crutch and cast to the unleveled snow. Carmen and Maria stood in front of them. The two women were of a size, so it was easy for the men to see over the tops of their heads.

A man with a waxed handlebar mustache climbed into the back of a flatbed trailer that had been festooned with greenery, bright orange bows and a cardboard turkey. He held a bullhorn to his lips.

"This is the quarter-mile slalom, done the Snowdown way. For you newcomers to Snowdown, we race a bit different here."

A loud roar came from the crowd. Whistles, whoops and shouts kept the man from speaking for a few minutes.

"Not only do these boys ride hell-bent-for-leather around this quarter-mile track, but they will be towing a sled with their partner on it."

"Are they crazy?" Chill looked at the horses. The big animals were fidgety, nostrils flaring, eyes white rimmed, haunches bunching with effort. The nylon line connecting to the sled looked fragile as a cobweb against the bulk of the horses.

"The first rider over the finish line, with his partner still on the sled—and I mean *on* it and not being dragged behind it—will be the winner."

More cries and cheers rolled over the snow. The loud pop of the starting gun brought a momentary hush. Then, like a painting bursting to life, the horses lunged forward. Hooves dug into the snow. Powerful muscles bunched, gathered and exploded with strength.

Chill had never seen anything so insane in his life. Coming from California, that was saying a lot.

Carmen had given back his sunglasses. Now he ripped off his shades, as if that could somehow alter the scene. The horses thundered down the track. A flurry of white snow followed them, showering the men and women standing on the sleds. Rooster tails showered the spectators as the participants whizzed by. Chill was put in mind of Roman charioteers, the way the sledders held the lines, bent their knees and braced themselves. It was only a blink of an eye, and they were coming into the first turn.

A big bay gelding lost his footing coming out of the turn. He went down on one hip, slinging the sledder off. The man tumbled, boots over shoulders into the crowd, taking out at least four onlookers. Chill tore his gaze from that unfortunate scene to the lead horse, a fine-boned palomino who took the turn too tight and sent the sled careening into the safety barrier. The sledder slammed up against a bale and sat there, stunned.

"Yeah!" He pumped his fist in the air. "Yeah, whooo hoo."

One guy was grandstanding and doing tricks before he was suddenly shot over the ice on his belly like a curling stone. He skidded off the track only moments before a horse thundered by him.

"Widowmaker is in the lead now." Carmen clapped her gloved hands together, the action making a hollow thwack when the soft leather met.

"Millie must be here someplace, watching. She dotes on that boy, as much as Millie dotes on anything besides her heeler." Maria pulled her collar up tighter against a cool breeze that had come up.

"I didn't realize you knew Millie, Mom," Carmen said.

"Our families are old-time Taos County. She's a little older than I am but, yes, I know Millie. Knew her brother, Wes, and her nephew, Cay. Wes's death was strange, Cay had a hard adjustment. Millie took him home with her. Surely you have met Cay, living on the same road as Millie?"

"No. No, I don't think I have." Carmen knew almost nothing about Millie's nephew, beyond the fact that he was a local cowboy poet of some renown and took care of the ranch in Red River.

"Surely you remember his father's death. It was the top story for more than a month about five or six years ago."

"I don't remember. Are you sure I was here?"

"Maria, wasn't that the year Carmen went to England to meet her overseas publisher?" Tony shifted his weight, obviously uncomfortable. Chill glanced down. Several of Tony's exposed toes were purpling.

"Yes, now you mention it, I think she was in London. Well, it was front-page news for a while. Wes Ross cut quite a figure in town—tall, tough—a real cowboy. Great looking in tight shotgun chaps, with a quick smile and rough charm, but there were rumors he had a dark side. Millie and he barely spoke, but when he died, she was there for his son."

"What made the death so noteworthy?" Chill murmured.

"Wes was one hell of a rider. He could handle the meanest bronc. But you know when your number is up it is up. They had a closed casket because of the damage to his face. Evidently he hit a rock when he was thrown. Always seemed funny that an experienced cowboy like Wes would have rocks in his round breaking pen. A good cowboy tills the ground eight inches deep and drags it for stones." Tony used the end of his cane to rub Tyson's sleek haunch.

Chill glanced back at the flyer in his hand, then at the tall, lean youth riding the big roan. He remembered the path running by Penny's place. The shadows on her windows.

And the autopsy reports.

"I need to have a talk with him." Chill had to yell to be heard over the cheering crowd. The roan had crossed the finish line, the winner by a length, with the sledder still on board.

"Now? With everything that is going on?" Carmen studied his face as if she could find answers there.

"Especially now."

"I think you'll have to wait until later. They are headed for the paintball course." Tony used the cane to prod a thin crust of ice, testing it before he hobbled onto it with his full weight. Maria and Tyson flanked him, walking slowly to accommodate his stride.

Chill fell in beside them, unseeing, while his mind was playing connect the dots. But if this new theory could hold up, then his original theory was wrong.

Could it be that simple? Could it have been right in front of his nose all along?

He wasn't going to say anything to Carmen until he was sure. He flipped open his phone and speed dialed Vicki Smith's cell phone. She was somewhere in the crowd, but he wasn't going to waste time looking for her.

"Yeah, it's Chill. I need you to go to the office and find me a copy of the autopsy report on Wes Ross—death by accident about five or six years ago. I don't care if it is Saturday. Roust whomever you need. Drive to Albuquerque if you have to, but get me that report. And, Vicki? Make some time in the next few days. We have to sit down and have a talk."

CHAPTER THIRTY

"That camo really works doesn't it?" The paintballers were dressed in winter camouflage. White and gray splotches blended well with the snow and shadows of the landscape. They all wore thick neck pads and protective face coverings. Chill wouldn't be able to identify Eloy in this kind of armor. Their faces were hidden, their bodies padded to absorb the shock of being shot.

It was a near perfect disguise.

The teams split up, each group roughly thirty people, heading in opposite directions, ducking behind bales of hay stacked to form bunkers in the vista as far as Chill could see. The blinding white of the snow made it difficult to stare at the course for long, even with shades on, so he concentrated on the players.

Some of the guns they used were camouflaged, too; others were painted in bright colors. There were black, green, and even an electric purple that glared in the sunshine. Chill tried to remember what color the one hanging on Millie's wall had been, but he couldn't dredge up a clear picture through the fog of his cold-remedy hangover.

"Do women play this as well?"

"I guess. Frankly, it is a little too physical for me." Carmen fluffed the pink boa around her neck and winked at him. "We romance writers don't go in for such violence."

He was glad she was feeling lighthearted enough to joke. Unfortunately, he didn't share her mood. He was waiting for the shoe to drop.

The paintball war began. Within moments the armies had exploded into action. The force of the O2 canisters splattered the round balls on contact. Orange, red, and yellow paint dotted the camo clothes. The offensive group moved in a loose mass toward another bunker set up at least a mile away—perhaps farther—where a black flag flapped in the breeze.

One of the paintball-soldiers on the field took a shot to the head. The paint burst across his face, making an abstract painting of his protective helmet. He fell down as if he had been coldcocked. Chill watched him lie there for a full minute, before the man wobbled to his feet, shook his head like a bare-knuckle fighter and returned fire.

"Ouch, that looks like it really hurt," Carmen said. Tyson was sitting at her feet, watching the carnage in good-natured canine silence.

"I'd like to see one of those paintballs close up," Chill said aloud.

"Hey, I need to find the head. What say we take a walk? I think I saw a booth selling paintball gear up this way." Tony gestured with his cane.

"I don't think we should leave these two ladies alone." Chill's cop-radar was pinging.

"Nonsense. I can assure you we will be all right for a few minutes," Maria informed Chill with a tight smile.

"Uh-uh. I don't think so."

"Madre de Dios!" Maria exploded. "We are not helpless. It is broad daylight, Chill, and we have the dog."

"Yeah, stop trying to play Mr. Macho. Go." Carmen grinned. "But while you are gone, can I borrow your glasses again? The glare is giving me a headache."

"Sure." Chill slid them off and put them on her face. "Stay put, okay?"

"We won't budge from this spot," Carmen promised. "What

could possibly happen in broad daylight in this crowd of people?"

Tony hobbled toward the dark blue porta-potty. Chill saw the paintball booth a little farther up the path.

"I'll meet you back here in five," Chill said.

"Take your time. I'm not setting any land-speed records today." Tony disappeared into the fiberglass outhouse.

Chill hurried on, his boots crunching on the snow. There were a few patrons, and he was obliged to wait a moment before he could step up and examine a cluster of bright neon-yellow balls. He picked one up and rolled it between his thumb and forefinger. It was firm, but not hard.

"Hey, can I interest you in a hundred of those?" the guy manning the booth asked. "Our prices are better than the sporting goods stores, since we buy in bulk."

"What's the casing made of?"

"Casing? Oh, the outside. It is a gelatin-based coating. These are high quality. They don't gum up the barrel like some of those cheap brands."

"Can you get molds for these?"

"Molds? What would you want molds for?" The guy squinted at him suspiciously. "Hey, who are you?"

Chill dug out his badge. He squinted at a couple of guns. A crude cardboard sign proclaimed them to be non-jamming, smooth action.

"Can you shoot anything besides these balls through one of those guns barrels? If a guy wanted could he use a different kind of ammo, could he do it?"

"I don't know where you are going with this, but the clubs have strict rules. We use regulation paintballs. We have rules."

Chill was still holding a bright fluorescent ball in his hand. "What about freezing these things? Would they still work?"

"Freezing? Hell. Look, like I said, we have rules. If a guy is caught using frozen paintballs, he is kicked out and blackballed. Ice balls are deadly."

"Ice balls?"

"Yeah. Freezing these things makes them like a real slug. You get me?"

"Deadly? Just how deadly?"

The guy stepped back from the counter and lifted his sweater, exposing his bare torso.

"This is what you get even when you wear full gear using regulation paintballs."

Chill eyed the welts and bruises. Most of them were about the size of a blackjack chip: raised, angry welts with black and purple edges. The approximate size of the holes in both his vics' heads.

"Thanks." Chill headed back toward the porta-potty. Tony was hobbling along the path.

"Tony." Chill slowed his step to match Tony's slower gait. His phone rang. It was Vicki Smith. He flipped it open.

"Talk to me." He listened, while she read from the report, the information sizzling through his brain. A shiver worked its way up his spine and burrowed into the base of his brain. "Thanks. Get the rest of the officers we have available and get up here to the paintball course as soon as you can."

He snapped the phone shut. "Tony, I don't want to leave you in a lurch, but I need to get to Carmen."

Tony's eyes narrowed. "Hurry."

Chill saw the cluster of people standing where he had left Carmen and Maria. He started to run, elbowing his way through, his heart in his throat. Maria was slumped on a bale of straw. Tyson sat beside her, growling, as a woman dabbed at Maria's face. One of Chill's deputies was already there.

"What the hell happened?" Chill went down on one knee and

gently turned Maria's head. She was conscious, but stunned and clearly out of it. There was an unfocused, faraway look in her eyes, and she was murmuring something over and over in Spanish. A trickle of blood ran from beneath the wet fur of her fashionable hat, a black bruise coming up at the edges where the fur ended.

"Maria. Maria? Can you hear me?" Chill rubbed her hands, then he turned to the deputy.

"Report."

"I didn't see. Ms. Alvarez was just standing there and then she was down in the snow. By the time I got over here, there was already a crowd around her. At first I thought she had been shot, but I don't know. Maybe a rock got kicked up."

"Where's Carmen?" Chill patted Maria on the shoulder, trying to comfort as well as rouse her. She had clearly taken a helluva blow, the thick fur of the hat deflecting most of the impact. And the spot where she had been hit was wet, wetter than the rest of the hat.

"Well? Where is Carmen Pollini?" Chill glared up at the officer.

"That's what I'm trying to tell you. By the time I got here, Maria was out cold and Carmen was gone. I don't know where she is."

CHAPTER THIRTY-ONE

As soon as Vicki Smith and two other deputies arrived, Chill sent them off in different directions. The paintball war was still in high swing. There was no way to tell if any of the players were missing, since they were strung out from the entrance, in tight groups of a half dozen combatants all making for the black flag bunker.

Most everyone was oblivious to the drama that had played out near them. Most people focused on the paintball war.

The rescue vehicles on-site had moved quickly. Tony had gone with Maria in the back of an ambulance.

Chill was certain now what had killed Jake and Ethyl. And it made perfect sense that there was no forensic evidence. He knew how it had been done, but he was still unsure of which stalker had pulled the trigger.

Tyson whined and scratched at a bloodstain in the snow. Chill had forgotten about the dog. He would have to put him in his car. He was about to grab Tyson's collar and pull him away from the droplets of blood when he halted.

Tyson was digging something up. A bit of black appeared in the white snow. Chill bent down and picked it up.

His own sunglasses.

"Good dog." He rubbed his fingers over the ear-piece, trying to reconstruct what had happened. Unbelievably, nobody had seen a thing; they'd all been focused on the melee. Tyson had not been able to stop whatever happened—or he had stayed with Maria because she was injured.

"Did Carmen lose them in a struggle, or is she leaving us a trail?"

Tyson barked as if he understood. Chill saw the gleam in the boxer's eyes. It was a long shot but. . . .

"Find Carmen, Tyson. Find Carmen now."

Without hesitation, Tyson bounded through the snow, heading due north from the bale of straw. Chill followed him, dodging people as he broke into a run. He only hoped the boxer was the bloodhound he thought he was.

Carmen first became aware of a burning in her nostrils. She had done enough research and written enough mystery plots to conclude it was residual chloroform that made her sinuses burn and her eyes water. She didn't move while she tried to gather the shards of her memory.

She had been standing with Maria, watching the paintballers. There had been a pop. Maria fell at her feet. Before Carmen could react or get anyone's attention, someone had put his hand over her face. After that it was blurred, vague, disjointed. She couldn't even be sure that what she saw in her mind was a memory. Perhaps it was simply her writer's imagination.

"Mom." Was she dead? Carmen swallowed a moan and blinked back her tears. It wouldn't do any good to break down. She had to fight, regain her strength, learn who had done this and make him pay for hurting Maria.

But how?

Her hand was near her face. She stretched out her cold, numb, fingers to her neck—she had taken off her gloves? A vague memory of dropping them flitted through her mind—or was that just something the perfect, indomitable heroine would have done? In any case, her gloves were gone. The feathers of her boa were wet, straggly. Well, she had wanted to be the bait and evidently at least one shark in the water had smelled her blood.

She took a deep breath. Her cell phone!

She moved slowly, trying not to attract attention to the fact she was awake in case someone was watching her. She patted the pocket of her coat but the comforting bulge of the cell phone was gone. Had she lost it or had her abductor been smart enough to look for it?

Finally she opened her eyes. She was staring up at the sky, bales of straw surrounding her.

A bunker.

She cautiously levered herself up enough to peek over the low straw walls. She was in the middle of a field of snow. It was not level; here and there short, brittle stubs of winter grass poked through rolling rises of snow. Bales of straw surrounded her in a crude construction, much like the bunkers on the paint-ball course at Snowdown.

Some deep instinct for survival told her not to stand or raise her head above the protection of the bales. She kept her head low, peering out through a chink between two rough, snow-covered bales that made up one of the bunker's long sides.

She saw nothing but New Mexico wilderness spreading out for miles. There were trees in the distance, and the gray and purple sweep of the mountains, dusted in ermine.

The wind had picked up while the sun had dipped low. It had been hours since she had been taken. Late evening was falling. So was the temperature.

She had the sensation of being watched. She could almost feel the burn of eyes upon her.

"Now I know what the deer and elk feel like during hunting seasons. If I get out of this, I'm going to lobby against hunting," she whispered to herself, startled at how loud her voice sounded in the vast expanse of the prairie.

She glanced at the sky again. The sun was going down fast. It would be cold soon—too cold to survive out in the open.

Carmen peeled the wet boa from around her neck. She balled it up, wringing some of the water out. Then, without leaving the shelter of the bunker, she tossed it as far as she could into the field.

Something zinged through the air. The boa exploded into bits of pink feathers that wafted on the wintry breeze.

She shivered against the thought of what that shot would've done to her head as the image of Jake dead in the snow returned with the force of a fist.

"Well, at least I know one of my stalkers is out there, waiting for me, and I don't think it is Lover Boy, unless he has serious issues with foreplay."

Chill pounded over the snow. He was no tracker, but he had finally figured out that the half-moon shapes in the snow were the tracks left by a horse. Between Tyson and his own clumsy skills, he was able to follow, but the pace was damnably slow.

He realized too late that he should've found a horse, or a snowmobile, or something. But it was too late to turn back now; he would lose valuable time.

Hell, he hadn't even had the presence of mind to call and have somebody bring him a four-wheeler. Of course, he didn't have a clue where he was anyway.

His cell phone rang. He yanked it from the hip holder on the run.

"Blaines."

"Maria is coming around." Vicki Smith's voice took his thoughts from the trail and his shortcomings for a moment.

"What did she see?"

"Very little. She felt a blow to her head, and that was about it. Something interesting, Chill."

"Tell me."

"The doctor said if it hadn't been for the thick double fur on her hat, she would've sustained an injury consistent with those that killed Jake and Ethyl."

"The son of a bitch was trying to kill her?"

"Or Carmen."

He crawled on his belly through the snow. She wasn't moving. That could mean she wasn't able to move or that she was too smart to reveal herself.

"Too smart."

Carmen Pollini had been nobody's fool. But now she was out of options. If a well-placed shot didn't kill her, then the plummeting temperatures and the coming night would.

He couldn't believe it had come to this. He had been watching, waiting, fully expecting her to come around, but at every turn she misunderstood his intentions, rebuffed his attempts to aid her.

Now she had no choice. He could finally show her that he was truly the man she needed in her life—not that bumbling cop.

He had left the ski-doo a mile away. He had been forced to wait, but when night fell, he could whisk her to safety.

"And then I will introduce myself."

Not far away behind a stand of sage and scrub oak another man watched the bunker where Carmen hid. He was full of rage, the kind of fury that only killing could quell. He had felt that rage three times before.

But today, when he killed Carmen and proved his claims, would be the end of it. He would finally get the recognition he deserved.

★ ★ ★ ★ ★

"Tyson, find Carmen." Chill's deputies had found him. Coming on ski-doos that had picked him up and followed Carmen's bread-crumb trail. There had been a scrunchy from her hair, but Chill and the boxer had run out of clues.

The sun was going down and the wind had picked up, scrubbing away the prints in the snow. Desperation clutched at Chill's chest. He had told Vicki to keep well back. The last thing he wanted to do was to burst in and spook the abductor. Now he had left the ski-doo and was on foot again. He had to find Carmen, and assess the situation first. He had seen a lot of well-trained SWAT situations go all to hell.

"Carmen isn't going to become a statistic on my watch."

Tyson sniffed the snow, weaving back and forth as if he had been trained to track. Suddenly he started to dig in a soft shoulder of snow. He pulled something up and shook it.

It was one of Carmen's white gloves.

"Good boy. Find her, Tyson, find her."

Before the sun goes down and she is alone in the cold, dark, night.

Chapter Thirty-Two

The wind had turned the droplets of moisture on Carmen's coat to ice. She had tucked her bare fingers under the cuffs of her coat sleeves as much as she could, but they were starting to burn, just like her nose and cheeks.

She couldn't just sit here and freeze to death.

She looked around the small, protected space. There wasn't much there; just brittle winter-killed grass and a couple of stones. She used the edge of her boot to scrape down farther, exposing the hump of a huge anthill beneath the snow. The ants were well into their hibernation, warm and snug below the earth.

She scraped away some more snow in another area and found a small cluster of stones about the size of golf balls.

"Hello." She thought of the women she had created on paper in her novels. Sometimes they did outrageous things—heroic things—desperate things to survive.

"At least they try," Carmen murmured. Then she took a deep breath. Every one of those women were actually facets of her own psyche. She was a part of every character she created. All she needed to do was to tap into them, and she needed to do it now.

The sun had dipped below the tops of the great pine trees, turning the late afternoon into false night. The wind whispered through the trees, brooming along the field, sending wisps of snow spiraling into the air.

His breath was coming in hot little gasps, forming small clouds that left condensation in his neat goatee, condensation that had started to freeze.

With a tug he pulled his cashmere scarf up over his mouth in an effort to hide his presence. Stealth was vital if his plan was to succeed.

Suddenly he caught the flash of movement in the air. Half a heartbeat later there was a rapid explosion of pops as the other one fired at the bunker.

Carmen was becoming pro-active.

A smile twitched at the corner of his mouth. Her bravado and intellect never ceased to amaze him. It was why he admired her.

The swoop of an owl's wings overhead brought his mind back to the task at hand. With single-minded concentration, he started crawling on his belly like a snake, toward the bunker.

Toward Carmen.

Chill was mighty glad he'd given up cigarettes. This full-out run in icy weather was no cakewalk. He and Tyson were still on the trail, though, since they had found another set of hoof prints that had been visible in the deeper snow.

Of course now all the snow was deep, since they were traveling through open spaces far from any roads, tracking over powder that hadn't been touched by hikers, skiers or anybody but the maniac who had Carmen.

He knew whom he was chasing, of course. Not by sight, but by reputation.

"How could I have been so stupid?"

Chill's mind had reshuffled all the evidence, and this time the puzzle pieces fell into place, forming a completely different picture hell and gone from his original theory.

He had believed Carmen's unknown admirer, Lover Boy, had

killed Jake and Ethyl because Carmen had a beef with them. He had assumed the male model had been kneecapped for the same reason.

But he was wrong.

Jake had died because he delivered packages, manuscripts and padded envelopes. He had begun to keep a record of those deliveries as his feud with Carmen escalated. He could confirm her delivery dates on her books.

And Ethyl had died for the same reason. As Carmen's agent, she could verify the very week Carmen came up with a plot idea. It would've been child's play to shoot down the claim of plagiarism once Jake and Ethyl had been asked.

"So they both had to die."

And for someone who had already killed, it was a minor thing to kill again.

"He had motive, opportunity and prior experience."

Chill shivered. He was dealing with a stone-cold killer, someone who had avoided killing Carmen for his own twisted reasons. But now Chill was afraid those reasons were gone.

Carmen tossed a couple of rocks into the air, watching as something glittery blew them in different directions. She frowned, trying to figure out what kind of ammunition he was shooting.

"Who cares? This is not a plot I need to research. Get with it, girl. Stop thinking like a writer and start thinking like someone who is going to stay alive."

Carmen grabbed up a few more stones and flung them hard in the opposite direction. Right on cue, a barrage of something hit the spot where they fell.

Night had folded over the land like a curtain. There was a fingernail of a moon, turning the snowy landscape into a gray world of shadow and ice.

It had been a long, painstaking journey, but he was within two meters of the bunker. Two meters more and he would finally reach Carmen. It would be over tonight.

That thought gave him a sudden burst of energy. He scrabbled over the empty space, slithering over the walls of the bunker.

A smile was on his face. He would be the hero of the hour. This would impress her!

"Carmen—"

The bunker was empty. Carmen was gone.

A sound made him jerk to the left. The impact struck him on the jaw, driving him up. Another pain caught him in the area of his collarbone, spinning him around in the opposite direction. He heard a sharp crack and a sound so completely feral he could barely believe it bubbled up from his own throat. He realized with bitter clarity that he had been shot.

Chill and Tyson were still running full out, using the moon as their light, when the sudden appearance of the horse brought them both to a skidding stop. The roan whuffled softly, pawing at the scrub oak where he was tied. The ground beneath his hooves was churned up; brown mud caked his hooves.

"Easy boy. So you've been here a while, huh?"

Chill heard the noise the same instant Tyson reacted by growling. It was the unmistakable sound of a human in pain. Heat and cold ripped through Chill's chest while he sprinted toward the sound, dodging snow-covered bushes, drawing his weapon. He ran, ignoring the sting of icy air in his eyes, the stitch in his side, the burn in his windpipe.

"Carmen?"

The night had gone silent as a grave. Without sound Chill had no idea which direction to go, but Tyson never wavered. He plowed through the snow, a small brown speck against the endless background of white. Chill scrambled to stay with him.

They slid down a steep embankment, clamoring to the bottom.

Then Chill heard the sound of someone fighting for life. Something exploded a hundred yards ahead. He could make out the shapes of two people grappling over a weapon.

"Halt! Police!" Chill steadied his gun with both hands, but to shoot would be pointless. He couldn't tell who he was shooting at.

Tyson, however, didn't hesitate. He lunged at the two figures, bringing them to the ground. He growled, snapped and leapt at them, biting, grabbing arms, hands, fierce in his attack. One figure staggered to his feet and ran away, disappearing into the shadows of the night.

Chill ran to Tyson. The dog had someone in camo gear down, trying to bite his throat, but the heavy protection prevented the dog from getting a hold.

"Tyson! Tyson, sit!" Chill yelled at the dog, but it was useless.

Suddenly the figure reared up from the ground. He grabbed Tyson around the neck with both hands and flung him away.

"Don't you dare hurt him!" Carmen screamed from nearby.

The camouflaged killer pulled up the paintball gun and took aim. Chill squeezed the trigger. An oomph of pain and the drop of his shoulder was the only evidence that Chill had hit the mark. Quick as a striking snake, the shooter put the weapon in his other hand. He pulled up the gun and took aim again.

This time Chill's bullet hit the shooter in his camo-covered headgear. Slowly, like cold molasses pouring out of a jar, he went to his knees. Then he tipped forward, face down, a dark stain spreading out beneath him in the snow.

"Carmen, are you all right?" Chill kept his gun on the perp, circling the body until he reached Carmen, who was kneeling in the snow beside Tyson. "Is he hurt?"

"I think his leg is broken. That bastard hurt my dog!"

Carmen stood up, her face a mask of fury. She stomped over to the fallen body.

"Carmen, stay back," Chill warned.

"I want to see who it is. I want to know who has made my life a living hell, hurt my mother, and hunted me like an animal." She reached down and grabbed a handful of the camo head gear. She ripped it away, blood dripping from the cloth as she did so.

"I don't believe it. Why? Why? Why would Cay Ross want to kill me?"

The body was airlifted out after Vicki Smith showed up with the deputies and a horse trailer for the roan. They brought in real tracking dogs to find the wounded man who had run off, but Chill didn't think there was a better search-and-rescue dog in Taos County than Tyson.

"I just don't get it." Carmen was wrapped in a blanket provided by the search-and-rescue crew. She sipped hot chocolate, watching while they splinted Tyson's back leg.

"What don't you get?" Chill's pulse was still racing, and he didn't have a fresh stick of gum on him.

"I don't get how my rescuer, my knight in shining armor, my hero, is a boxer, and the runt of the litter, at that."

Chill was deflated. Not that he expected any big hoopla. After all, he was just doing the job he was hired to do. Still, it might've been nice to hear Carmen acknowledge his contribution to her rescue.

Vicki Smith handed Chill a new pack of Teaberry gum. "Here, you look like you could use this."

"Thanks."

"Don't mention it."

The press was a tight tangle of bodies, microphones and cameras by the time Chill drove into the station parking lot. Vicki Smith was in the passenger seat. Carmen had insisted on sitting in the backseat with Tyson.

"What say we swing by the hospital in Santa Fe and check on Maria? The rest of the deputies can handle this mess. I don't feel like having a microphone and camera shoved in my face."

"I feel exactly the same way," Vicki Smith whispered.

Chill did a quick U-turn, sending up a rooster tail of snow and gravel as he sped down the highway.

"Vicki, we need to have that talk—and soon."

CHAPTER THIRTY-THREE

"We have an update on the kidnapping that occurred at the Taos County Snowdown." The news blared from the TV in the lobby of La Señora.

Chill had come down early to find everyone else already up. He used to think rising at six in the morning was almost heroic, but here in this place, it was sleeping in. Tony hobbled in from the kitchen with cups of steaming coffee on a tray held in one hand, headed for Maria, who wore a thick bandage on her head. Carmen looked tired as she fussed with Tyson, who was now wearing a heavy cast on his hind leg.

"This looks like the painting of 1776," Chill quipped. Truth to tell, they all looked pretty damned satisfied with themselves—especially Tyson.

Chill made a mental note to find a breeder. He was going to have to get himself a dog like Tyson. When he left in the summer, he wanted a boxer in the passenger seat.

"The victim, Cay Ross, was shot by Taos County Sheriff Hugh Blaines. A search of the Red River Ranch revealed evidence the police are not yet prepared to divulge, but sources close to the investigation tell us it implicates Ross in the double homicide. On a lighter note—"

Tony switched off the television. "I brought a cup for you."

Chill glanced at the tray and saw an extra cup. "Thanks."

"Hey, it comes with a price. Up to now you have been pretty damned tight lipped. We have decided we want to be . . . what

260

is the word? . . . debriefed."

Maria, Carmen, and Tony, even Tyson, were watching Chill expectantly.

"Okay. This is what I have so far. Remember, none of this is official. You understand that? It is all off the record."

"Sure, off the record, strictly on the lowdown." Tony plumped a pillow behind Maria's back. "Spill it."

"Wes Ross was the first victim. When I saw the autopsy reports and compared the injury, I got a hunch."

"Might've been nice if you had shared," Carmen grumbled.

Yep, she had a mouth on her, but he liked it.

"It was only a hunch. After I interrogated Millie last night, she finally came clean and told me the whole story. Wes evidently had a mean temper—used to beat the boy. One day the kid had enough and shot him with the paintball gun. Millie helped him clean up the paint, then disguised the cause of death by putting him in with Widowmaker."

"I knew a guy like Wes wouldn't have rocks in his round pen," Tony said.

"But what did Cay have against me?" Carmen stroked Tyson's thick, muscled neck. His eyes closed; in a moment he was snoring.

"What is *A Hot Brand of Love* about, Carmen?"

"Oh, it's set in New Mexico, on a ranch. A wild cowboy meets his match, and they end up together."

Chill grinned. "Evidently that plot is not too unique—no offense. Seems Cay actually did have a story with some similar points. Now don't get all prickly on me. It was a completely different book. But the guy was sick, Carmen. He watched you for months from the vantage point of Millie's ranch. Then somewhere along the line, he spiraled out of control. When he made the plagiarism accusation, he must've realized it wouldn't hold up, so he decided to eliminate anybody who might be able to provide a timeline for your story. Jake was the first one. I don't know how Cay knew that Jake was keeping a log of all the mail, parcels and packages he picked up and delivered to your house, but we found Jake's log at the ranch in Red River."

"The Taos Telegraph," Carmen murmured.

"Maybe. It does seem to be the most reliable source of information in the valley."

"And Ethyl?"

"She was your agent. Cay didn't know you two were on the outs and that she was holding up your money. He just knew she could back up your claims of when you submitted ideas and stories to your publisher. How is your attorney doing with the court order to free your funds?"

"Gloria called. It looks like my money will be released in a couple of weeks."

"Good."

"She said it was due to you solving the case. The New York judges couldn't see any reason to keep any of her clients' royalties tied up if her murder had been solved and none of the literary clients had any connection to those who committed the crime." Carmen grinned.

"And the other stuff? The windows, the E-mails. All just to rattle her?" Tony asked.

"Seems that way. Except for the gifts and the deposit to your account. Those are from a different person. I had deputies posted at hospitals and emergency medical facilities in the area, thinking he might go for treatment. I'm convinced that was who was fighting with Cay. I think he had planned to rescue you, but Tyson beat him to it."

"And—?"

"And he was either not badly injured or he took care of it himself, because I have checked out every admission in every hospital nearby. Your secret admirer is still secret."

"Swell," Carmen quipped. "So Lover Boy is still out there."

"At least we know he is not violent. Everything has been checked and rechecked. Cay was our guy, all right."

"What about Dax's kneecapping?"

"Ah. Seems Dax was flirting with the wrong woman. A local guy has been charged with assault."

"So now what happens?" Carmen's eyes skimmed over Chill's face.

"Business as usual. In fact, I have a breakfast meeting with one of my deputies and I don't want to be late." Chill slipped on his shearling coat and headed for the door.

"Chill?" Carmen's voice stopped him.

"Yeah?"

"How about dinner? I'm making flan and margaritas."

"See you about sundown."

The drive to the police station gave Chill a chance to go over it all in his head. He rehearsed what he was going to say, fumbled, restarted, gave up and decided just to wing it.

After all, what did a guy say to a ghost?

Chill walked into the small diner that sat cheek by jowl to the police station. It was decorated in southwestern schlock, different from the Spanish Territorial décor of the Blue Coyote. Hunters, skiers and locals were slurping coffee and wolfing down greasy hash browns and eggs. At the very back booth, well out of the line of traffic and view, sat a lone figure.

He strode past the other tables, focused on the white-blond hair he could just see over the high back of the booth, slid in and nodded.

"I took the liberty of ordering you coffee."

"Thanks, Vicki."

"Don't mention it. Now what?"

263

"I have been trying to decide what I would say, but I think the best thing would be for me to just listen. You want to tell me why you sent my C.V. to the county commissioners? But first maybe you better tell me how you rose from the dead."

There was a pause, and Chill used the time to study her eyes: dark, expressive, unique eyes.

"Jetne Sisco had to be stopped. The Feds promised to protect me, but I knew they could only do that one way."

"Witness protection."

"Give the man a cigar." Vicki Smith grinned at Chill; straight white teeth flashed. So much about her face was changed. Gone was the ethnic nose, her teeth were straight and white, evidently due to veneers, her cheeks were more sculpted, her chin longer. But no amount of surgery could change what was in those eyes.

"I had only one caveat before I entered witness protection. I wanted to go into law enforcement. So after the trial, after my testimony sealed Sisco's fate, the car crash was staged and I was taken to a hospital at a secret location for plastic surgery." She grinned and a blush crept up her face. "The doctor who did it used to do procedures on Rodeo Drive. He made me a lot prettier than I ever expected. My teeth were fixed, electrolysis changed my hairline, and I became a blonde. I became Vicki Smith."

"How did you end up in Taos County?"

"It seemed perfect, a small county with an established sheriff. Only after I got here and began to work, I found out Jim Dunn was corrupt. I had a real problem. I could expose him, but that would mean witness protection would pull me out and give me a new identity. Or I could just keep my mouth shut."

"Not likely." Chill grinned at her.

"I was afraid that someone would recognize me before I could find a solution. The press was starting to hang around a lot, and Jim kept shoving me in front of them. Things were heating up.

Jim was going to be charged. I was determined to see him answer for what he had done. The clock was ticking."

"You could've called up the Feds and turned him in."

"Yes, but I didn't want to be relocated. Making a new life once I could do, but I couldn't face that possibility again. You understand. Don't you? I mean, you walked away and left everything in California after your partner wrote that book. You left everything but your name."

"It wasn't just the book that made me walk away. It was the death of a brave young woman who was willing to risk all to tell the truth about a murderer."

"I see."

She blinked rapidly, but tears welled in her eyes. Damn it, he hated to see a woman cry. And she was right. Pulling up stakes, starting over, wasn't easy, and at least he had been able to remain who he was inside. He couldn't imagine how hard it must be for someone like Vicki.

"How did I play into it? I was just passing through on my way to nowhere."

"You got a ticket." She grinned. "When I stopped you and ran your plates, I realized who you were. I remembered you and your partner Eloy very well. Straight cops—incorruptible. I went on-line, got your credentials, worked up a résumé and sent it to the commissioners. They knew a good thing when they saw it."

"So what now, Vicki?"

"I hope you will just forget the past and let us continue as we have been. I'm a good cop, Chill. I like working with you. As long as I don't have to do interviews, I'm safe."

"Why didn't you just tell me who you were?"

"I did. I'm Vicki Smith. If I had another life, it is dead and buried. I want to keep it that way."

"I thought the young woman who took the stand to put a

murdering, drug-dealing monster away was the bravest person I had ever seen. I always regretted not being able to tell her so. If she were sitting here right now, I would tell her that I have her back. She is safe. And the past will remain the past."

"I'm sure she would be happy to hear that and to thank you."

When Chill walked into the dining room of the Blue Coyote, he was shocked to find it empty save one small table where a lone candle burned.

Carmen stood in the doorway to the kitchen, an apron wrapped around her trim waist. She had her sleek hair pulled back at her nape.

"Welcome."

"We have the dining room to ourselves?" Chill walked to the table, suddenly feeling a little awkward.

"Maria needs rest. Tony insisted. I concurred. Besides, it is time to show you that I can cook." She grinned and disappeared into the kitchen.

"Guess that is my cue to sit down, huh?" His voice seemed loud in the big empty room.

"Yes, it is. I have prepared my specialty. I hope you like it."

Chill wasn't sure what to expect. Chili? Enchiladas? Burritos? That would be it, burritos. They were fairly simple.

Carmen walked through the door with a big serving platter balanced on one hand. She pulled out a stand and put the tray on it.

Chill stared in surprise. Two platters held juicy, sizzling T-bones, baked potatoes and a fresh salad topped with croutons. Two thick slices of Texas toast sat on a plate in the middle.

"Steaks? Your specialty is steaks?"

"Uh-huh." Carmen put the platter before him. "Dig in. Then I have another surprise for you."

"Smells good." Chill sniffed luxuriantly. Then he took up his knife and sliced off a piece of steak. It was tender, flavorful, cooked just right.

"Is it good?" She fished for a compliment.

"Great." And it was. A glass of iced tea sat beside him. He ate and drank in silence until they had consumed more than half of their meals.

"Okay, what is my other surprise, because, Carmen I honestly didn't think you could cook."

"I know." She smiled at him. "I have one or two other things that I can make very well." She got up again and disappeared into the kitchen. When she returned she was carrying two stemmed margarita glasses.

"Surprise number two."

Chill sipped the drink. It was a perfect blending of sweet and sour. "Magnificent. And for dessert?"

"Flan. I do know how to make flan."

Chill scraped the plate and got the last sweet bits of flan on his spoon. It was like heaven in his mouth. He was full to bursting. Two nice T-bones sat on a paper napkin. Right on cue, Tyson thumped into the dining room.

"Poor little beggar, he wants a T-bone, Carmen."

"Yeah. Well, they are too sharp, but I trimmed off some fat and he can have it later."

"By the way, I have been meaning to ask you—do you know where I can buy a boxer pup? I have decided to get myself a dog like Tyson."

Carmen averted her eyes and a pretty blush crept up her face.

"What? What did I say?"

"Oh, it is just funny that you bring up Tyson. I have decided to tell you about my arrest record."

Chill leaned back in his chair. "Really? So you finally trust me?"

"Yes, I do. Anyway, it involves Tyson and his mother."

Now Chill was really interested. The mystery of Carmen's arrest and the continuing story of her crazy temper had become almost mythic. But he didn't want to rush her. She might clam up again if he pressed.

"I was in the park one day. Lots of backyard breeders bring pups to sell in the summer. I wasn't really looking for a boxer, but there he was, the runt of the litter, half the size of his litter mates. I bought him on sight. The guy gave me the puppy papers and I paid him. I was halfway to my car when I realized I had stiffed him ten dollars."

"So instead of keeping the ten, you went back."

"Right. Only when I got back he was doing a demonstration of dog training techniques on Tyson's mom."

"Good was he?"

"The cruel bastard had one of those electronic shock collars on her, but he had amped it up somehow. Instead of delivering a mild shock, it was knocking her to her knees in a sort of seizure. Her tongue had been bitten through and her eyes were rolling back in her head."

"Son of a—"

"There were even some young toughs cheering him on. It was horrible. I couldn't stand it. I put Tyson on my sweater under a tree and confronted the guy."

"Without backup?"

"I wasn't concerned with my safety. I just wanted to save Tyson's mom. He wouldn't give me the controls. So I kicked him in the gonads and took it from him."

"While everyone watched? I bet they loved that."

"As a matter of fact, they did. It seemed like seeing him in pain was even more fun than watching him torture a defenseless animal."

"That's all? That's all you did? And Dunn arrested you? It was justified."

"Well, I wasn't exactly finished. You see, after I got the controls, I removed the collar from the dog's neck, and while he was still writhing on the ground, I sort of . . . well I put it on him. Tyson's mom was a big girl. She had a nice, muscled neck."

Chill was laughing now. "Oh, Carmen, you didn't!"

"Uh-huh, I did. I turned it up and let him have it. I didn't realize that a body could do things like that. He was like a puppet, but after he bit his own tongue and I saw the blood, I turned it off. Vicki Smith showed up. She slapped him with cruelty to animals, a felony in New Mexico."

"Well, I still don't get it. How did you end up getting arrested?"

Carmen's gaze slid to the ceiling. It was the first time Chill could remember her not looking him straight in the eye when she talked.

"It seems that while the guy was being treated by the EMTs for the rupture of one testicle, electrical shock and a nearly severed tongue, his dogs disappeared."

"Carmen?"

"I was charged with theft. I spent a few days in jail. Jim Dunn was sure I would talk and tell him where the boxer and her remaining pups had gone if he softened me up a bit."

"He didn't know you very well, did he?"

She grinned. "Nope."

"So where is Tyson's mom and his litter mates?"

"What makes you think I know?"

"Hey, I know you."

"Just let me say they are all in places where they are loved, cared for and happy. In fact, I might even know that in a few weeks a puppy just like Tyson will be looking for a home. But, Chill, Maria will never let you keep a dog at La Señora. She has adopted a no-pet rule."

"Oh, that's no problem. I'm moving."

A shadow of something flitted across Carmen's face. Was it disappointment?

"Moving?" She took a sip of her margarita. "I thought you were joking when you said you were leaving in the summer, but I guess after the city, Taos County can't compete."

"Yeah, that was sort of the original plan, but I've had a change of heart. I'm just getting my own place."

"They must be paying you really well if you can afford a house here."

"I got a good deal on a place because of some exigent circumstances. In fact, you and I will be neighbors soon. I bought Penny Black's place."

Chill saw Carmen's face alter, but before she could say whether or not she liked the idea of having him for a neighbor, there was the sound of someone entering the front lobby. Almost as soon as the door opened, it was shut again.

"What the . . . ?" Chill rose from his chair and hurried to the front of the restaurant. His footfalls were muffled by the venerable wool rug. When he reached the lobby, it was empty except for a long, white flower box.

"What is it?" Carmen asked behind him. She picked up the box and lifted the lid. Inside were a dozen white roses. The lovely scent wafted into the room.

"Looks like flowers." He plucked off the card and handed it to Carmen.

She opened the envelope and read the card. Then she handed it to Chill. He read it.

White roses, like the snow. Carmen. I want you to know I am still watching you—and I will always be your number-one fan.

270

MARIA'S FAMOUS BLUE COYOTE FLAN

Ingredients
Carmel:

1 cup sugar
1/4 cup water

Custard:

12 egg yolks
two 13-ounce cans evaporated milk
14-ounce can condensed sweetened milk
1 teaspoon vanilla

Cooking Instructions
Carmel:

Caramelize sugar in a sauce pan by boiling the water and stirring continuously over medium heat until sugar is melted. Pour caramelized syrup into flan mold or custard cups, tilting the mold to make sure the whole surface is covered.

Custard:

In a large bowl, combine all custard ingredients. Stir lightly when mixing to prevent bubbles or foam from forming. Strain slowly while pouring into caramel-lined flan mold. Preheat oven to 325 degrees. Cover mold with tin foil. Put molds in a bigger tray filled with water. Bake in oven for one hour or until mixture is firm. Cool before unmolding on a platter.

CHILL'S FAVORITE MARGARITA

1-1/2 ounces tequila
1/2 ounce premium triple sec (preferably Cointreau)
1 ounce lime juice

Rub the rim of a cocktail glass with lime juice, and dip in salt. Shake all ingredients with ice, strain into the glass, and serve.

AUTHOR'S NOTE

La Señora del Destino and the Blue Coyote are not real, and I have taken a few liberties with a few other details. I hope you will enjoy book two of the Carmen & Chill mystery series where Chill, Carmen and Tyson become embroiled in art theft and lost fortunes.

Linda

ABOUT THE AUTHOR

Linda Lea Castle knows about the quirks and beauty of New Mexico. She is a third-generation native New Mexican and has cowboys, artists and writers in her family tree. *Taos Chill* is her nineteenth published novel. She has been nominated twice and finaled once for the Romance Writers of America RITA. She has won the *Romantic Times* Reviewers' Choice Award, is a double LORIE winner, chosen best historical author of the year in 2002, and has been a double finalist in the Daphne du Maurier mystery awards.